The Big House

Born and brought up in Co. Mayo, Áine Greaney now lives in Massachusetts where she writes and teaches. She has published many features, essays and award-winning short stories. *The Big House* is her first novel.

Visit www.ainegreaney.com

The Big House

Áine Greaney

POCKET BOOKS

TownHouse

First published in Great Britain and Ireland by Pocket/TownHouse, 2003
An imprint of Simon & Schuster UK Ltd
and TownHouse and CountryHouse Ltd, Dublin

Simon & Schuster UK is a Viacom company

1 3 5 7 9 8 6 4 2

Simon & Schuster UK Ltd
Africa House
64–78 Kingsway
London WC2B 6AH

www.simonsays.co.uk

Simon & Schuster Australia
Sydney

TownHouse and CountryHouse Ltd
Trinity House
Charleston Road
Ranelagh
Dublin 6
Ireland

A CIP catalogue record for this book is available
from the British Library

ISBN 1-9036-5050-X

Typeset by Palimpsest Book Production Limited,
Polmont, Stirlingshire
Printed and bound in Great Britain by
Cox & Wyman Ltd, Reading Berkshire

Acknowledgements

Robert James Scally's *The End of Hidden Ireland: Rebellion Famine and Emigration* (Oxford U.P., 1995) and John Fitzmaurice Mills' *The Noble Dwellings of Ireland* (Thames & Hudson, 1987) were most useful for background for this book. My thanks also to Austin O'Hare, contracts manager, Tinnelly Demolition, Newry, Co. Down for helping those walls to go down. Thanks to Treasa Coady and TownHouse for reading, accepting and encouraging. And heartfelt gratitude to Ken for his support and love.

Part 1

Part I

Chapter 1

The wipers thwacked back and forth. Ten minutes. This country estate agent was ten minutes late already.

A car came around the turn at the end of the village. McHugh checked himself in the rear-view mirror, set his features into a suave but disapproving expression. This, after all, was what he did best – prospect property.

The driver slowed at the gateway where McHugh was parked. Veered off the road into the mud to peer at McHugh's rental car, then sped up again and continued off down the Rathloe–Ballyshee road.

McHugh checked the car clock again. A quarter to three. Not like he had all bloody day. Tomorrow he'd drive back to Dublin again, turn in this rental car and then fly back to London.

If he decided to make an offer on this place – and certainly the price was right – he'd have to find some place to stay tonight. Surely there'd be some kind of hotel, B & B? And then . . . ? Come back later in the month, he supposed. Pack up a few winter things. Rent some kind of holiday cottage until he built his own house on this land.

He peered through the fogged-up windows at the high, demesne gates held together with rusted wire, propped up each side by big, agricultural boulders.

Beyond the gates, an overgrown avenue, a fretwork

of bare branches against an October sky. Two distant chimneys, a rooftop above the trees.

Could this be the one? Back in August, he'd dropped tools in London to jet over to a small horse farm in the Midlands. Last April, it was a sheep farm in Wicklow. In February, a miserable, waterlogged place along the Monaghan–Cavan border – all misrepresented by the newspaper property pages. Paper doesn't refuse ink. His mother used to say that. Funny the expression should come back to him now.

Her funeral was his last real visit home – to the seaside farm forty miles north of here where he was born and where his mother had died of old age in her sleep. Peacefully. Or at least, that's what his brother Seamus had told him. Five years ago.

Afterwards, safely back in London, he would remember the trip as an unreal few days – the funeral with its sandwiches and handshakes, Seamus and Seamus's wife Rita's bungalow packed with vaguely remembered faces.

In the five years since, McHugh had had a repeating dream, once a month at least, in which he was running, racing to catch a train, a boat. He would stop to make phone calls from payphones that wouldn't work, numbers that wouldn't dial.

When he woke in his luxury flat in Notting Hill, the dream's galloping anxiety would still linger. He had forgotten, mislaid something. Walked away from it back there in Carraig-by-the-sea, his home parish.

Since her death he hadn't even come for Christmas – couldn't somehow, no reason for him and Seamus to sit across a Christmas dinner table from each other in his brother's house with the velveteen couches and flowered carpets. In the summer, Rita ran a B & B, her deadpan face and voice suddenly coming alive for American, English and German tourists.

He'd spent the last few Christmases in Pinner
with Jimmy, his building manager, where Jimmy's
wife Phyllis fussed over him and vowed that one of
these days she'd match him up with just the right
woman.

He searched for a lever to let back the car seat.
Only compact vehicles left at the rental car place this
morning. He switched the engine off. Stretched back at
an uncomfortable angle, then shut his eyes against the
dripping day.

Of course, he remembered driving through this village of Rathloe en route to Galway City. They were
young, him and Seamus, their father already dead.
Their mother hired hackney cars for trips to a hospital,
to a clinic for children's hearing tests, Seamus being
brought for new eyeglasses. Before McHugh left for
England, Seamus had bought his first car – a grey,
egg-shaped thing that McHugh remembered pushing
down a hillside *bóithrín* to get it started that morning
in 1964 when Seamus brought him to a bus that would
take him to a train, a boat, then another train to Euston
Station and the London building sites.

The knock on the car window woke him. A red-faced
man was grinning and waving through the glass. He
sat up, rolled down the window.

A damp, beefy hand. 'How'rya? Mr McHugh, is it?
Dan Tierney. Bad oul' day, hah?'

Pointedly, McHugh checked his watch.

Tierney was already squeezing through a stone stile to
the left of the gates. This estate agent extraordinaire was
wearing huge, black wellingtons, a stained, green anorak
with the fur trim around the hood balded in places. 'You
weren't waiting too long, were you?' Tierney called
back over his shoulder.

McHugh stepped up on the stile. 'Well, actually . . .'

he started, but Tierney, waiting on the other side, was eyeing McHugh up there: beige mackintosh, well-tailored slacks, black polo neck and hand-stitched Italian moccasins. The hair and trim beard flecked with grey, the piercing blue eyes.

A professor, editor or some bookish type, people thought when they first met McHugh, heard the carefully enunciated words, the almost English accent. Never a navvy turned wealthy property developer.

Tierney jabbed a thumb towards the ramshackle avenue and fields beyond. 'Arrah, have you no wellingtons or an oul' jacket or something? It'll be mucky . . .' A smirk on the big, florid face.

'Packed in rather a hurry once I got off the phone with you in London yesterday,' McHugh said irritably. 'Sure I'll be fine. Done this before, you know.'

'Now, as I told you on the phone, Mr McHugh, it's twenty-five acres altogether, but even a blind man'd tell you this land's been badly neglected. Old fella called Cronin owned it, died a few months ago below in the county home. Like, that's where they put old people who can't afford—'

'I know,' McHugh snapped, trudging and skidding after Tierney in his leather-soled shoes. 'As I told you on the telephone, Mr – ah – Tierney, I'm actually from here, originally, well, not here but the county anyway – parish of Carraig . . .'

'Hah? Well is that so? A Mayoman? Well, I'd never have pegged ya . . . Oh, a lovely spot, lovely spot, Mr McHugh. The wife and myself and the kids go down to the seaside of a Sunday in the summer. Woeful rough and lonely on a winter's night though . . . But sure like everyplace else nowadays, cleaning up on th'oul foreigners and artists and herb gardeners.'

'Well, it's only natural—'

'Hah?' Tierney interrupted again. 'A wonder you

didn't go looking for something down that way yourself? A savage loves his native land or so they say, am
I right?'

Before McHugh could answer, Tierney said, 'Though
there isn't five *not to mind twenty-five* decent acres down
there . . . No, I don't blame you wan bit, so I don't, not
wan bit.'

They had left the avenue behind, were tramping
across a huge, open field.

'Best shaggin' walls in the country.' Tierney waved a
pudgy hand to take in the checkerboard of symmetrical
fields and high stone walls that stretched before them.
'But then, if th'oul landlords hadn't mighty walls, who
would? Isn't it true for me? Hah? They didn't build
them with their own hands anyways, that's for sure.
Am I right?'

Tierney was off through the wet grass again, wellingtons
thuck-thucking, McHugh hurrying after him breathlessly. He could feel the wet grass through his socks,
his drenched trouser legs plastered to his ankles.

'Now, of course, the beauty of this place is that
you've access from th'oul road below here as well.'
Tierney pointed to where a high wall marked the end
of the landlord's demesne. It abutted a narrow roadway
that led off east from a crossroads. On the opposite,
westbound road stood a white, pebble-dashed primary
school with Venetian blinds, playground, football fields
with goal posts. Beyond the demesne were farmers'
fields with their straggle of stone walls, sheep, cattle,
gaps with rusty barrels for gates.

High, new houses sprouted here and there. One was
painted bright lemon with a sparkling white moulding.
It reminded McHugh of a wedding cake. Another had
Italianate balconies.

Tierney looked to the sky and said, 'Jaysus, there
isn't a feckin' hope of it letting up, hah? D'you want

to walk all the way down to th'end there or what?' He was hoping for a no.

'A field is a field, I suppose. All drained?'

'Oh, bone-dry, Mr McHugh. Just you can see yourself, like badly neglected. I'd say anyone wanting to work this place now'd have to pull out a few bushes, stones, throw th'oul bit of fertiliser down anyways—' He stopped abruptly.

McHugh remembered this look, a countryman's terror of someone else's – even a stranger's – opportunism. 'Or . . . maybe 'tisn't farming at all you're after it for?' Tierney eyed him cagily.

McHugh stared him down.

Back on the avenue again, Tierney had stopped to wait for McHugh. He was lighting a cigarette, sheltering his lit match with one side of his anorak.

'Well? What's the verdict?' he asked, exhaling smoke through his nose.

McHugh was used to these bluff, estate agents' questions. 'So far so good, Mr Tierney. But let's continue. Like to see the residence.'

'Aw, haw, haw, haw.' Tierney's laugh was forced and theatrical. '*Tráth*, now I'd hardly call it that. Talk for years of the county council or someone making that oul' Cronin tear it down, a deathtrap to children and the like. And sure, Cronin, th'oul cranky bastard, said that if the shaggers would stay off his land, there'd be no danger in it. But you know yourself, Mr McHugh, th'odd tourist or historian down from Dublin, America, even the teachers in the school below – all like to show the youngsters an oul' landlord's house on their own back doorstep.'

The woods had thickened, then the avenue turned and disappeared under what was once an arbour of yew hedges, now a wild tangle of undergrowth. Again

Tierney stood waiting for him, gingerly holding aside a huge, vicious-looking briar.

'Thanks,' McHugh said acidly.

'Well, there y'are. Rathloe House. The big house. A pure deathtrap.'

They were standing in a pebbled clearing before a square, stone house, eight steps to the front door, an eyebrow of ivy over the top windows, rafters through a hole in the roof. The door was boarded up with warped and graffitied plywood.

On each side of the portico were two set-in pillars, mottled white and yellow with lichens. An ornate fanlight peeped above the plywood, its glass and timber shattered like broken teeth.

The first- and second-floor windows were also boarded with ill-fitting plywood. At ground level a row of squat windows, exposed except for rusted iron railings. Servants' quarters, he supposed. A kitchen, cellars.

McHugh crouched in the wet grass before the cellar windows, shaded his eyes to peer into the darkness. Inside, water dripped on to a mud floor. A stench of dry rot and animal droppings.

Tierney had already dashed off around the side of the house, but McHugh walked back across the clearing again for another eyeful of Rathloe House.

He'd known all along, hadn't he? What in God's name had he expected? An Ascendancy mansion – a big house – waiting just for him, nothing to do but pop into Galway City for a few new curtains, a touch of paint along the landing? Oh, it was laughable, his notions of grandeur. But now, a strange, hollow feeling of . . .

'The gardens . . . ?' Tierney's hooded head appeared around the corner of the house, the voice, face, straining for patience. 'Ye'll want to be careful on these oul' steps. Not much to see anyways, especially on a day like today.' McHugh followed him under the dripping bushes, three steps down into the rear garden – a wilderness of briars and scotch grass. At the end, more steps to a second, lower garden that ended at the orchard wall.

There was a stone urn in the first garden, miraculously intact and elegant, though the stone was mottled and it was full of greenish water. The back of the house was completely covered with ivy, five windows up, five down, steps down to a boarded-up back door, another set of subterranean windows with their rusted iron bars.

His trousers and feet drenched now, McHugh crossed the garden to a line of stables – roofless, walls crumbling. Inside, mud, hoofprints and fresh cowdung. Someone's cattle had wandered and sheltered here.

'Are you right there, Mr McHugh?' Tierney was holding the sides of his green hood together, his face puckered into a tormented, drenched look.

'Look, could I suggest that you go on ahead? Home . . . or your office in Ballyshee or wherever. I'll be fine here. Just need a moment, you know . . . to walk around, see things for myself.'

'Ah, Mr McHugh, we always stay with the client, like 'cos . . .'

Something in McHugh's expression stopped Tierney. Here was a man used to getting his way, a wilfulness almost vicious.

'Look, I'll contact you from my hotel tonight or before I leave for London, all right?'

Tierney nodded, shoved his hands in his pockets and turned to tramp back around the front of the house.

Almost impossible to gain a footing in the orchard

wall. Shoes scuffed. The belt of his mackintosh caught in a stone.

At last he jumped down on the other side. Crouching, he walked like a sniper between the orchard wall and the old apple trees. Trunks discoloured and twisted. A smell of nettles. Rotting apples.

Rain ticked in the leaves above his head.

Where the orchard wall ended, he found a huge crab apple tree. Swung himself up into the 'Y' of the trunk.

Ever since he was a boy he'd done this – found himself some secret spot among his mother's mountainside fields, or in the dunes at Carraig. Watch the people, tourists, on the beach below.

Thirty-five years ago, those early days in London, the other lads would clamour around the lunch van, then sit on upturned buckets around the building site to jeer and whistle after passers-by in the street. But McHugh would stay perched among the scaffoldings and girders, tea from a flask, munching a sandwich he'd made that morning in his bedsit flat in Shepherd's Bush. Watching, staring out over the rooftops and spires of London, weighing, plotting.

'That luck of the Irish.' Over the years his London business acquaintances, even Jimmy his manager, would tease about his astute property investments.

But McHugh, the expatriate Mayoman, didn't believe in luck. An immigrant sense of what was and what wasn't. That was what built his London property empire. Luck was for the foolish or the silver-spoon types.

From his tree he looked out over the gardens, the ivy-covered house, a swathe of pewter sky between the roof and the high copper beeches. It was a rule of his: never decide on a property without sleeping on it.

But God, this was different, wasn't it?

Of course, he'd level and rebuild – a modern, custom-design with long windows looking out on his gardens.

11

In the front, he'd cart away the yew hedges for an uninterrupted view across his twenty-five acres, which he would reclaim, re-seed, best breeds of cattle. Horticulture. Tierney's voice came back. McHugh laughed out loud in the orchard. *Foreigners and artists and herb gardeners. Cleaning up.*

A trickle of rain down his neck. A tree branch biting into his shoulder.

Between the big house and the roadside gateway, he would keep all these old copper beeches and horse chestnuts. Plant a few extra.

Protection from that peering little village.

Chapter 2

Susan Brown Whitaker was reading a poster in the glass display case at the Cripton train station.

'Come for the craic; stay for the job.'

The poster sported a collage of glossy photos: a centrepiece of young Irish people drinking pints of stout in a pub, smiling like Hollywood starlets; young executives around a conference table, a white-coated woman peering down a microscope.

Monster Christmas Career Expo. Ballsbridge, Dublin. IT, engineering, pharmaceuticals. On-the-spot interviews with the best companies. A telephone number and website for more information. A separate telephone number for companies to reserve an exhibit booth.

She turned to walk back down the station, high heels clicking, mackintosh belted, briefcase strap snug on her shoulder.

It was a bright, October morning. A threat of frost; perhaps she should have worn gloves. On her morning walk to the station, she saw the trees had already turned yellow in Cripton's town park.

Cripton was like a dozen other dormitory communities on London's outer rim – forty minutes by train to Liverpool Street Station, a High Street with a Boots, Sainsbury's, pubs with their faux antique fronts and flower boxes, a glassy shopping arcade with an atrium café. On the outskirts, a web of link roads, overpasses and roundabouts, schools, a library, shopping centres with their tarmacadamed car parks.

The town and the district council touted Cripton's reputation as a traditional market town with quality of life. Vibrant, they said, yet entirely independent of the clank and sprawl of London to the south.

Yet, here now were fifteen men and women, waiting for a London train already late, pacing like monks at their vespers.

She exchanged a can-you-believe-this look with a man in an anorak and too-large glasses. Almost time for her winter coat, except that, come lunchtime, the Indian summer would have her and everyone else sweating and shedding suit jackets inside their London offices.

The anorak man crooked his body away from her to answer a call on his mobile phone. 'Yes, yes; no, late again,' he said. He glanced down the tracks. 'Look, try and keep him there . . . can't be much longer . . . this blasted . . . British Snail, ha, ha, ha . . . Right. See you then.'

He dialled another number.

A headache throbbed at Susan's temples. Familiar, every morning for over a month now, ever since Gerald, her husband of twenty-three years, announced he was leaving her.

Announced was hardly right.

On a damp Tuesday in late August, he'd broached it over the spaghetti dinner she'd bought from the Italian delicatessen near the train station. Refilled his glass of Merlot and asked, 'So, what do you think about us splitting up, then?' As if it were a topic they had discussed last week and they were just now getting back to it.

No tears, of course, no ranting like someone on a soap opera or a chat show. And now, almost two months later, she couldn't remember the exact words that evening, just their stiff voices in their vaulted-ceiling kitchen.

They had not forced each other to admit anything too vicious, like that they had fallen out of love, had become housemates of a sort. They did not say that for months, years, their marital intimacy consisted of absent kisses on the cheek – she enquiring about his day in his upstairs home office; he if the London train was crowded.

Above all, they did not confess how tired they had grown of each other – not a petulant disenchantment, but, over the years, a slow retreat into their separate ends of the house.

After their evening dinners – always arranged by her via telephone from the train – he would go upstairs again to click away on his computer, while she went to their lounge with the French doors that looked out on the side garden. Absently, she would glance at the television as she leafed through memoranda, acquisitions proposals from iTemps, the chain of London employment agencies she co-owned with Anna, her business partner and best friend since university.

He presented her with quiet logic: *nothing acrimonious here, Suze, but really, hardly spent any time together*; separate holidays every summer, she was always so occupied with iTemps and Anna. Look, they even had separate friends.

She had not meant to be churlish, but in a seething, strangled voice she reminded him that he, Gerald, didn't have any friends – rather difficult when he sat caged upstairs in that office of his all day, surfing and e-mailing and chatting to so-called clients he built databases and e-commerce websites for. Were they the friends he had in mind? Or was it these imaginary friends of his in all these damn chatrooms?

And there, quite accidentally, she had stumbled upon Gerald's real reason for leaving.

Yes, he admitted, a touch defensively and breaking off a chunk of French bread. He had, in fact, met someone on-line, but not on-line *per se*. Of course, there'd been visits, coffees, wine bars, dinners – here. Gosh, not *here*, *here* – he laughed and waved a hand to take in their kitchen, the half-empty wine glasses, their crumpled serviettes – but in London, yes, and a weekend or two away. Brighton. Edinburgh. Cornwall. And now he . . . or rather, *they* . . . his friend – Alison was her name – well, they were giving things a shot. Had to. Surely she, Suze, could see that? These things, you know . . . Beastly to have regrets later . . .

Outside, the late summer light was fading over the privet hedges. The clematis had withered against the white painted trellises. Funny that, she thought. Mad but funny.

She asked if he could at least be discreet about this woman, not tell people where they'd met, or indeed, his real reason for leaving. Surely he could give her that?

'Who would I tell?' he asked, with the boyish, quizzical grin that had made her fall in love with him, and, through the years, made her support his string of cocksure business schemes.

'Daddy, Anna, people at my office, your sister . . .' She fluttered a hand, little twirling motions as if to crank out a jolly list of mutual friends, acquaintances, family.

He caught, steadied her hand. Like trapping a frantic bird. 'Of course not, Suze.' Here now was his most gallant expression, under which lurked his undisguised glee.

Gerald Whitaker was finally escaping Anna, his wife's bull-terrier business partner and meddling friend, plus the disapproving, tweedy father-in-law. The same father-in-law who, in fact, could disapprove of nothing now, except to slurp his rice puddings at the Manor, a country nursing home for Alzheimer's patients with money or private insurance or both.

Oh no, thank you very much, the face across the table from her said, *won't miss those one bit.*

Now, these post-Gerald days were numbing, a distracted busyness that was almost enjoyable, punctuated by her morning and evening train journey. Each day, work, teleconferences, meetings. Anna or Peter, the iTemps marketing director, insisted on some cheer-Susan-up lunches. Over plates of risotto or penne pasta, they coaxed and coached her. Absolutely no way that Gerald should get a fifty-fifty split; after all, hadn't she, Susan, been the breadwinner?

She laughed, fobbed them off. Yes, yes of course she was going to stand her ground.

But the truth was that Susan Brown Whitaker was too exhausted, too headachy from sleeplessness and late-night glasses of wine to quibble with Gerald's relentless e-mails and telephone calls. Every night, a message on her answering machine saying that the last thing he wanted to do was rush her, but . . . look, where did things stand with their house? Any punters? Another trilling message from the estate agent saying how much that day's couple had loved it; loved what they'd done with the bedroom, the en suite, but . . . of course, still looking, shopping.

Alone again in her office or on the evening train, she knew she would apportion the house – three gardens, a shed – into the simplest things: pounds sterling. Half for you and half for me.

The anorak man was on his mobile phone again. A finger in one ear to block out the racket from the building site across the street – warehouses mutating into luxury flats. Clink of metal on metal. The rat-tat-tat of a jackhammer.

Every morning this summer these builders had appeared like rock climbers among the scaffoldings and rooftops. A sign was pasted on the newly concreted walls: *Railroad Place, luxury one- and two-bedroom flats.* A telephone number to view the model unit. Pre-order your home like a takeaway pizza.

It was the builders and property developers, she thought acidly. The builders and not the marriage counsellors or psychologists of England who knew the ins and outs of late 1990s marriages. Knew that people like her and Gerald would just wear each other out, trade in lives, homes, trade down to the bright-eyed, the young and the eager.

And there they were – tanned young men in jeans and hard hats, ready and waiting with your new, après-divorce nest.

She walked back up the platform. Behind her throbbing temples, an idea was forming. She stood to read the Christmas Career Expo poster again. *Come for the craic.*

At iTemps she saw them come and go, these Celtic Tiger Irish – computer mercenaries – trendy young creatures who answered their mobile phones during employment interviews, turned their Irish accents on and off as the need arose.

Everything Irish was hot these days – that ridiculous Riverdance thing that played for God knows how long in Hammersmith, the plays in the West End, the Hollywood films with those Northern Irish men with the brutish, relentless accents.

She could, she supposed, claim some Irishness herself. Well not really, but Daddy's father had had a stint over there as some sort of land agent – caretaker – on a country estate for a distant cousin landlord. Left wife and child in the family house in Kent, went haring off to hunt foxes, collect land rents in some godforsaken place. Batty, people said, completely mad when he came back in 1922 when the Irish no longer needed caretakers or land agents.

Where was that estate? Perhaps she'd ask Daddy on her next visit to the Manor. God knows he didn't remember much else these days. The distant past. That's what the nurses kept telling her. History more real for him than the present.

She bit her lower lip.

Years ago, at Newbury Academy for Girls, the head-mistress used to say this habit made her look too pensive. Unpleasant.

Anyway, the Irish estate was probably a tourist hotel now. Or a housing estate with semi-detacheds, a playground and allotments.

Up and down the platform, people were hastily terminating mobile telephone calls, clicking laptops shut and leaving their benches to hurry across for the approaching train.

She found a pen in the front pocket of her briefcase. Scribbled the number for the career expo on the back of a Visa receipt. December 29. She wouldn't bring anyone from the marketing department. Host the iTemps booth herself. Fly over a few days early. Perhaps even look up that estate where her grandfather was land agent.

That was the thing about divorce, wasn't it? Come Christmas, birthdays, no place to be. The last child left uncollected from the school playground. Conspicuous. An object of pity.

She settled into her usual seat, loosened her mackintosh belt, propped the briefcase on her lap. The benches and the waiting room slid away behind. Here came the converted warehouses and the builders halfway up into the sky.

She retrieved her pen, found the Visa receipt again and wrote down the Railroad Place telephone number as the cat's cradle of girders and scaffoldings slid out of sight.

Chapter 3

'Lotto,' Mannion said, staring at the telly on its high shelf behind O'Neill's pub counter.

The four men had just arrived – always the same time, same bar stools each afternoon. Four fresh pints of stout.

Mannion, bald, always kept his tweed cap on. Sweeney, always on the stool nearest the door, had taken to wearing a white, gabardine hat which the other three sniggered at and said it was something like you'd see on a fisherman or a Yank. Walsh had a sweep of grey hairs that fanned out across his bald spot. O'Brien had raven-black hair, which everyone around Rathloe parish knew was dyed. Ridiculous, they said behind his back, pure lunacy a man dyeing his hair this hour of his life, when the whole parish knew his exact age anyway.

'For a fact I heard lotto,' Mannion persisted. 'Within in the hotel in town.'

Kitty O'Neill was arranging cans of lager in the tall fridge at the other end of the bar. Sweeney, O'Brien and Walsh kept staring at a repeat of *Here's Lucy*. Long ago, they'd given up begging for the telly sound to be turned up.

'Enough blaring tellies throughout this country, in every hotel, pub, and sitting room,' Kitty always said. 'Kills conversation.' The chat and the laugh, she said; these were the mainstay of the pub business.

'That's what I heard anyways,' Mannion broke the silence again, this time with a wink and twitch of the head as if he were propositioning Lucille Ball. 'After the mart in Ballyshee last Thursday. A known fact that this fella bought the big house and the land below with his English lotto winnings.'

Surmising, theorising about land purchases, exact acreage and prices had become a daily topic for the foursome.

On the side and main roads around Rathloe, an unfamiliar car would appear of a Saturday or Sunday in a farmer's roadside gap. A young man or couple would be sighted striding after a surveyor or estate agent, window-shopping for a housing site in a field that nobody had even known was up for sale.

They came and went then, these blow-ins, all biz with excavating, digging, builders' sand heaps and waterpipes. Before the villagers' eyes, it seemed to appear: a high, shiny house, dormer windows, balconies, Australian gateways, a landscaped garden with rain-ravaged palm trees.

The twenty-mile drive to Galway City was nothing, these newcomers said, nothing at all compared to the gridlock of Dublin, Cork or Limerick. And country schools. Who could beat the pupil–teacher ratio out the country?

Native sons and daughters had also returned from a stint in Dublin, New York, London, Toronto. Back now with a spouse or live-in lover, a house built on a father's or grandfather's land, from which they emulated the city or suburban life they'd left behind.

'Sure, how the hell . . . ?' the four men would ask around O'Neill's pub counter. 'That miserable *fieldín* is never worth that . . . A fool and their money . . .'

Last month, September, when Tierney the estate agent's sign had appeared among the briars above the big house wall, all land-purchase debates were escalated. Every afternoon the four surmised, argued, relayed tidbits about the future of the big house land.

A housing estate for young families with fifty semi-detacheds and a big playground, Sweeney heard.

A retirement village for people from England and up the north, Walsh and Mannion countered.

A picnic area and petting zoo, O'Brien offered. All theories were dead-cert facts.

But then came the sightings: cars, vans, men and women trudging across the best twenty-five acres in Rathloe with that Tierney fellow leading the way, or helping some fancy-looking woman to climb through that old demesne stile.

But now, late October, the news was out: a tall lad. McHugh, a returned Paddy from England. Seen this past week coming and going to the big, high gates in a Volvo stationwagon with English number plates.

Money to burn, Margaret O'Neill reported to her twin sister, Kitty, over their nightly cup of cocoa when their respective businesses – Kitty's pub and Margaret's village supermarket – were closed up for the night. Both premises were painted a matching, bright lavender with a deeper purple trim. Buy in bulk, the sisters always said. Cheaper. Handier.

Margaret reported that McHugh had bought the world of toothpaste, bathroom and kitchen cleaners, bread, cheeses, sausages, washing-up liquid, and an expensive duck liver pâté that a salesman had left as a free sample. And, the story went, he didn't blink an eye or haggle over the weekly rental price for his tourist cottage on the Ballyshee road. Oh, and dressed like Astor's pet horse.

'Must have been a big win,' Mannion gave it one last try.

Kitty slapped the fridge door shut. 'Arrah, will ye

give over, lads,' she said. 'Look, wherever he got his money, he got it and bought the big house and land and that's that.'

Sweeney turned his gaze from the telly and said coyly, 'A lad within in the barber's was telling me, knew someone that was a neighbour of McHugh's above in Carraig.' He turned back to the telly.

They waited. Sweeney always made them wait. Loved tormenting them.

'They say there was nothing in the world as greedy as him beyond in London: houses, flats, shops – 'tisn't known all he bought . . . left nothing for anyone else . . .'

'Will you shut up!' Kitty hissed at him. Sweeney flinched. Nettled. Hated to be interrupted. And abuse where he spent his hard-earned money.

'Look, I just—' he started.

But Kitty was already around the counter and crossing to the pub window, her slippers padding against the floorboards.

A Volvo stationwagon had turned into the car park. A spray of pebbles against the beer barrels outside. Sweeney, Mannion, O'Brien and Walsh angled on their stools for a better view.

'In the flesh, lads.' Sweeney thumped the counter. 'The iceman bloody cometh.'

McHugh stooped his tall frame in the doorway.

Safely back behind the counter again, Kitty had a white linen tea towel slung over her shoulder, her sweetest smile ready.

'Afternoon.' McHugh nodded to the men.

They kept watching *Here's Lucy*.

'Mr McHugh, isn't it?' Kitty shook hands over the counter. 'You're heartily welcome to Rathloe. Not a bad evening now for October, the last of it, I suppose. Oh sure, nothing ahead now but the winter evenings drawing in, but sure, I suppose that's the way it goes, isn't it, good with the bad, we have to take it the way the man above sends it, isn't that the only way to say it?'

'Yes, keeping mild enough,' McHugh said, a puzzled look on the face. 'Not much doing up at the shop today, then?'

Kitty stared at him. Then a coquettish, high laugh. 'Oooh, Mr McHugh, I bet you thought I was Margaret. Ha, ha, ha, ha. Oh, 'tis many's the wan thinks I'm Margaret above and that Margaret is me.'

McHugh stared at the sixty-something barmaid: high, hairsprayed hair, blue eyeshadow, arched, pencilled eyebrows, a high-necked blouse.

'Twins. Identical, like. Since we were born. I'm Kitty. Hee, hee, hee. Now, what'll it be there?'

'A pint of lager, thanks.'

The men watched as he peeled a twenty-pound note from a leather wallet. 'Cheers, Kitty. One for yourself? For the bin?'

'How do you mean, like?' Kitty's face, eyes, simmered with suspicion. Throw good beer in the bin?

He shrugged. 'Just something they say in England. Buying the landlady a drink, that's all. For later on, when she's finished work.'

'Oooh, well thanks very much.' The smile was back. 'Arrah, I never touch it, really. Better off without it at my age, or that's what they maintain anyways, on the telly and in the magazines, like, though a person has to have something, I suppose, or life wouldn't be worth living at all.'

She counted out his change, 'Now, five, ten and two pounds . . . Lovely. Poke up the fire over there and throw on a bit of coal for yourself. Evenings turning coolish enough.'

The four men glowered. Jesus! Kitty O'Neill was ever

full of oul' chat, especially when there was money to be made. Bord bloody Fáilte herself.

Mannion shunted his bar stool to the right so he could watch McHugh in a bar mirror. There he was, tucked into the lounge seat beside the fireplace, the *Irish Times* spread open, the long oul' legs like two pokers.

'Gentleman Jim on his throne,' he muttered to the other three.

Kitty shot them a look.

Sweeney raised his eyes to heaven.

Oh, he'd seen it all now in this parish of Rathloe. Bad enough that you'd all these young blow-ins snapping up land and building on top of your big toe. And half of them never seen up in the church of a Sunday, except for christenings and communions when they appeared in a flurry of designer outfits and zoom-lens cameras.

His own son, Richie, had moved back two years ago with his wife, Claire, and two kids. Richie was an engineer now with the county; Claire some sort of network administrator above in Galway, whatever the dickens that was.

Yet, when it came to a house, Sadie, Sweeney's wife, had tormented her husband with 'poor Richie this' and 'poor Richie that' until at last Sweeney had to hand over a fine bit of land on the Rathloe–Galway road for a building site. Guff about passing things down and family heritage. Not a red penny in Sweeney's own pocket while the rest of the country was cleaning up.

And now, here was this English Paddy, aping the big shot with his newspaper and big car.

'I knew plenty of his likes when I was over there myself,' he said to the other three.

In the 1950s, Sweeney had had a brief stint in London. Interrupted when his late father got sick and he was

summoned home to Rathloe to take over the Sweeney
land.

He said, 'Musha, a lot of them lads are nothing
but—'

A high-pitched ringing came from the fireplace.
Mannion edged his stool down even further, angled,
craned his neck for a better view in the bar mirror. But
the curiosity had got the better of O'Brien and Walsh,
so they swivelled around towards the fire. McHugh
reached into his jacket pocket and flipped open the
smallest phone they'd ever seen.

'Hello?' McHugh said. 'Uh-huh. Right-e-o. Yes, I see.'
The head was nodding, long, delicate fingers around
the toy phone. 'Well, can't you take care of it? You
know I trust your judgement, Jimmy. Two hundred and
twenty-five thousand? Uh-huh. Yeah. Highish, don't
you think? For what it is. Do what you can and let me
know, then. But . . . look, I can be over there tomorrow
afternoon if things get . . . Right. Yes, yes a lot to be
done here. Bit of a shambles . . . What? Well, just give
us a shout then.' He clicked the phone shut and faced
the jury of four staring men. 'Everyone here all right
with that, then?'

A great shuffle of boots, wellingtons, stools scraping
off the wooden floor as the four whipped back around.
Suddenly, O'Brien pointed up at the telly, let out a
purposeful, screeching laugh at Lucille Ball typing a
letter in an office.

'Pup,' Sweeney said, loud enough to be heard down
at the fire.

Kitty shot him a look.

Sweeney ignored her. His eyes were narrowed.

Walsh looked sheepish. Mannion sneaked a look at
O'Brien.

Oh, they knew this mood of Sweeney's, all right.
Never a man to be crossed.

Chapter 4

Ever since he retired from the town library four years ago, Johnny Monahan's life had settled into a pleasant routine: mass on Sundays at Rathloe church, chairman of the church grounds committee, and every afternoon he and his brother, Micheál, left their cottage just south of Rathloe to walk into O'Neill's supermarket to see how the rest of the world was faring.

Every Thursday, Johnny's daffodil-yellow Mini Minor nudged out through their yard gates onto the Rathloe road, slowing before the turn at the end of the village, then off into Ballyshee. In town, the brothers renewed their library books, stopped at the chemist's for toiletries, the hardware shop for coal and, in the summertime, gardening supplies and border plants. At half four on the dot, they retired to the lounge of the Hermitage Hotel on Main Street for their afternoon tea.

Every August, the yellow Mini Minor made the journey to a seaside B&B in Sligo, where the landlady welcomed them royally, and never raised her voice or spoke extra slowly at Micheál, the way people often do with the simple-minded. Indeed, she treated him no differently from her other summertime guests, and, for this, Johnny felt eternal gratitude.

There were weeks, even months, when Johnny could almost forget his family secret, let it fade among the rhythm of their days in their cottage and gardens set back from the main Rathloe–Galway road. Sometimes he deliberately put his secret away, like hiding something in the back of a drawer.

Over the years there had been bitter reminders, incidents that left Johnny fretting and wondering if, like nearly everything else around this parish, people already knew every dark, hidden thing about the two Monahan brothers.

A Thursday afternoon three years ago, the brothers had settled in for their tea at the Hermitage Hotel. It was cattle-mart day. That morning the usual cars, tractors, cattle jobbers' lorries had rattled through Ballyshee's streets on their way to the low, concrete building just north of the town. By afternoon, the clatter of gates, cattle trailers and the tinny, amplified auctioneer's voice could still be heard all the way up on Main Street.

Five men were sitting at the Hermitage bar – jaunty in their overcoats, ties and pinstriped suit trousers stuffed into oversized wellingtons. Through the town shops, pubs, streets and alleyways they carried the whiff of cattle, cowdung, feedstuffs. The two men at the end had propped their blackthorn sticks against the counter as if they were auditioning for some stage-Irish theatre production.

In their usual lounge seats by the fire, the Monahans were letting their tea draw in its white porcelain pot, and, as his Micheál had never much cared for mustard, Johnny was fastidiously spreading mayonnaise on his brother's toasted ham sandwich.

With each round of drink, the men at the counter grew more uproarious. They discussed cattle prices, the rise and fall; politics, the morality and social responsibility of politicians above in Dublin, the demise of Church and priestly influence in small places such as the parishes they themselves had left that morning. One man began a rambling, hilarious story about a timely retort made to an overbearing parish priest. A man with a greasy, checked cap snorted in amusement.

The two men with the blackthorn sticks beckoned the young barman for another round and, while their pints of porter were settling, they went in search of a Gents' toilet, thucking across the flowered lounge carpet in their wellingtons.

Afterwards, Johnny Monahan would remember the hopsy smell of fresh drink, a stench of cowdung as the men stopped at the Monahans' lounge seats. He would recall the bloodshot eyes, glowering, seething with dev-ilment. But mostly he would remember his brother: a happy, simpleton's face suddenly furrowed with terror, as if his brother could sniff impending badness.

'*Gaimses*,' the first man said. He thumped the end of his stick against the floor. 'Fuckin' imbeciles, the both of ye.'

The second one eyed Johnny's neat, grey suit, the starched shirt and the paisley bow tie he always wore to town. 'Queer as a fuckin' nine-pound note,' he said. 'Bent as a fuckin' hairpin.'

The two men laughed. A hail of warm saliva in Johnny's face. The men at the counter screeched and sniggered.

The first man teetered backwards slightly, then stead-ied himself to lean on his blackthorn stick. He was posed as if for a vaudeville song or recitation. 'The bad drop,' he announced to his friends, the red velvet lounge seats, the fireplace, the embossed wallpaper. 'Me father, God rest him, always said, "a man is just like a horse," he said, there's them with breeding and those without. There's them with the bad drop in them . . . there's purebreds and then . . .' He leaned closer to the brothers, 'There's fuckin' mongrels.'

The other man slapped his thigh delightedly. 'The bad drop,' he chorused. 'Makes nothing but pansies and imbeciles.'

The two men trooped off then, out into the tiled corridor in search of a Gents' toilet.

Johnny was twenty-two and in his first librarian job in Dublin when his father died. John Senior was a tall, broad-shouldered man with wavy black hair, who, in Johnny's memory, did everything fast: wolfed down his midday dinner, clattered his cutlery against the plate, a heavy tread across the kitchen floor, a slap of the back door.

Johnny had loved his late mother, Gretta, with a deep unquestioning devotion. What was there not to love? And when he prayed to her now at night, he never invoked the image of a frail, dying young woman, but the beautiful mother she was – before her sickness. To this day he could picture her winding a bobbin of thread for a new dress, or reaching to brush back a lock of his or Micheál's hair and saying, 'Surely, no mother in Ireland has been blessed with such fine little gentlemen?'

His parents' wedding portrait still hung above the parlour sideboard, and it always reminded Johnny of that black-and-white King Kong film – a huge, dark-haired man looming over a young bride with laughing eyes.

When Johnny was thirteen and Micheál seven, Gretta died in a tuberculosis sanitorium. He could remember the funeral – neighbouring women who wept, lamented that never was there such a lovely woman, a fine family in the parish of Rathloe. He remembered the wake, the house full of loud talk, the clink of whiskey glasses, the relations, friends, men who played cards with his father on Saturday nights.

Tuberculosis was the scourge of Rathloe and other parishes in the 1940s. The Monahan house was not exempt, and after her diagnosis the marital bedroom had to be scrubbed, her bed thrown out, the cottage reeked of sulphur for days. He remembered the day Gretta his mother was transferred to a sanatorium by the sea. 'Just a little holiday, a touch of sea air for old Mum,' she'd said. Back in no time to her two fine little gentlemen.

At the sanatorium, Gretta told Johnny the secret that would haunt him to this day.

Her mother, his dead grandmother, had been sent as a servant girl to Rathloe House when the big house was still in its heyday. She was just sixteen, a refined girl, could cook and sew anything.

His grandmother, Gretta told him on that awful day, her face dwarfed on the starched sanatorium pillow, worked in the big house for this agent, an Englishman – not even the real landlord, everybody said, but an agent, a fellow who couldn't tell the difference between night and day, roamed around the demesne, the orchards and gardens half the night, then slept by day. And oh! Those around Rathloe parish who took advantage, bigger farmers who sublet to those poorer than them, but reneged on their own land rents. Nobody was easier to bamboozle than this agent fellow, a Richard Brown.

In the end, during the Troubles or civil war, he was rarely seen at all, holed up in the big house, terrified for his life, until he returned for good to England.

Gretta's mother worked in the house for two years. At eighteen she was sent home again – pregnant, expecting the agent's own child. Oh! it wasn't uncommon, not uncommon at all. A well-known fact that these men, lonely, irascible creatures – there were stories, rumours about others in near and faraway places, further north in Mayo, in Roscommon, Galway – employed the prettiest, the most refined girls, then subjected them to lust.

Nobody knew, Gretta told the thirteen-year-old Johnny. Nobody must know. For wasn't it easy to let on that she, Gretta, the baby of this unseemly union, was a sister, not a daughter to her mother? For hadn't the twins, Johnny's uncles, been born only four years earlier? And here now was a little sister for them, a little girl with lively eyes.

Did Johnny even understand it that day, standing at his mother's deathbed inside the high, cavernous windows with their view of the sea? In the fifty-six years since, did he ever fully understand about fathers and grandfathers and a family's vigilant secrecy?

On that day, he'd blinked back boyish tears, told himself that it was this room with its disinfectant smell, the stark whiteness of it, the ghostly emptiness of its corridors.

It wasn't until he was studying for a scholarship to the university at the Christian Brothers school in Ballyshee, swotting history, dates, land wars, that it became real for him, a story, a picture in his head. The Monahan brothers had a grandfather – a half-grandfather – someplace in England. The man was probably dead by then.

Sometimes when he drove past Rathloe House, especially when the winter trees revealed the high windows, he would find himself replaying his mother's story. Inside which window did it happen? Were the shutters closed that night? Was it at night? Perhaps during the day, when this Englishman slept, hibernated like a bear or a fox in preparation for his nocturnal prowls. Had Johnny's grandmother, in some girlish way, fancied some affection from the older man? What had he said – with deliberate, rounded vowels the way English people do – to inveigle a girl into his arms, his bed? There they were, these thoughts buzzing around in Johnny's mind.

Sometimes after Micheál was tucked up in bed, Johnny would sit by the fire in their parlour and watch the dying flames quiver and flicker against the diamond-paned windows, the framed photographs on the walls, the two china dogs on the mantelpiece. At this hour, they became the same girl, his mother and grandmother, one frightened young woman for another, cowering in the shadows of a high house.

Chapter 5

'No, no. Absolutely not,' McHugh said into his mobile. He was sitting at the Formica table in his rental cottage. The table was strewn with new phone books, papers, a pocket calendar, a Sunday newspaper, pamphlets from the Department of Agriculture. 'Sorry, don't work that way, Mr O'Connor. No paying by the hour. Come and give me a quote for the job or nothing.'

O'Connor Brothers' Excavation was the fourth company he'd called. The others either hadn't returned his messages or complained about the too-short notice.

"Tell me, will you be on the job or the premises yourself the whole time, like?' Joe O'Connor asked on the other end.

McHugh didn't answer.

'Ah . . . hello?' O'Connor's voice grew nervous.

'Ye-es.'

'Oh, I thought you were gone off there for the bit of Sunday dinner or something. D'you know it's Sunday, Mr McHugh?'

McHugh looked out at the grey skies, the rain spitting against the cottage window.

'Look, Mr O'Connor . . . Yes, yes, I do know it's Sunday. And yes, I will be on the job. I have to tell you I believe in running a tight ship—'

'A ship? Ha, ha, ha. Didn't I think 'twas a bit of land you were after buying,' O'Connor said. McHugh knew this game. Take him down a peg or two. Lambast him with this glorious, west of Ireland wit.

'Ah . . . h-hello? Mr McHugh?'

'Yes?'

'Oh, you're there. Listen, ah, what time in Rathloe tomorrow so? They're promising more showers in the morning I see.'

'Eight o'clock.'

Silence. Then, 'London you're home from, is it?'

'Thank you, Mr O'Connor.' McHugh clicked his phone off. Tilted the kitchen chair back to switch on the gas cooker under the kettle.

He'd never had so much tea as in the past two weeks – a damn compunction more than a beverage. He thought of films, news clips – policemen waiting for news of kidnap victims, distraught families in hospital waiting rooms – drinking tea, smoking, waiting. What was he waiting for, then? Things to happen: land excavated, seeded, export beef cattle, foundation dug for his house.

He switched on a floor lamp in the corner. The light glowed off the whitewashed walls, made shadows on the slanted ceilings of his loft bedroom – for the tourists, the real Irish cottage and all that. Last night's ashes were still in the fireplace, his coat still slung across the back of a brown plaid couch, more papers and pamphlets on the cheap coffee table.

Suddenly, he longed for his own flat near Notting Hill – the spacious order of his high, pale rooms, the predictability of Sunday afternoons. Back there, time became muted, manageable among the leafy, Victorian streets.

He checked the round, green alarm clock on the mantel. Just gone three. Back there – should he call it home? – he would have had someplace to be: a matinee in the West End, or a languorous brunch with fresh-ground coffee and the Sunday newspapers with one of his Saturday-night dates.

Not this blasted cramped bleakness, his suitcase still half unpacked under the eaves of his loft bedroom. Living like a damn refugee back in his own country.

The kettle steamed. He emptied old tea leaves down the tiny sink, poured water into a battered aluminium teapot.

Stop, he told himself. Temporary. All temporary until things got going – scrub, briars, bushes pulled up by the roots, stones hauled away, new grass, his new house on the demesne. He poured the tea. Sick of its strong, tannic smell.

London you're home from, is it? He recalled Joe O'Connor's voice. Patronising. Smug.

Derision. It was everywhere in London when he'd arrived at Euston Station in 1964, raw and exhausted from the Dublin boat, five hours on the train from Holyhead. His landlady in Shepherd's Bush who made them take off their boots inside the front door; the woman in the corner shop. 'You'll 'ave to speak up love. Pint of milk and wha' else?' On the tube home from the building site, the girls with their wet-look mini skirts and Beatle boots avoided his eyes. Older Englishwomen with their shopping bags and poodles – he felt them recoiling from his smell, the concrete on his boots, trousers, his cement-raw hands.

When he was holidaying with some woman on a Caribbean island, or at a London black-tie charity do, suddenly there they were: those 1960s memories. On the building sites, the gaffer roared like a bull, the other Irish lads sniggering, waiting for their chance to bamboozle, get one over. They were like boys in an orphanage, twittering, plotting, muttering over their lunchtime sandwiches and cigarettes. He could picture the scaffoldings against a winter sky, hear the thump-thump of men's boots across half-finished roofs, floorboards, the crank and shudder of cement mixers, jackhammers, pickaxes. And all the chat and *craic* – how many days, hours until payday, the pub and dances on Friday, Saturday nights; off home to th'oul sod for the Christmas holidays. Hangovers and sexual bravado on Monday mornings.

It had all sickened him. The lads knew it. He arrived neat as a pin every morning, his flask of tea, homemade sandwiches, stayed sitting on a rooftop to eat his lunch, aloof and apart. They mocked him, nicknames. The sour resentment of men who feel betrayed by their own kind.

He turned down all their invitations for the pub – McGinty's, the Irish Rose, the Blackthorn. Even the names sickened him. Instead, he went home every evening to his bedsit in Shepherd's Bush, set himself a perfect tea table inside his third-storey window, read the *Guardian* and ate beans on toast, poured himself English tea from a china teapot. On Fridays, he treated himself to a grilled steak on his two-ring cooker, spent Saturday and Sunday mornings studying for his A level exams.

On weekend afternoons he took the Tube – random, unplanned trips: Bayswater, Kensington, Highgate, Hammersmith, Hounslow. Turn left or right out of the Underground station to roam through unfamiliar streets. Looking for something.

It was a Saturday in early spring when he found it: a 'For Sale' sign outside a grotty house on the fringes of a pleasant, middle-class area.

He withdrew everything from his savings.

All that summer he worked on the house: evenings after work, Saturdays, Sundays, enlisted some serious young Irish lads just arrived off the boat, paid them time and a half, hammered and sawed until just before the last Tube home.

He finished before deadline: airy one-bedroom flats, serious renters only, no smokers, references, first and last week's rent, one late rent brought an eviction notice.

After that, it was a two-up, two-down in Kilburn, two more houses in Camden Town, converted lofts, a paint factory, a warehouse turned into chic apartments, shops, multi-use timeshares in Brighton.

He assembled his own, hand-picked building crew – blacks, Spaniards, Irish, Yorkshiremen, Welshmen, Scotsmen – paid them above the going wage, two weeks' paid at Christmas and summer, but ten minutes late, slack off on the job once, and they collected their last pay packet that Friday.

His tea had grown cold. Perhaps this O'Connor fellow was right. A spot of Sunday dinner would lift this gloom – something plain but nicely done, a bottle of good Cabernet. That hotel in the town – Ballyshee. All the British travel articles were raving these days about the new Irish restaurants with their organic goat's cheese salads and wild salmon dishes.

Too late to drive up to Carraig to his brother, Seamus's. They'd telephoned, of course, him and Rita. Wouldn't he come for tea, stay the night? They hadn't seen him since he'd been home. Only right a returned emigrant would want to come and see the old homestead. Something testy in his brother and sister-in-law's voices on the phone. Resentful. The prodigal brother comes home to play pretend farmer.

He leafed through his phone book and dialled. It rang and rang. A woman answered breathlessly. No, they don't open until four anyways, when their barman comes on duty, and even then it's just à la carte on Sundays, or maybe a toasted sandwich in the bar. Would that fit the bill? Had he far to travel? Bad oul' day out, wasn't it?

He emptied the last of his tea down the sink. Zipped

up his coat, searched for a cap among the couch cushions. He would walk into the Hermitage Hotel in Ballyshee, shake off this crankiness, this feeling of yawning, empty gloom. A carafe of wine, a hot sandwich; get another Sunday paper.

He lifted the latch on the emerald-green painted door, crunched across the short, gravel path and turned right for the town.

The light was fading over the fields, the winter bushes like giant dandelion clocks against the sky.

Chapter 6

Susan slammed the car door and walked up the curved driveway towards the Tudor-style house. The pale, November sun made it look pleasant – white walls, wood trim, curtains drawn back neatly.

The matron had telephoned from the Manor yesterday. Crazily, Susan thought the woman knew about Susan's news already. Calling to warn, admonish: please don't upset your poor father. Please tell him about your impending divorce gently, properly or better yet, not at all. But all the woman wanted was to ask if Susan could bring Daddy's winter wardrobe – that is, if Mrs Whitaker intended coming down to visit this Saturday. Sweaters for these chilly evenings, and pyjamas – no more than two of each. Choices. Can't give them choices. Well . . . they just confuse . . . So, could Mrs Whitaker please bring some things? His own, naturally. Not new. All the better if he has some comfy favourites. Important to keep things familiar.

The front lawns had been raked, leaves and branches carted away.

She never thought of it as her house. Couldn't. It wasn't anyway, except on a signed piece of paper in a Hargrove solicitor's office. In a day, an afternoon of lucidity last June, Daddy had insisted. Wordlessly, she'd driven him down there, no words exchanged about what they both knew but couldn't, wouldn't say aloud.

41

He would not be coming back here. And yet, here it stood now, the brass door knocker polished and shiny. Everything in perfect order as if someone had just slipped out, gone down the shops in Hargrove village.

Susan had kept on Mrs Lawson, Daddy's cleaning woman from the village who came faithfully to dust, air out rooms. On Fridays, Mrs Lawson's husband came and cranked up lawn mowers, hedge trimmers, meticulously clipped and pruned in gardens front and back.

Last month, Susan had sent a gift voucher for a restaurant with their fortnightly cheque. Guilt money. Keep my father's house looking trim and lived-in. Sane.

A thing. That was how she'd come to think of it, this Alzheimer's. There Daddy was, walking to his mahogany office at Hargrove General Hospital every morning, or summoning a car to Heathrow to fly off for another symposium, a three-month lectureship at an American university. But there *it* was, lurking, waiting, marking time. Then pounce.

She turned the key in the front door. The house still smelled of bleach and disinfectant – from last spring and winter when he still lived here. When home-care nurses came and went – foreign young women whom Susan sometimes met on Saturday mornings with owlish, sleepless eyes, weary of trailing Dr Brown through the house, the gardens at ridiculous hours of the night. Yes, and scrubbing up after him when he opened kitchen and scullery cupboards to pee among the mops, brushes.

In the lounge, a Persian rug in the middle of the wood floor – vivid reds and blues, his leather armchair angled towards the wide fireplace. A black, antique fireguard with an etching of a peacock. House plants in the front windowsill – watered, dead foliage snipped – begonias, hyacinths, a potted red geranium. Under the window, a massive brown leather couch with satiny cushions. On either side of the fireplace, built-in bookshelves – old, heavy volumes up top: anthologies, medical texts. On the lower shelves, novels, travel guides, the collected poems of Thomas Hardy, biographies of Churchill, Lloyd George.

Framed photos stared back at her from the shelves – Daddy receiving awards, handsome face, wry smile, hospital functions with tweedy colleagues. Snapshots with him in sunglasses, bright golf shirts, shorts – his tan dark against the elegant white hair, the same, tanned woman on his elbow in each photo. Indonesia, Florence, Barbados, Zanzibar. Since he moved to Hargrove fifteen years ago, he took two or three holidays a year, not counting work tours.

Here were Susan and Anna, her business partner. Nineteen-seventies pageboy haircuts and high-necked, frilly blouses. She had the same photo at home – or at least, wrapped and taped up in a box and waiting for her move next week. She remembered: the snapshot was taken on opening day at their first iTemps office. They looked young, rather daft really, like two women from a Penelope Keith comedy.

There was a teabag in the kitchen sink. An upturned mug in the dish rack. It made her oddly glad, knowing that Mrs Lawson enjoyed her cup of tea while here. Some life in the house.

In an upstairs airing cupboard she found the pyjamas – flannel stripes, all newish, two still in Selfridges Cellophane. She carried them across to the master bedroom.

Still the whiff of cleaning fluid, bleach. In his armoire, navy-blue blazers with gold buttons, dress shirts starched and dry-cleaned. Dressing gowns – a white terrycloth with a hotel crest and name above the pocket, his and hers matching silk kimonos.

In the bottom drawers she found two V-neck Pringle sweaters, both embroidered with 'Hargrove Country Club' and two crossed golf clubs. They would have to do. She could shop for cardigans next week. Old men's cardigans.

It was a sunny room, pea-green walls, deep beige carpet. His shoes lined up under the window – sandals, runners, golf shoes, hand-stitched leather dress shoes.

More framed photographs above the bed. She swallowed. Mummy and him sitting in the grass, a picnic cloth spread out in front of them; Mummy with her legs folded under her. Twenty-four, twenty-five at the most. A shirt-waist dress, small, pert face, a red lipstick smile like a World War II photo. There was an official portrait of the three of them, the colours slightly faded – a parents' day at Newbury Academy for Girls; Susan in her V-neck, school sweater, a navy-blue tie, face in a twelve-year-old pout. Mummy at her back, one hand on her daughter's shoulder. Daddy handsome, perfect posture.

She remembered the morning when the housemistress came for her – escorted her down the tiled corridors to the headmistress's office. What misdemeanour was thirteen-year-old Susan Brown guilty of? Cheekiness in the refectory? Her French marks had been down this term.

Mummy dead. Brain tumour. Unimaginable until the car came for her, a little suitcase the housemistress helped her pack stowed in the boot, then whisked through the gloomy, dark afternoon, the fading light over trees, fields, towns. Then Mummy's funeral at a small, drafty church in Kent – old cousins she'd never met before, a country servant woman who fussed over her and brought her cocoa.

Two days later, back again among the girls, the classrooms with the high windows, so that Mummy's death was something to put away – a nagging, guilty thing that only revisited at night in her dormitory or in dreams. Waiting until the Christmas holidays. It would become real when she was home.

She never went home that Christmas, but to a new house with a narrow garden outside hospital walls. A new medical posting in Gloucestershire, where their furniture looked odd in the unfamiliar rooms, like looking at a stranger in your own, favourite dress.

She knelt on Daddy's bed to look at the other photos – Mummy again, a petite, cheerful woman with a dusting of summertime freckles from gardening. Here she was at an outdoors luncheon on a patio, finger sandwiches, a high cake stand, Mrs Elizabeth Brown the doctor's wife in a lavender linen dress.

Susan crossed to the dressing table where she'd piled Daddy's things. The mirror told her that she had nothing of her mother's petite prettiness. Instead, Daddy's high cheekbones, his longish features, wispy hair and pale green eyes that gave her a translucent look.

Downstairs, she rummaged through the kitchen drawers for a bag for his things. Outside the kitchen window, a house sparrow sat on the holly bush – twittering, hopping, then disappeared under the eaves.

Chapter 7

The village woke to the grind and rattle of machinery. It trundled and bumped across the big house fields, high, mechanical arms rising above the walls, angling, dipping, rising. Buckets with jagged teeth swung and arched against a November sky, then swooped to the ground to scoop up old stones, clay, roots.

Young Rathloe families woke before daybreak; the children startled by the racket. Commuting mothers and fathers rushed their children through breakfast, drank a fast cup of tea, let the babysitter in, then backed their cars out of garages. It was two, three miles along the Galway road before they released their whitened grip on the steering wheel and slowly, gratefully relaxed to the morning DJ on the car radio.

At twelve o'clock on the dot the noise stopped. But this lunchtime reprieve only made it all the louder when it started up again on the dot of one. The older villagers clanked doors, windows shut. A scourge, the elder parishioners lamented. A scourge upon the whole bloody parish.

'Nothing but show if you ask me,' said Mrs Sadie Sweeney, standing in a group around Margaret O'Neill's supermarket checkout. 'Sure there was nothing wrong with that land below the way it was?'

'Ah, hold your horses, now, there Mrs Sweeney,' Mrs Babs Mannion said. 'Isn't this the kind of progress the whole country's after, has us all the way we are? Times never better.'

Bridgie Walsh, who, like the other three women, had a husband sitting at Kitty O'Neill's counter at this very moment, started to say something.

But Babs Mannion folded her arms across her huge bosom to add the final word: 'I heard within in the hairdressers' that this McHugh is building some class of a new-wave house. Every mod con. The likes of it, I heard, was and will never be seen around here—'

Sadie Sweeney persisted. 'But the racket, girls. The bloomin' racket, no let-up, and like, it's a pity to pull down . . .'

The two Monahan brothers had been foraging among the supermarket shelves, Micheál picking up packets of tea, biscuits, bathroom cleaner, and Johnny patiently reading each label to him.

Now they were finished and had come to stand at the edge of the women's foursome. His wire supermarket basket over his arm, Johnny pretended to read the headlines on the daily newspaper, for he couldn't let the women see that he was listening for the updates on Rathloe House.

Margaret O'Neill said, 'Ah, hello there, Johnny; sure I never saw you there at all. And Micheál. How are ye all keeping up your way?'

'Lovely, grand now, Miss O'Neill.' He nodded to each. 'Mrs Sweeney, Mrs Mannion, Mrs O'Brien and Mrs Walsh. Micheál, say "hello" to the nice ladies.'

Micheál grinned at them. They smiled back. Automatically, as if someone had pulled a puppet string in the backs of their necks.

'I'll take you here, Johnny,' Margaret O'Neill said, reaching past Babs Mannion for Johnny's basket. 'These ladies are all finished; we're just chattin', discussin' this how-do-ye-do below at the big house. Sure, I suppose ye can hear the racket up as far as your place, Johnny?'

'Ah, just a touch, Miss O'Neill. Just the touch. And sure, maybe 'twas meant to be . . . whatever it is this Mr McHugh likes to build for himself, sure who are we . . . ?'

The women eyed each other. Jesus! A little went a long way when it came to Johnny Monahan's old guff and sweet talk. Sure, the bloody man was like a nun.

Sadie Sweeney said, 'But he just barged in here, *all biz* and JCBs, and soon it'll be builders for this new house of his, and where the dickens will it all stop?'

Nobody answered. Sadie tightened the knot on her headscarf.

'Now ten pounds and fifty-eight pence there when you're ready, Johnny,' Margaret said, the hand out and waiting. Micheál was packing their groceries in a striped shopping bag.

'But perhaps . . .' Johnny said, but felt his cheeks grow hotter, the flush spreading to his whitened hairline.

The women waited.

'We-eell?' Babs said.

'Um . . . nothing,' Johnny said, dropping coins on the floor as he peeled Margaret's money from a wallet.

The women watched the brothers through the window. They stepped around the puddles in the supermarket car park, Micheál swinging the striped shopping bag.

'Ach sure, harmless as babies, the two of them,' Sadie Sweeney said.

Chapter 8

'Seems to be his favourite spot,' the weekend matron said, nodding to the wing chair by the bay window. The voice indulgent, as if Daddy were a mischievous house cat.

The woman had grey, shoulder-length hair and a flared, print dress to give a country, earthy look. A hand fluttered somewhere around Susan's shoulder. Solicitous, as if expecting the visiting daughter to bolt back down the polished wood corridor.

Around the drawing room were coffee tables with magazines. Paperback books on a shelf. It reminded Susan of a furniture showroom – contrived islands of homeliness, the chairs facing each other or the windows.

She avoided the other families' eyes – visiting wives with oversized handbags on their laps, all trussed up in their winter coats. Adult sons, daughters, a child with her legs swinging. Bored and trapped.

At the centre of each group, a Manor resident – important, according to the matrons, to call them residents, not patients – pallid faces above buttoned-up shirts; women with haunted eyes, stockinged legs obediently together.

She bent to kiss his cheek. 'Hello, Daddy.'

'Hello,' he said, turning from the window. The face animated as if someone had suddenly come up with a jolly little game. Someone had dressed him in his burgundy blazer with gold buttons, a matching tie with polka dots.

'Elizabeth,' he said, the smile determined, gleeful. Aunt Elizabeth had been dead for over twenty years.

'Susan, Daddy. Not . . . Elizabeth. I've come to visit. How are you, Daddy?' Her voice high, too shrill.

He blinked at her, frowned, turned back to the window.

She followed his gaze to the long, narrow garden with the perfectly sculpted hedges in the shape of people, teapots, animals. Topiary. A word she'd forgotten. Once, there was a topiary garden near one of Daddy's houses on a country road outside a university town.

She was nineteen, almost finished at university, and brought Gerald home for a weekend. After a Saturday lunch, she'd brought him for a walk, used the excuse of showing off the neighbour's topiary.

It was 1966. Free at last from Daddy's scrutiny – they were already living together in Earls Court – they gambolled along the country roads like children, mocking the bourgeois ridiculousness of the neighbour and his hedge teapots, giant birds, garden gnomes. In defiance of Daddy's imposed separate beds, Gerald had suggested sex behind someone's potting shed. Hurried. Giggling.

Now the memory rose and soured in her throat. She pictured Gerald's puffing, ejaculating face, not as a lover but like a little boy masturbating.

'I brought your things,' she said to Daddy, rustling the plastic duty-free bag, forcing them both back to this room with its hushed voices and huddled families. A tableau, she thought, a wax museum of the stricken and the dutiful.

He fingered the tissue paper. Stared at the pyjamas inside their Cellophaned packets.

'Selfridges, Daddy. A shop. A store. Very big.'
Befuddled. Resentful.

'Your V-necks,' she said, leaning towards him to pull
out the two Pringle wool sweaters. 'The matron said you
could choose.' She held them up with flourish. 'Red?
Yellow?'

She was a tourist in a foreign country, flinging random
words, names, things, willing this face across from her
to flicker with comprehension.

He was studiously peeling the tape off the pyjama
packet. She leaned towards him, cupped her hand over
his to stop him. 'Gerald has moved out.'

He unfolded the striped pyjama top. Long fingers
fussed, fluttered impatiently as he held it up against
him. Grinned at her over the buttoned-up collar. Another
game. He reached for the yellow sweater.

In a coaxing voice she said, 'Lovely. Good colour,
warmer for these nights. You remember Gerald, Daddy?
You two didn't like each other very much.' Gently, she
handed him the red sweater, took the pyjama top to fold
it back into its bag.

He had turned from her, lips moving as if in prayer,
eyes fixed on the window panes, the garden outside.

An attendant came to click on bright lamps around
the room. They glinted, reflected back at them from the
window glass – made the winter afternoon darker, later,
the hedges eerie in the light.

'Have *you* seen Elizabeth?' he asked, the face furrowed with worry.

Chapter 9

They arrived by mid-afternoon, tugging at rain-drenched coat collars and winter caps. Kitty O'Neill had already lit a fire in the grate and was padding around in her slippers, furniture polish and duster in hand.

Walsh, always last, clicked the door shut, and she stepped behind the counter to pull their pints and plug in the electric kettle for a hot whiskey for O'Brien who, for days now, had been sniffling with a head cold.

Walsh nodded at the bright, yellow poster under the dartboards.

'A load of shite,' he said, too loud. Kitty's head whipped around. He mumbled an apology for bad language in a lady's company, but when she was back slicing a lemon, he whispered, 'The greatest bollix of an idea . . .'

The poster was one of many that had appeared around the village: on electricity poles, in Margaret O'Neill's supermarket, the Rathloe church hallway – plus an advertisement in the *Western Telegraph*, the weekly paper. 'Inaugural meeting. Rathloe Preservation Committee. Rathloe Village Hall, Thursday, 22 November, 7 p.m. All welcome,' the advertisements read, with a digital photo of Rathloe House.

Above the bar, Lucille Ball was still frolicking around the telly screen with her wide eyes and lipsticked smile.

O'Brien wrapped his hands around his hot whiskey

glass, breathed in the clove-scented steam. Though they would never admit it to her, nobody made hot punch like Kitty O'Neill. O'Brien took a deep slug and, half-turning to Walsh, said, 'A cheek putting that up there. They should tear that bloody house down to hell.'

Mannion, second from the door, glanced delightedly at Sweeney, then back at Walsh and O'Brien, for every-one knew it was Sweeney's young daughter-in-law, Claire – married to his son Richie – who'd helped put up these yellow preservation posters.

The couple and their two young children had moved back to Rathloe three years ago, built a house on Sweeney's roadside land.

Claire's best friend was Edel Quinn, another young thirty-something, except that Edel and her husband, Jarlath, had no roots in Rathloe whatsoever, but had moved here for the easy commute and cheaper housing sites.

The two women often shared lifts to the city, babysat each other's young children, and they were seen with their husbands every Saturday night in O'Neill's – sportily dressed; Richie Sweeney with a congenial air and a word for all the locals, young and old, Claire blonde and petite, while Edel Quinn was almost six feet tall, animatedly flicking her shiny black hair over her shoulders.

'More like a Spaniard or an Italian than one of our own,' the older women would tell her when she stopped after work at O'Neill's supermarket, the car still running outside, while she bought milk, bread and children's breakfast cereal.

Walsh turned to glare at the poster again. 'Well I remember me poor father, God rest him, telling me about those English bastards and how they swanked around this parish, with their rent collectors for rents that should never have been paid to them in the first place.'

O'Brien, not to be outdone, said, 'What are you

saying? Sure, didn't me own grandfather get brought up by the RIC – the cursed constabulary – for hunting hares on the demesne land below?' He jabbed a thumb over his shoulder in the direction of the big house. 'And what was the poor man doing? What was he doing only like any of us, providing for his family when the bloody English landlords wouldn't take the coal off your foot?'

On his bar stool, Walsh straightened, in readiness for a suitable retort, when here came McHugh's Volvo across the pub car park; driven off the excavation job early by the rain. He stooped his tall frame in the doorway, nodded at Kitty in that cool, maddening way of his and said, 'Usual, Kitty. Thanks.'

They waited. Had he seen it? The yellow poster. The Gents'. Sooner or later he'd have to pass it by on the way to the Gents' toilet.

At the fireside, McHugh shook out his mackintosh, brushed the rain from his grey hair before installing himself in his usual seat and opening up his *Irish Times*.

Sweeney took his gaze from the television, turned and narrowed his eyes at the man behind the newspaper.

Sweeney would be seventy-one next birthday. Even he knew that his life had not been tragic, some would say even lucky. Yet, since McHugh had come swaggering into Rathloe, Sweeney was haunted by his own lost chances.

Sometimes at night, he fantasised about a different life if he'd been let stay over there in England: a two-up, two-down in a leafy London suburb, annual trips to the seaside in Wales, down the shops of a Saturday – an unfettered life with chosen friends, visits back to Rathloe where people could see that he, Patrick Sweeney, had done well for himself.

Sometimes he still looked at Sadie's lined, florid face across the supper table, and imagined his London girlfriend all those years ago – Maureen her name was, a buxom, red-headed nurse from County Armagh – and he wondered where she was now and what would have happened if . . .

'Now you're feckin' talking,' Walsh's voice cut across Sweeney's thoughts. Walsh and O'Brien still out-telling with tales of landlords, evictions, bailiffs, families by the roadsides with nothing but their settle beds.

Mannion's head swivelled from one man to the other, a spectator at a tennis match or a dog waiting for treats.

O'Brien, forgetting about Claire Sweeney's involvement, thumped his forefinger into the counter and said it was time, past shaggin' time for these young blow-ins and upstarts to stop taking over the parish anyways. For what? What? he demanded, would these shaggin' yuppies know about history?

Sweeney stole another poisonous look at McHugh and his smug, lean face. Ah, yes, why hadn't he thought of it before? Sweeney nudged Mannion, pointed to the poster under the dartboard, nodded towards the fireplace and winked.

Mannion frowned. What? Sweeney stared at him. Slowly, realisation dawned across Mannion's face. Whatever the two men's real loyalties were to Rathloe House and all this old guff about history and landlords, here was a chance to knock the stuffing out of McHugh and his grandiose notions.

Another round was drunk. Walsh and O'Brien rambled on. McHugh finished his pint and, to the great disappointment of all, never even ventured towards the Gents'. Instead, with a cursory nod, he ducked out of the door into the rainy night.

Two other men arrived, cars and trailers abandoned in the car park, perished with cold and already smelling of drink. They were on their way home from the cattle mart in Ballyshee. Walsh and O'Brien immediately inveigled

them into the conversation, dispatched them to read the
blasted poster for themselves.

A round for the house, the men demanded. *Yes, yes*, they
insisted. Wouldn't hear otherwise. Such an auspicious
night might never come again. A mark of sensible men's
solidarity against such cocked-up nonsense as they'd
just read on that poster.

Sweeney paused. It was half past six. He pulled on
his white gabardine hat and announced to all, 'Nothing.
Not a drop for me and Mannion here. Off up to this
meeting. Only right to support people when they're
doing their best in the interests of this parish. Ready
there, Mannion?'

Sweeney and Mannion slammed Sweeney's car doors.
The engine started.

O'Brien's face appeared at the driver's side window.
'You can tell them two glamour girls above in the
hall what we said, and plenty around what agrees
with us.'

Sweeney shoved the car into gear.

'History my arse,' O'Brien screamed after them as the
car sped up the village.

Edel Quinn and Claire Sweeney were sitting at a long table
under the hall stage. In the front row of tubular chairs sat
seven older women – members of the Rathloe Altar Society who had stayed after their own, earlier meeting, curious to hear what this preservation thing was all about.

Mannion and Sweeney installed themselves in the
back row nearest the door. Sadie Sweeney, sitting next
to Babs Mannion in the front row, swivelled in her chair
to eyebrow her husband. Obediently, Sweeney removed
his gabardine hat. Mannion followed suit with his tweed
cap as if they'd just entered a church.

Father Briscoe arrived, nodded to all, then whispered

and produced some papers and notes for Edel and Claire before taking his seat with them at the long table.

The Monahan brothers came, paisley-patterned scarves peeping above their overcoat collars; Johnny ushering Micheál to a place next to the Altar Society women.

On stage, in front of the faded, red curtains, were donations for the annual 8th of December sale of work for the St Vincent de Paul: toys, tricycles, knitted and crocheted baby blankets, boxes of groceries, fruitcakes, a set of gardening tools. At floor level were left and right stage doorways sporting the same, faded curtains, beyond which were two short flights of stairs to the stage area.

By seven o'clock, the fold-out chairs were almost full: younger people, blow-ins, some still in their work clothes, the rushed, harried look of night-time traffic on their faces. Young women shook out umbrellas inside the hall doorway, scanned the room for a friend who promptly waved them to a chair.

Young men arrived – one still in his gym wear; two others with toddlers squirming in their laps. People chatted from chair to chair, lamented how the mornings were so dark now; early frost made their commute tricky, and oh, the Christmas break just couldn't come soon enough.

Skiing, one young woman said. No trek across the country to the in-laws for her, just the husband and kids this Christmas. Packing up and heading to Switzerland for a fortnight's skiing.

At twenty past seven, Edel Quinn rang a little bell. Flashing her best smile she said, 'First, let me welcome you all and I suppose you're wondering why Claire and I and Father here invited you all this evening.'

Heads nodded. Babs Mannion whispered something to Sadie Sweeney. Edel continued, 'Well, I don't think it's news to anyone here that' – she paused – 'under its current ownership, the future of Rathloe House is in jeopardy.'

A woman arrived late, tiptoed up the aisle between the rows before installing herself in a chair halfway down.

Edel shuffled some of the papers on the front table. 'Now, we've done some preliminary research. And the records show Rathloe – the big house – dating back to . . .' She turned to Claire.

Claire, caught unawares, flushed slightly and announced, '1740.'

Edel said, 'Of course there were many, more famous big houses like Westport, Castletown, Strokestown, but we believe that Rathloe and its grounds may be one of the finest remaining examples of one of Ireland's smaller, Palladian-style houses. And, as such, it's a living history lesson for our children, our children's children and indeed, for ourselves, as part of our parish's heritage.'

A hand was raised. The woman planning the family ski holiday asked, 'How do you mean, Palladian?'

'Well, myself and Claire hope to do more research in due course, but basically, there were a few Irish architects, notably a Mr Richard Cassels, a German who later anglicised his name to Castle, who designed some of these smaller houses, based on their larger counterparts such as Westport or Castletown. These larger houses followed what we now call Irish Palladianism – influenced, of course, by Italian Renaissance architecture. And the Italians had borrowed backward again from the Greek tradition.' She held up a large, glossy coffee-table book, opened to a centrefold of a large, stone house. 'Basically, you'll notice that many of these houses had ornate doorways or porticos, a symmetrical style, though of course, Rathloe has nothing like the grandeur and linked pavilions of this particular example . . .' She smiled at the woman, 'I hope I've answered your question.'

The woman nodded yes.

'Now, what we'd hoped to accomplish tonight,' Edel continued, 'is to launch the preservation committee, but most important to hear your thoughts on the future of this house.'

Another hand rose from the left side of the hall.

'Another question,' Edel said. 'We like questions, don't we, Claire?'

A young man raised his voice over his toddler's gurgling. 'Look, I'm going to play devil's advocate here for a minute. Let's say, for argument's sake, that we *have* a measure of success, that we actually stop the demolition of Rathloe House such as it stands now; but what then?'

'Excellent question,' Edel said, 'Claire, would you like to take this one?'

Claire Sweeney cleared her throat and said, 'Well, obviously, myself and Edel haven't had much of a chance to make any real projections, but basically, it would depend on the will of the people, you, and what you all wanted, voted for—'

Edel interrupted, 'But mainly our best-case scenario would be that Rathloe House be (a) saved from being torn down by its current owner and then (b) restored to its original – or close to original – condition, opened to the public, to tourists and locals as a visitors' centre.'

She leaned forward, grinned conspiratorially. 'We could be looking at a very valuable asset to the village of Rathloe – economically and culturally.'

'Who knows?' Claire added. 'We could certainly restore the gardens and orchards, possibly plant herbs, organic gardening enterprises, eventually have all types of gardening classes, demonstrations in flower-drying, herb- and fruit-preserving . . .'

'Other questions?' Edel asked. ' Remember: information is key to . . .'

Johnny Monahan had already tucked his paisley scarf inside his own overcoat, and was leaning over to button up his brother Micheál's. Quietly they scraped back their chairs, nodded apologetically to Father Briscoe, and then to Claire and Edel.

'Something to say or you're leaving us for the evening, Mr Monahan?' Edel asked, smiling at the brothers as if they were slightly curmudgeonly but lovable pets.

Everybody waited.

'Actually, Miss Quinn, Miss Sweeney, we were just . . .' Johnny glanced edgily towards the door. 'We . . . well, perhaps it's best if . . .'

'If you've something to add, given your long years of experience in this parish and as a librarian, I'm sure we'd all value your input,' Edel persisted.

'Well,' Johnny said, sagging back into his chair. He beckoned to Micheál to sit. His voice came high-pitched, like a wrongly accused child. 'Now, I don't want to be, I believe the word is *derogatory*, of your efforts here, but I would just like to suggest—' He held up a gloved hand. 'Of course, not to take away from your marvellous work and intentions, Miss Quinn and Miss Sweeney, and of course, the good of the parish comes first . . .'

The older women shuffled their feet. The younger people looked at their watches. 'Bah!' a toddler called out into the silent, waiting hall. 'Bah! Bah!' Sweeney nudged Mannion. Would that eejit Monahan ever come to the point and stop his *seafóid* or blathering on like an old woman?

'I suppose what I'd like to say or suggest is that we take our time, proceed here judiciously or at least, at the very least with . . . and sensitivity. There are those in the parish for whom . . .' He stood up again. Micheál stood, grinned around at everyone, and Johnny added, 'I'm sorry but my brother and I really must be . . .'

'By Jay, Monahan, leave it to the educated fella to speak out the truth.'

Everyone turned to the bellowing voice in the doorway. There was Walsh, leaning against the door jamb.

Behind him in the hallway were O'Brien and their two new friends from the cattle mart. Walsh's face was purple with opinion and drink.

'Would you and your friends like to come in and sit down, Mr Walsh?' Edel asked testily.

Walsh stamped his wellingtoned foot. 'No I would not like to come in, we'll stay where we are and say our say. That oul' rookery of a house should be levelled to hell, man; and it isn't now but years ago that every stone of it should have been mowed down and taken away. When Cronin was alive, God rest him, nobody in this parish wanted to interfere with an old man and his land, but now that we have someone willing to get rid of it to hell, this bloody parish should mind its own feckin' business and leave all the oul' soft chat about restoration and heritage to someone else.'

Edel swallowed, readjusted her features. Claire kept staring at the table. Father Briscoe lit a cigarette and left it smoking in the ashtray in front of him. The Monahan brothers, frozen in their spot, stared straight ahead at the stage.

'Now, I've said what I've come to say, and I'm sure you'll find that there's plenty like me,' Walsh roared. Then, he and the other three men turned and trooped back out past the cloakroom and the ticket office.

'Please, folks. Please.' Edel's voice was barely heard above the chatter.

Once the Monahan brothers had left, everyone young and old had started talking, hands waving to make a point, people leaning across from chair to chair. Up front, the Altar Society women whispered loudly, their headscarved and permed heads nodding emphatically.

Mannion and Sweeney nudged and watched.

Chapter 10

The golden retriever pup lunged at him, ears erect, tail wagging frantically.

McHugh bent to rub the head and laughed, 'All right then. Let's see what you've been destroying around this house today, eh? You going to let me inside to see?'

The dog went to bolt across the yard, but instead turned to lead the way into McHugh's rented cottage.

On the living-room floor was a chewed-up sock. On the loft stairs, a man's underpants. An old tea towel on the couch. 'Oh! Not too bad, not a bad day for mischief, was it? Good dog. All right, calm down. Sit. Let's go for nice walkies, eh?'

She stood on her hind paws to lean against his thighs, lick and pant in his face.

He'd had her for a week now – saw a breeder's ad in the paper and spent a wet Sunday driving to a Midland town to pick her up.

A dog hadn't been in his plans. In fact, except for the mongrel dogs his family had had in his youth, this was the first dog he'd owned.

One of these days he'd select a real name for her. On the Formica kitchen table was a book from the library in Ballyshee, *Naming Your Pet*. He was hoping for something perfect for this golden face he'd already fallen in love with.

Even in bad weather they went for their evening

65

walks, the two trotting the half mile along the Rathloe road into Ballyshee.

On the outskirts of town was a school with its playground abandoned for the evening, cut-outs and coloured letters pasted in the Venetian blind windows. Next came bungalows with privet hedges and glassed-in front porches.

The road became a street, the terraced houses with their rectangles of light above hall doors, the bluish flicker of televisions in sitting-room windows.

On they went, McHugh pulling his coat collar up from the damp cold, the pup trotting, straining on her lead to stop and sniff at doorways and drainpipes.

On Main Street, the evening bus stood coughing diesel fumes while waiting for the last passengers to get on or off. Cars were parked haphazardly along the pavement, engines still running while someone ran into the newsagent's or a late-open shop for the evening paper, cigarettes.

They passed the electrical shop, closed on the dot of six. In the window, early Christmas lights, retail displays of food mixers, CD players, stereo systems, electric carving knives.

Next came the shoe shop, Christmas tinsel snaking through furry ladies' slippers, cut-out price tags clipped to the winter boots. There was a menswear shop, then a bookmaker's, a ladies' drapery with mannequins in glittery blouses, packets of women's stockings in the window.

From the Hermitage Hotel came the hopsy smell of beer and cigarettes. Through the wide front window he saw a freshly lit fire in the lounge fireplace.

At the corner of Main and High Street was a takeaway chip shop from which three teenage boys came, balancing paper bags as they picked up bicycles from the foot-path. Abruptly, the pup stalled. Ears alert, begging.

'Here,' a boy said, holding a fat, vinegary chip to her. But he sensed something foreign and stern in the dog's owner. He asked McHugh, 'Is she allowed?'

'One can't do any harm,' McHugh said.

'She's a gorgeous pup.' The boy looked up at him shyly. The dog spat her sizzling-hot treat onto the footpath, nosed around it, then wolfed it down noisily. 'What's her name?'

'Don't actually have one – yet.'

The boy bent to scratch the pup's ears, crooned at her, 'You're a grand pup; d'you know that? Do you? A *lovín*, a pure *lovín*.' He gave the dog another chip.

'Did you say thank you?' McHugh said. 'Did you thank this nice boy for the treats, then?'

The boys giggled. They were right. Only a foreigner – an Englishman – would talk to a dog like it was a baby.

They turned down High Street, McHugh's steps quickening down the hill, the dog straining on her lead.

They turned into a ramshackle town park where McHugh bent to unclip her lead. She bolted, the tail high and quivering, head busily sniffing, then off after some new curiosity.

There was hardly anyone down in this park, a river walk, except for the odd group of teenagers with skittish eyes, cigarettes cupped in their hands. Some evenings, he met an older couple in long winter coats.

Lately, especially since these posters and this cursed Rathloe preservation meeting, he was glad of this place. Across the grass, away from the river, was a square of cement for a children's playground. Weeds sprouted from among the cracks. It was littered with broken glass, and the swing seats had been removed so that three sets of rusted chains dangled as from a gallows.

Three benches were set at intervals along the river.

Hardly even a river, just a swollen stream where plastic shopping bags, old branches clogged up the brackish waters. There was a riverside path overgrown with weeds.

The pup had disappeared among the bushes.

He walked a while, then sat on the middle bench to listen to the rushing water, to watch the silhouetted trees, the backs of the houses on Main Street.

Oh God! How could he have expected this Rathloe House preservation nonsense? A spanner in the works, if ever there was one. Those two perky young women and those old men in O'Neill's with their smirking, whispering faces. Maddening as hell. Was it too much that a man be left alone to his own damn property? Had this whole damn country, all thirty-two counties of it, east to west, just changed since he'd left thirty-five years ago, colours, forms mutated like a meadow under a passing storm?

Their children's heritage. A major tourist attraction. He'd seen the stupid posters, read the newspaper articles, the cleverly pitched quotes from Edel Quinn.

Last Sunday afternoon he'd even met Claire and Richie Sweeney strolling through the big house rear gardens, their children hoisted shoulder-high, the parents more baby-voiced than the children, pointing out all the interesting things.

They'd stopped for a jovial little afternoon chat as if it was the most natural thing in the world to have a family – the family that was trying to take away his own property, mind you – parading through his land. It sickened him. Heritage. These Celtic Tiger yuppies only wanted history if it came with a designer label.

He ground his hands into his coat pockets, then got up to follow the river path as it grew grassier, wetter, ending at a stone wall beyond which were open, country fields.

Of course he hadn't come back here to make friends.

Not the type for mad, nostalgic dreams of immigrant-come-home-again, back-slapping and welcome-homes in the pub on a Saturday night. Friends, like historical preservation, were the privilege of the rich or the fool-hardy. He had one good mate – his property manager, Jimmy in Pinner. Others – even his own brother – had, over the years, somehow let him down, had failed to pass some undefined, McHugh test.

The same with his women. Trouble-free, that was the way to go. Divorcées were best – cool, jaded enough not to cling.

The thing was, women liked him, said the subtle remains of his Irish accent made him more real, exotic, savage. In London, he'd been to all the best dinner parties, black-tie charity do's. Twice, three times a year, he had exotic holidays in the Mediterranean and Caribbean. But never had he acted foolishly, impetu-ously – surprised a woman with late-night phone calls, whispered promises the morning after.

Since moving back, he'd begun to miss women. Sex? No, not so much. Just their presence, the vain need – satisfaction at having been chosen. A glance, retreat, a jousting of bodies, minds.

In Galway City he'd found a rather nice jazz club in a city-centre hotel, even scouted out some decent restaurants for his solitary dinners. But not his type, these nouveau riche Irishwomen. Too much make-up, fidgeted with ill-fitting clothes, chattered and peered predatorily over their beer glasses.

He reached the end of the path, the broken-down wall. A smell of old weeds, drenched roots, cowdung in the fields beyond. He whistled for the pup – Lovín.

She's a real lovín, the boy outside the chip shop had said. It was as good a name as any. He whistled again. Waited for the flash of white – her nose, underside of her tail.

It pleased him, the name. This Irishism he thought he'd left behind years and years ago – the West of Ireland habit of adding *-ín* to the ends of words to make them affectionate or roguish. His mother, Seamus his brother, their neighbours in Carraig did it. Lovín she would be.

She came at last, chasing past him towards the river, then doubling back to pant around his legs. 'Come on, then. Come on, Lovín, you great white hunter. Let's get back home, eh? Don't you want to go home and lie before that nice fire?'

They headed back through the park.

They were approaching the gateway to the High Street when along came the older couple, long overcoats, the wife picking her way among the weeds in her sensible walking shoes.

As usual the man said, 'Not a bad evening, now.'

'Keeping dry anyway,' McHugh said, and stopped to clip on Lovín's lead.

Chapter 11

She emptied her fridge onto the kitchen breakfast counter: containers of crumbled goat's cheese, baked brie, Stilton, a takeaway portion of stuffed mushrooms, a salmon pâté. A bottle of brut champagne.

Here came the movers again, thump, thump, up her front steps and across her hallway.

They'd been here all afternoon – their heavy steps across the landing, calling to each other as her bed, couches, dining table were hoisted high and delivered into a dark, metallic truck. Swing it left, right now, lift it higher, higher, angle it around to fit it out through the door. One of them Irish. A handsome fellow with James Dean features and long, gangly legs inside Levi's jeans.

Tomorrow she'd be in her new flat – installed at Railroad Place, her boxes of dishes, glassware. Waiting for BT and British Gas to arrive.

Anna had begged her to stay with her in her flat in Bloomsbury. Lots of room, though she, Anna, wouldn't be there until late – another date with the new boyfriend, Georges. French, but living here now.

'Don't, Suze,' Anna had said yesterday at lunchtime. No last nights in that empty house. Too weird. Too many silly regrets. 'Do come stay with Panny.'

Now she crossed to her kitchen cupboards to search for crackers, crispbreads. Smiled to herself. Anna had resumed her old, university nickname for herself lately. Trying to humour, persuade Susan, the curmudgeonly divorcée. But no, Susan Brown would camp out tonight on a fold-out bed in the lounge. One last night. A last hurrah.

'Honest, you could fit my whole house just in 'ere,' one of the moving men – Tom with the cockney accent – called from the lounge, his voice echoing in the empty room.

'A drink, you two? You must be hungry . . . ?' she called back to him.

They came to wash their hands – just the two fellows left now; the others already gone to Railroad Place with her bedroom and dining things.

'No beer, I'm afraid,' she said. 'Must be thirsty . . .'

Tom eyed the little buffet she'd assembled. 'Weren't expecting all this,' he said. 'Should I do the honours with the champers?'

All day yesterday, last night lying awake, she'd hoped Gerald would come. Say goodbye to the house, to her. To the idea, a memory of them together in these rooms that were now stripped of curtains, pictures, photos, rectangles of pale wood where their rugs used to be.

In a cupboard next to the fridge she found paper cups with a Christmas holly design. More unchilled champagne. Remnants of an iTemps office party. Last year, the year before. She couldn't remember.

'Well, here's to your new pad,' the Irish fellow, Cillian, said. Laughing, the three toasted their paper cups.

Cillian Brady was from Dublin. A nixer, he assured her, this moving job of his – searching around for something in marketing, that's what his college degree was in, and the moving gig gave him time to search, go to morning job interviews. 'Plus build up th'oul muscles,' he grinned at her, flexing his biceps.

'Dig in,' she said. 'Sorry there's nothing substantial –

just whatever was left.' Tom, the cockney, was already munching on a cracker and brie.

Cillian laughed. 'No, this is brillo – brilliant. Save me microwaving th'oul frozen dinner tonight, wha— ? Susan, isn't it?'

She nodded.

He said, 'Always like to use people's names if I can, like.' The brown eyes twinkled at her again. 'Lovely drop of bubbles, by the way.'

'There's lots more,' she said gesturing towards the cupboards. 'No point in leaving it for the newcomers, is there?'

'Splitting up? Divorced?' Tom asked. She didn't mind him asking, did she? Only, naturally, him and Cillian *had* wondered . . . They could see there'd been a man here once. You noticed these things as a mover . . .

They were on their second bottle of champagne now. She was getting tipsy.

Divorced himself, Tom was, once. First marriage, when he was very – too – young. Stupid really, but then, you just don't know, do you?

'You'll be all right,' Cillian said, leaning across the counter towards her. The voice lilting and kind.

She met his eyes. Shrugged. 'I'll be fine.'

'Great place, your new flat,' Cillian said. 'Brilliant concept, use of space. Better than tearing things down . . .'

Outside, the brief winter twilight was fading. A light was on in the neighbours' kitchen. Tomorrow, tonight, she knew she wouldn't go over there to say goodbye.

Over the years they had nodded to each other over the back fence, a wave from driveway to driveway as they each got into their cars. Gerald used to chat with the husband sometimes. Went over to fix their kids' computer once or twice.

'Another?' she asked, and poured for the three of them.

Cillian was standing before her fireplace, an elbow resting on the mantel. He was telling another story. This one about a family he'd once moved in a Dublin suburb. The ex-husband following them into the van removing everything they'd just carted out. Cillian laughed. What the feck did him and the lads care? Lucky they were being paid by the hour. Oh, and listen, in the middle of it all, outta nowhere comes this boyfriend. A thick, country yob. Starts roaring like a bull. Wife cursing like a banshee. Fisticuffs between hubby and boyfriend on the front lawn of the house while Cillian and his mates are left standing there with a shaggin' couch.

The three of them laughed. She was leaning against the door between the kitchen and the lounge. The two men had been entertaining her, outdoing each other with tales, confessions of a moving man. Tom was sitting on an upturned crate.

She was drunk. Mad things rising, tingling in her head. Effervescent thoughts. Fizzle. Bubble. Goodbye, this window. That door, this door jamb. Goodbye, house. So long, Gerald.

The kitchen phone rang. She hesitated. Went to pick it up just before the machine.

'Suze? It's me. Look, I just thought I'd call and . . . well, everything went all right, didn't it? Oh, and thanks for the stuff.'

Last Thursday, Gerald had e-mailed his last-minute list: a winter coat from the attic, a box of computer CDs he couldn't seem to find among the other stuff she'd sent.

He said, 'Arrived in perfect nick.'

'That's all right. It wasn't terribly difficult.' Words clotted drunkenly on her tongue. Cillian came in his stocking feet across the darkened kitchen. Light from the fridge as he looked for their latest open bottle. He caught her eye and mouthed at her, 'Ex?'

She chewed her lower lip. Nodded yes.

He gave her a cheeky thumbs up, offered to top up her drink.

Gerald said, 'Look, is something . . . wrong, Suze?'

All these nights, his other calls, she'd imagined him in a lofty, London flat curled up on a couch with this Alison girl.

But now, in this empty kitchen, she pictured him no place at all. Except a bother, an annoying voice on the end of her phone.

She said, 'Look, I'm having a bit of a party, so I really should get back . . .'

Silence.

At last he said, 'So long then. And Suze, we *will* keep in—'

But she had already hung up.

It was after eleven o'clock. An hour ago, Tom, stumbling as he negotiated her front steps, had gone home in a taxi. Tomorrow they would come for the van outside her house, locked up now with the last of her furniture inside.

She was dry-mouthed. A champagne headache.

'Bleedin' amazin',' Cillian said.

She had just told him about her grandfather and the estate in the West of Ireland. He touched her arm. Long, piano fingers, tiny black hairs below the knuckles. 'Susan, would you not think of taking a jaunt over there? Look up the old *Oirish* roots like they all do, visit where he actually lived and all that?'

'I'm going at Christmas, actually. A career expo in Dublin. Might drive out West, but . . . ?' She hesitated.

75

They were facing each other on the lounge carpet now, cross-legged like some caricature Indian squaws.

'Well, we – people like my grandfather – were hardly the men of the hour, were they? I mean, even now, you hardly have the red carpet out for people like us . . .'

'Ah, now Susan. No offence there, but sure, you're talking about some old, forgotten Ireland, twenty, fifty years go, like. All living on each other's shadow, who did what to who, stepped on whose corns, took whose land. Sure the Irish are more interested in microchips these days than chips on the shoulders.'

He stood in a pool of light on her front step. A mist was falling, halos of light around the streetlamps. In her front lawn, the estate agent's sign with the triumphant 'Sold' across it. At the kerb, a taxi ticking over, waiting for him.

Drunken words in her head. *Look, Cillian, I don't want to spend the night alone here, so would you stay?* Unsaid.

'Keep th'oul faith anyways, Susan, right?' He turned away, but then came up the steps to kiss her cheek. Teasingly, like a grown-up son.

'Always wanted to kiss British royalty,' he laughed.

'Right. Brilliant night. Look, think about what I said. The wilds of Mayo. Do you good after all this – the man, the move and everything.'

'Good night, Cillian,' she said, closing the door.

She stood in the too-bright hallway. All her lampshades packed. Went to check her appearance in a large hall mirror that wasn't there any more. In its place, a rectangle of wallpaper darker than the rest.

She had wanted him – a young man half her age – to kiss her.

Silly, silly woman.

She said it aloud in the empty house.

Chapter 12

Santy's Playhouse was propped under the heavy red stage curtain. It was a plywood affair, the roof swathed with cotton wool and evergreen branches frosted with spray-on snow.

For years, Johnny Monahan had played Santy Claus for the annual 8th December sale of work for the St Vincent de Paul, because the women always maintained he had the gentlest voice and wouldn't frighten the children.

He wore a pillow stuffed underneath his threadbare red jacket, a black belt taped together from a cut-up binliner, a theatrical beard that he and Micheál had to patch and sew every year in time for the 8th December sale of work.

Jinglebell music tinkled from inside the playhouse.

Every year, the Rathloe Sale of Work Committee vetoed Johnny's suggestion for classical music or Christmas carols. Carols just not Christmassy enough, the women members said, and after all, the Santy visits were by far the biggest money-maker of the whole sale of work.

At floor level, mothers, fathers, babysitters queued up at the stage door. Bridgie Walsh ducked in and out from behind the narrow curtain, in a green elf's outfit she'd worn for years, and wavering in and out of her squeaky

Santy's elf voice. 'Now, who's next to see Santy Claus? How many tickets there, ma'am?'

Down the left and right sides of the hall, the rest of the committee had set up their long tables.

Babs Mannion was running the baked goods table: Christmas cakes, iced buns, apple tarts, sponge cakes, plum puddings, – every penny a clean profit.

This year, Mrs O'Brien had chosen household goods.

Two younger women had volunteered for the toy tables where Teletubbies, Ninja Turtles, Power Rangers squeaked, clanked, babbled, as children tried them out, whined and begged to have this toy or that, fought over them, and wore down the batteries.

The noise grew. Toy bugles, wind-up soldiers, crying babies, burst balloons – a cacophony that rose up to the slatted ceiling, reverberated among the gold and red Christmas decorations.

'Look, it's all for a good cause,' Mrs O'Brien snapped at a shopper who had returned to the household goods table for the third time. He was deliberating over a Christmas salt and pepper set, peering myopically at it and asking Mrs O'Brien the price over and over.

'We've labelled everything,' she said.

'Left me specs at home,' he said, and listen, Missus Whatever-Your-Name-Is, there's absolutely no need to be so ratty about it. A free bloody country.'

The truth was that none of the women had expected such crowds, a bigger turn-out this year than any-one could remember. People from Rathloe, Ballyshee – families whom nobody had ever seen before – came crowding through the little cloakroom, the hallway, then spread out among the crush of shoppers, browsers who wheeled buggies and ushered children up and down the makeshift aisles.

'And what about the gentlemen?' Father Briscoe screamed into a microphone from the parish raffle table in the very centre of the hall. 'Come on, now. Donated by Ballyshee Menswear, a lovely tweed hat and scarf set. Buy your tickets.'

Across the end wall opposite the stage hung a white banner with bold blue letters: 'Rathloe Preservation Committee'. Edel Quinn and Claire Sweeney held court, talking, politicking, giving away free cups of cocoa and biscuits. Sadie Sweeney, Claire's mother-in-law, circulated between the preservation table, household and baked goods, where she tried to help all, and ran to make change for twenty- and fifty-pound notes.

From her own, small table, Sadie sold hand-knitted caps, mittens, babies' booties, crocheted slippers and bibs. All proceeds from the knitwear went to the Rathloe Preservation Committee.

Claire presided over the cocoa and petitions – sheets of lined paper on clipboards, purple Biros with 'Rathloe Preservation' along the side – free for the taking once you signed the petition to preserve and rebuild Rathloe House. Or over there, you could do it electronically, just type your name in on the lovely computer. Or better yet, buy a raffle ticket.

Edel, in skintight leggings and a long, crimson sweater, solicited, enticed people towards the hot pink computer monitor with a scrolling marquee across the screen: 'Win Me for £50.'

'Try it,' she told the people, her dark eyes twinkling. 'Go on, the very latest PC – a personal computer for yourselves. And look, all these software programs pre-loaded – free to the lucky prize winner. Click,' she said. 'Just click and see.'

She cajoled, praised, urged them to click the mouse, enter the preservation website with its digital photos and buttons: 'Enter', 'Who We Are', 'The Preservation Committee and You', 'Bulletin Board', 'Drawing-room Chat'.

Children demonstrated for parents and grandparents who peered over each other's shoulders to watch, to marvel and to rummage in their handbags for a cheque-book to buy a raffle ticket.

Johnny Monahan stared past the children's heads and arms at the blip and flicker of computer images, the constant queue of people waiting to buy the fifty-pound computer raffle tickets, the huge banner for Rathloe Preservation Committee. The children fidgeted on his lap, were petulant and cheeky, as if they sensed Santy's edginess this year.

He nodded his head to a blond boy on his lap, mumbled absently that he shouldn't be surprised if Santy wasn't very, very good to him this year and, of course, not to forget the boys and girls less fortunate than himself.

Whoops of delight rose from a big family who had gathered to view the website. A visiting grandfather was insisting: a good win on the horses yesterday, so he would, yes he would pay the fifty-pound raffle money for each of his grandchildren to have a chance at the pink computer.

On stage, the little boy eyed Johnny. Waited. Tugged on Santy's beard.

Johnny grimaced at the child and said quickly, 'Now, tell Santy what you want for Christmas this year.'

The boy said, 'Ah for feck's sake . . . amn't I only after telling you that, Santy? Is it bloody deaf y'are or what?'

Johnny drew his gaze back from the Preservation Committee banner and tables to smile at the boy and said, yes, yes, of course, of course he remembered; it was just that Santy liked to play little jokes sometimes.

By three o'clock, Father Briscoe had shushed everyone

to draw the winning tickets for the parish raffle. A boy from the Christian Brothers' National School in Ballyshee won the first prize of a bicycle. The hamper of food and spirits went to an elderly man with a pale face whom nobody seemed to know, though Bridgie Walsh said she'd heard he'd just had an operation and had come to stay and convalesce with a niece of his in Rathloe.

Richie Sweeney, Claire's husband, won the man's hat and scarf set, but then donated it back to be raffled again; all for the good of the parish.

The hall had grown hot and breathless.

Finally, Father Briscoe handed over the microphone and the floor to Edel Quinn for the moment they'd all been waiting for. Edel walked to the centre of the hall. Claire Sweeney followed her with a huge, glass fish bowl full of raffle tickets.

'Someone very impartial to draw the lucky ticket,' Edel said, flicking back her dark hair.

'Santy Claus!' a little girl shouted.

'Of course,' Edel laughed. 'Santy Claus would never, ever pick the wrong ticket, would he, boys and girls?'

'No!' A high chorus.

'OK, ladies and gentlemen, let's see who Santa will pick to win this lovely computer.'

Everyone watched as Claire held the glass bowl high above her head. A startled, exhausted Santa leaned over from his playhouse to reach in and pick a winner.

'Give them a good stir there, John – I mean Santy,' a man shouted from the floor. People laughed.

The little girl on Johnny's lap whispered in his ear, 'Pick my mum, Santy. Please pick my mum.'

'And it's . . .' Edel paused. Unfolded the ticket stub. Grinned around mysteriously. 'One of our own! Ms Kitty O'Neill. Kitty, are you here? Someplace? Or Margaret?'

People muttered, shuffled feet. What the hell would Kitty O'Neill want with a computer? Oh, but wouldn't it be the likes of her who would win it? Not someone who needed it. Unless, of course, she donated it back, just like Richie Sweeney with the hat and scarf set.

'Kitt-eeee?' Edel called into the microphone again.

Neither of the O'Neill sisters appeared.

Someone rang down to the pub on a mobile phone.

People had started buttoning toddlers into coats, gathering up their day's purchases when at last the O'Neill sisters arrived.

'The O'Neills,' Edel announced, presenting the two women in their matching hair sets, pencilled eyebrows, purple winter coats. 'Proud owners of a home PC – personal computer.'

People stalled in the doorway; shushed each other to hear what Kitty would say to her big win, all mock humility when she donated it back, sucking up to Father Briscoe.

Kitty's small lips were in an 'O' of embarrassed delight. She shook Father Briscoe's hand, Claire's, then Edel's and said, 'Oh, I just . . . I really. Well . . . Oh, 'tis just too much. We never expected half of this.'

'Well, Kitty, ready to give it a whirl?' Edel said, but the sisters, Kitty leading, were already halfway down the hall towards their new pink computer.

Kitty blinked at the scrolling letters on the screen.

'Pick up the mouse. Go on,' Edel coaxed. Everyone waited.

Kitty held the mouse high above her right shoulder. Click, click, click.

Stifled giggles.

She shuffled her feet in time to the mouse clicking. Click, click, click. A Spanish dancer with her castanets.

'On the *table*, Kitty,' Father Briscoe whispered.

'Oh!' Kitty said, and let the mouse clatter to the table. Colours, words, photos from the preservation website fluttered before her eyes. 'Oh,' she said again, blinking at the front page and the house photo. 'Oh, isn't that just a gorgeous snap?'

The last child of the day was sitting on Johnny's lap. Why wouldn't Santy answer him? Look at him at least? 'Look, will I start my list again, Santy?' the boy asked impatiently.

'Yes, yes,' Johnny said. 'Maybe you'd better start at the start.'

Chapter 13

A Saturday evening, and Sweeney was driving home from O'Neill's with his stomach rattling from the hunger, his head bothered as usual by those other three jokers and their old chat. The car heater hadn't been working lately, so even for the short drive up through the village to the Sweeney house, the December cold had him perished.

He thought there'd be peace in his house once this sale of work lark was over, but no. No such bloody luck.

For the days, nights before the sale of work, Sweeney had been tortured by the click, click, click of Sadie's knitting needles when a man was trying to watch his own telly in peace.

If anything, things were worse now – preservation meetings in their sitting room that kept Sadie up half the night, lists, numbers, petitions, a mailing list. They were even selling specially printed preservation Christmas cards up in O'Neill's shop. Phone calls flying back and forth between the women. Sadie gallivanting off to town with Babs Mannion – a woman who, in Sweeney's opinion, should never have been given a driver's licence.

Now, their house seemed littered with papers, printouts from the preservation website, phone numbers scribbled on the backs of envelopes, books borrowed from the town library: oh yes, he, Sweeney had had a bellyfull.

He drove in their back yard. The house was in darkness. In the kitchen, no signs of the tea, not a smell of a rasher, an egg, the Christmas post still unopened among her latest library books: *Irish Country Houses*, *Ireland after the Famine*, *The Country Houses of Ireland*, *From the Grassroots Up: How to Galvanise Community Support*. No table set for two under the kitchen window. He shivered in the usually sweltering kitchen. The fire in the range had been let go out.

He prowled up the corridor, where, sure enough, there was Sadie in the front hall, pacing up and down, her new mobile phone tucked under her chin and saying, 'Right, right. That's true for you. Right. Well, maybe if we . . .'

She was forever on that bloody phone now, ever since Claire surprised her with it as an early Christmas present.

He retreated into the front sitting room where, though there was only a week left to Christmas, the Christmas tree stood naked. The lights and decorations lay in a tangle on the carpeted floor. He switched on the telly loud. Sat on the arm of the couch.

He heard her hanging up. Starting to dial again for another phone call. But no, Sweeney wasn't a man to be caught twice. He shot out into the hall.

'What?' She eyed him rattily as if he were a sudden intruder.

'The tea,' he seethed. 'Where's the tea? Nothing . . .'

'I'm busy,' she said. 'Anyways, myself and the girls had a quick cup and a sandwich in the Hermitage Hotel.'

The girls, he mimicked. Babs Mannion and Bridgie Walsh and that Mrs O'Brien were far from girls. Couldn't she call them women?

But she silenced him with a look, as if he should suddenly know better than to ask for the evening meal she'd been preparing for him every evening for the past forty-five years.

'Look, if you're that anxious for tea, can't you go into the town and buy yourself something. Fish and chips. Whatever. Oh, and hey . . . look in the fridge while you're at it. Milk . . . butter . . . anything wanting for tomorrow's Sunday dinner.'

She dialled her number again. 'Ah, hello? Jarlath? Arrah, how'rya. Listen, is Edel there by any chance?'

Speechless, Sweeney backed the car out between the haysheds, then headed out onto the side road, the main road, then off towards the village of Rathloe.

If you're that anxious for tea . . . He mimicked her aloud to the windscreen. Of all the . . .

Probably no clean shirt left out for him for tomorrow either. There was none last Sunday. Had to wear the one from the week before. He pounded the steering wheel. Nothing, nothing infuriated him more than this casual attitude, that look, tone, as if he, Sweeney, should know better than to ask.

He sped down through the village, slowed for the turn at the far end of Rathloe, then sped up again for the town.

He stopped dead.

Was it the starvation making him hallucinate?

He reversed, then turned into the gravelled gateway of the big house. He left the headlights on.

Gone were the old, rusted gates and their scramble of wires. In their place now were custom-fitted, iron gates, high, elegant spokes reaching into the sky. A shiny new padlock. Tucked among the iron rails, a printed sign: No Trespassing.

He grabbed a rail, then another, and shook the heavy gates in their new hinges. He was an enraged prisoner, a man seeking deliverance.

The big house avenue had been newly surfaced

with small, marbleised stones. They glittered in his headlights. To the left of the avenue, the ploughed-up demesne fields were sodden now, but ready for re-seeding at the first promise of spring.

To the right, the big house trees stood skeletal, ghostly against a pitch-black sky. It reminded him of a documentary he'd once seen on French royalty and their chateaux.

He rattled the gates again.

So here he was, that pup McHugh just laughing at them, the whole parish of Rathloe racing hither and thither with their fundraising and sales of work and petitions, while Gentleman Jim himself was commissioning gates, resurfacing avenues, forging ahead with his grandiose plans.

Pebbles pinged off the axles and wheels as he started off for the town again.

Tomorrow there'd be the usual Sunday dinner with Richie, Claire and the kids – the last before their family Christmas dinner next week.

Sweeney's daughter, Eileen, a teacher in Galway City, would condescend to drive the twenty miles out to the country. Richie and Claire's children would demand, refuse, whine that they didn't eat this or that. They wanted it cut up smaller, shaped like flowers. No, no, they'd changed their minds. Oh, didn't Granny and Grandad remember since last time? No, they never liked that kind of vegetable, this kind of biscuit, that kind of fizzy orange. Hadn't Granny more choices to offer?

After dinner, the children would race up into the sitting room, where they'd hog his telly for their afternoon cartoons. Eileen, as usual, would wave away Sadie's homemade trifle or apple tart. Another diet. Low carbs. No sugar. All carbs. No fat. One foot out the door. City friends. A new boyfriend whom Sadie would enquire about; invite him down for the Christmas. But no, in her small, shiny car, Eileen would rush away. People to see.

What kind of a man resented his own children? Their college degrees, their independent, come-and-go lives, their moneyed, confident ways?

There it would be: when Sadie was still asleep beside him and he lay watching the chink of early morning light between their bedroom curtains. When he tramped through the Sweeney land after cattle, searching among bushes, rocks for a wandering sheep. He was tortured, beset by these whys and wherefores, the way the world gave to some; withheld from others.

Like there was McHugh with his Volvo and stupid, sissy dog. Owns half of London and then comes swanking back to buy up land in a parish where he had no roots whatsoever – on a whim, Sweeney was sure of it, buying twenty-five demesne acres like another man would buy a pair of socks.

Chapter 14

A Christmas tree winked on and off in the corner. The dining room smelled of roast turkey, sage and onion stuffing. The matron shepherded them all from the drawing room, seated them at named table places – white linen and shiny glassware – families, wives, husbands, grandchildren, adult daughters in their fluffy, Christmas sweaters, sons in best suits. Paper hats and Christmas crackers for all.

'Rudolph the Red-Nosed Reindeer' was piped through the walls and the high ceilings.

A faux gas fire flickered in the grate; red candles nestled in a fringe of holly along the mantel.

They were the only twosome, her and Daddy, sitting stiffly at their table under a glittering chandelier. No, over there, nearer the kitchen, a prim little husband and wife, the husband's face set in the same, gruesome cheeriness of all the other visitors'.

She caught his eye. Smiled at him wistfully. He smiled back. She wondered if she shouldn't ask to be seated together: two and two to make a foursome? Pleasant chat about Christmas shopping and weather. Comforting, perhaps. For him. And for her. But the man had already turned away to help his wife with her linen napkin.

'This is lovely, Daddy,' she said across the red carnation centrepiece.

When she'd arrived he'd been waiting, sitting inside his usual window in the drawing room reading a cooking article in a magazine. One of his good days – a sudden, unpredictable spate of lucidity. Her Christmas present.

'Yes,' he said, in a rehearsed, stilted voice. 'They do it every year . . . Settling in, then, at that new flat?'

Around them, the burr of muted conversations, the clink of plates and cutlery. A woman in a white apron set melon slices in glass dishes before them.

'Well, let's dig in,' Susan said gallantly.

He ate in a choreographed way. One false move and it would be gone, lost. She followed his economic movements. Fork, plate, turkey, stuffing, butter on the potatoes. A cough, a flourish of the hand could upset the entire apple cart.

'Going to Ireland tomorrow. Have I told you?' she said, brightly, her voice raised. 'Huge career fair in Dublin. And renting a car to visit that estate in the West. Grandad's. Do you remember, Daddy?'

The Manor staff were seated at a long table by the kitchen door – Mediterranean, pale eastern European, Balkan faces above white scrubs. Wine glasses clinking, the snap of Christmas crackers, screeches of laughter at the little gifts inside.

He said, 'We were there once, my mum, your aunt Elizabeth and I. Ghastly place . . . But once, they let me come on a fox hunt. You know there were things at the house in Hargrove . . . From there, from Father. Did you know that?'

More laughter from the staff table. Heavy, foreign accents intermingled with cockney. Birds, Susan thought. Migrating birds who had somehow veered off course down into Hargrove, the country backwoods, this house with its topiary garden and stage-set rooms.

The matron sat next to the Christmas tree with another

woman – the weekend matron; she just recognised her now – and two administrators, men in crisp suits and red Christmas ties.

'More turkey, Daddy?' she asked. 'I'm sure we could ask for . . .'

He shook his head.

Chatter dwindled as the matron clinked on a glass, then stood to make a speech.

In a fluting voice she said she hoped they had all enjoyed themselves; they, the administrators, certainly had. And the visiting families, they were the residents' – and indeed the staff's – most valued asset, a crucial link in the wellbeing of their clients. A long tradition here at the Manor, the family Christmas luncheon. And now, if everyone was quite finished, coffee and teas served back out in the drawing room with Christmas pudding and cream. And afterward, the activities director would lead them in the annual carol-singing. She wagged a finger at them. Oh, now, there were to be no excuses, for they had songbooks for all. And from past singalongs, she *personally* knew of some very fine songbirds indeed.

A break from the carol-singing to watch the Queen's Christmas message on a large TV. Old heads cocked, gazing at the screen, white, flattened hair under paper party hats. Her Majesty's deliberate words. Two women had come to collect their glass dishes with traces of Christmas pudding, smears of whipped cream.

He watched obediently with the others, his usual chair angled away from the window. His presents – two cashmere cardigans from Liberty's – and their wrapping paper strewn at his feet, a hymn book stuffed in his top jacket pocket.

She sat watching, listening, determined like all the other families to see this day through to the end.

Chapter 15

McHugh watched the back of his brother's balding head and wished he'd returned to London for Christmas. They were walking up the *bóithrín*, the side road that led from the house, up through the McHugh land on the side of a mountain.

His manager, Jimmy, and Jimmy's wife Phyllis had invited him. Hadn't seen him in so long, Phyllis had coaxed; so nice to have him over, fatten him up with a nice, traditional Christmas in their dining room in Pinner.

But on this, his first Christmas back in Ireland, he felt a duty to drive the forty miles to Carraig, presents stuffed randomly on the back seat of the Volvo, Lovín perched up front, eyes fixed on the road. His sister-in-law, Rita, offered him his pick of the Bed and Breakfast rooms; no guests this time of year.

McHugh's nephews, Lorcan and Tomás, were home from university – earnest, tall young men in faded jeans and hiking boots. Next June, Lorcan would graduate from Dublin City University in computer science; Tomás was finishing a Master's in Cork.

The boys had walked on ahead, up the *bóithrín* where the small, mountainside fields were washed pale by a winter sun. Lovín and Seamus's sheepdog, Shep, chased, sniffed around each other, then Lovín tore away to bark at something in the briars. Lorcan whistled after

95

her; the two boys were enjoying the antics of their uncle's new pup.

'Sheep you'll put in this Rathloe place?' Seamus asked.

All day, his brother's questions nettled McHugh. Too much sudden camaraderie, this forced, farmer-to-farmer chatter. Better, wasn't it, when they treated him like the visiting brother home from England?

'Cattle,' McHugh said. 'Been doing a lot of reading up on it.'

They had each picked up a stick to walk with, to lash at the briars and nettles, cut through the frosty air. McHugh remembered, it was something they'd always done as boys, but this, too, made him edgy.

Seamus stopped to unlatch a wide gate into the old farmyard.

Years ago, this was the yard McHugh had left in Seamus's car to catch a train for the boat to England. The ruins of the old, thatched McHugh house had been fortified and roofed with corrugated iron to make sheds.

'Like to do this right if I'm doing it at all,' McHugh said. 'Important in this market to plan for maximum efficiency, return on investment.'

'Ah, 'tis hard to beat the few sheep though,' Seamus persisted. 'Subsidies are mighty now altogether. Never beat the bitta government cash coming in your door, hah?'

In Pinner, it would have been peaceful. Jimmy and Phyllis believed in after-dinner cognacs and comfortable silences.

In the early years, for Christmas homecomings before their mother's death, it troubled him to walk this land: his childhood house turned to a shed, the yard tarmacadamed like a tennis court. Bushes, trees, copses of hazel rock had been flattened. Stone walls, gaps and galvanised gateways in unaccustomed spots. It was like waking up in a room where someone had secretly rearranged the furniture.

In the yard, Seamus stopped to break a disc of ice on top of a water barrel. Through a door in the house-turned-shed he called 'suck, suck, suck, suck' after calves, went in to spread fresh straw on calf beds.

McHugh was carrying bails of hay from a shed, hoisting them over the wall to where eleven cattle were jostling, their breath fogging on the air. He brushed off his clothes after each bail.

Seamus came trudging up through the field gate; in each hand, buckets of feedstuff for the sheep that Shep was stalking, nipping and driving from the far end. Lorcan and Tomás, already in the next, hillside field, stopped, turned in the far gap.

'Want a hand?' Lorcan shouted, his voice carrying across the frosty air.

'Go on, we're grand,' Seamus answered. The boys kept on walking, their tall, loping figures growing smaller on the mountainside.

Before dinner, Lorcan had been telling them about the hiking group he'd joined in Dublin. Great gas. Brilliant *craic* with all the friends in the Wicklow Mountains every Sunday.

The stock fed, the two older men were following in the boys' path up hill. 'Ah, sure, those two wouldn't know the back end of a bullock from the front,' Seamus laughed. 'And forty times better off. Not what we wanted for them, Rita and me. When they've the brains for better, that's what they should do besides all this.' He turned, waved his stick to take in the patchwork of fields and houses that fell off beneath them to the sea.

McHugh wanted to protest. Hadn't the land been good enough for Seamus himself? Good enough for their widowed mother with two young boys to feed? Today, he couldn't seem to contain his touchiness – random thoughts, malaise.

'Still an' all, I'd advise the sheep myself. Put in a few anyways. Ten or twelve hoggets, I'd say for a start.'

McHugh didn't answer.

'And you'd want a dog. There's a lad below in the village here with mighty breeding dogs. I could enquire for you. With sheep, a good dog is half the battle.'

'I have a dog,' McHugh said. He swished his stick through a clump of nettles.

'Well I meant . . . a working . . . like a . . .'

A right dog. That's what Seamus had intended to say, and McHugh tensed with a fierce loyalty towards Lovín, his only companion for this past month.

The afternoon shadows had lengthened across the mountain. The brothers had turned back for the house, their steps quickening down the sloping fields, the dogs trotting ahead. With his stick Seamus pointed out different houses. Delivered news, updates on McHugh's old neighbours.

'The Murphys,' he jabbed towards a small, 1950s bungalow with Christmas lights in the window. One of the old Murphy sisters died. A fortnight ago. Hadn't McHugh heard? Rita was saying that for sure he, McHugh, would come up to Carraig for the funeral. Did he not read the daily deaths in the paper?

Seamus pointed towards another house – a long, white bungalow with a plume of turf smoke from the chimney. Old Tiernan Walsh's place. Crippled with arthritis, the creature, kept going as long as he could, but now . . . rumours of him signing over to a nephew from Limerick.

And the Durkans? He remembered them, of course he did, why wouldn't he? One of the sisters in McHugh's own class at the national school, married a man from up the country. Her son now that had the place; talk of him turning some acreage into a holiday resort, a health place with thatched tourist cottages, walking tours, horseback riding down on the beach.

'What do you think of the likes of that?' Seamus asked.

McHugh went to answer, but Seamus interrupted, 'Sure, when all is said and done, might be as good as any. Oh, plenty around opposed to it, talk of the young lad getting a huge government grant for it, a lot of jealousy.'

'D'you not find them very standoffish up there in Rathloe?' Seamus asked. 'God, we heard ever that they had that oul' uppity way with them. Cagey. And mad for land, what?'

'Oh, no. Quite different now,' McHugh said. 'New people moved in, land snapped up for houses like hot cakes . . . In fact, they're saying—'

'Still an' all now, that's what I ever heard about the people of Rathloe. Used to meet the odd fella from up that way at the cattle marts. Cute as a shaggin' fox. Could herd mice at a crossroads . . .'

McHugh thought of his overnight bag left in his room, the long night ahead with tea, Christmas cake, the two boys showing off their Christmas presents: Lorcan got the packaged version of a new computer operating system he'd been dying to lay his hands on; Tomás a new laptop for his studies. A bit more than they'd planned on, Rita had laughed, but then wasn't that the way?

They had arrived at the front gateway of the house with its black lettering on the white pillars, 'B & B, Guests and Teas.'

'Look, I think I'll continue on down. Walk the beach,' McHugh said.

'But she'll have the tea ready inside and the dessert. Coffee kept hot for the lads, if you'd prefer coffee, like,' Seamus said, suspicious of his brother's rebuff. Who went to the beach on a freezing Christmas?

'I'll be fine,' McHugh muttered, already headed down the *bóithrín* and whistling for Lovín.

*   *   *

They left a trail of human and dog footprints across the wet sand. A shaft of pale sunlight lingered out over the bay. Seagulls wheeled, screeched, coasted on the rising breeze. Lovín chased them along the edge of the water, paws splashing into the tide.

Yes, he wished he hadn't come, had either stayed at home alone in his rental cottage outside Ballyshee or flown back to London.

For the first time since his return last September, he felt an old, immigrant loneliness, a desperation. He hated this.

It reminded him of those first, early Christmases home from London. The minute he stepped off the night boat, all these things rose from nowhere: nostalgia yet this inexplicable touchiness.

On those and later visits, he would walk among these fields and *bóithríns*, everything like a half-remembered dream. The briars, bushes, walls, the main road going into the village of Carraig – it all seemed to mock his London amnesia, a past suspended.

On those early trips home, the house would be full of visitors – neighbours who came dutifully to see the Paddy returned. Men sitting in over the range in the old house drinking bottles of stout, the chat seeping around the kitchen, everything repeated, agreed, you-never-said-a-truer-word, a relay race of words and cigarettes under the brown, wood-slat ceiling. Then, he would suddenly long to be back in London, even in his dismal room in Shepherd's Bush, because it was simpler; safe from these feelings suddenly laid raw and open.

But this year, he would not be retreating to his luxury flat on an anonymous street in a grid of other streets and Notting Hill cul de sacs. This year, it was for good, and his brother's banter made him feel helpless and desperate.

As children, they had only visited this beach after the summer tourists had all gone home. Down from their mountainside home they came, fishing with rods made from string and hazel sticks, sling-shots to hunt rabbits among the dunes.

He remembered: on a hot, summer day, their mother, Seamus and himself, forking, raking hay. He and Seamus stripped to the waist; their mother in a hand-me-down sleeveless summer dress, loud, American prints, charity from a cousin in Cleveland, Ohio, a pair of old, winter shoes cut open at the toe to make sandals.

Down below, they would watch the cars trundling down to the beach, the coloured blankets, picnics, children running in swimming togs. He remembered that youthful sting of envy, shame, a boyish wish that somehow, the McHughs could just taste something – anything – of this life, these people who could skip along the sand and drink tea from Thermos flasks.

From her thatched house and windswept fields, Mrs McHugh the widow saw a world of smart alec people – luckier, worthier, more blessed by the hand of God than them.

Late at night in that room in Shepherd's Bush, in a sudden, maudlin fit, McHugh would unearth photos of her. There it was: every feature of her stricken face, the fatalistic keening over dead stock, summer rain on a field of newly cut hay, ruined turf in the bog. And then, the final proof of God's capricious hand – her younger son took a boat to England.

Tucking her photos away, he knew then, as he knew now, that it was from that gloom, that keening that all his paths and life investments had led away.

He reached the stream at the end of the beach. He stepped, balanced from rock to rock in the rushing water. Lovín came, gambolled across, her underbelly already dripping. They would have to return soon. Already, the rising tide was eddying among the round, speckled stones, knocking them together like billiards.

He climbed a sandy path up through the dunes to a

narrow finger of land jutting out over the sea. The path ended at a stone wall, a garden gate, a house with its name, '*Súil na Mara*', in faded letters on the side wall.

Years ago, a stranger – some class of a poet, they said down in the village pub – from Dublin had commissioned lorries with concrete bricks, mortar, cement, to rattle down a *bóithrín* on the other side of this point. Built a house that everyone said would end up floating in the Atlantic.

A cantankerous oul' bastard, they said, brought women there by the score. Only came when it suited him, then off back again to Dublin.

McHugh walked around the front. The grey paint was flaking off the house walls, the wide, oceanside windows miraculously unharmed by storms. Between the house and the cliff edge was a lip of land, a rock garden started and then abandoned. A steep, treacherous path led down through the cliff to a small, half-moon beach.

Lovín came panting around the side of the house from the garden. He crouched to rub her ears, listened to the sea crashing beneath them.

It was time to go. Tide would be up; then impossible to cross back over that stream. Time for tea and Christmas television specials at his brother's house.

But dog and man lingered. It was bitterly cold, a crescent moon rising over the bay.

In London, the only thing he'd missed had been this wild beach, this hermit's spot at the edge of the world with its smell of seaweed, the screech of birds.

Turning, he saw that the mountain was shrouded in darkness now, Christmas lights twinkling from the houses. From here, the fields and *bóithríns* that just two hours ago had unsettled him, now seemed peaceful and harmless.

Without memory.

Chapter 16

She hadn't expected Boxing Day in Ireland to be a big party, but this was ridiculous. She had already unpacked in the big, upstairs room and now she was starving. Lunch, a sandwich, something.

She paced up and down the hotel lobby with its black and white tiles, approached again the high, wooden desk. Had she missed some vital clue? A note with 'Back in five minutes'? Directions for tourists who wanted a sandwich and a stiff drink?

In the lounge, a fire had been set, a television was on above the bar. On a seat under the front window, an old man fast asleep, his head lolling back against the upholstered seat. His false teeth looked as if they might clatter to the floor at any minute. She wondered if she shouldn't wake him, but something about his grey, flaccid face decided her against it.

It was a mad idea to come here to this town of Ballyshee – absolutely ludicrous, but too late now.

Back out into the hotel lobby again. Oh yes, this Hermitage Hotel was far from her vision of a cosy, country inn. The entire place a contradiction – this antique foyer with its tiled floor and antique desk; upstairs, her old-fashioned bedroom with a fireplace and high mantel. But then this bar and lounge with its smoked glass and blond wood, garish, crimson velvet seats – like something in a casino or a cruise ship. And no staff. No food. Not a whiff, no rattle of plates in a dining room someplace.

The rental car place at the airport had said this town and this hotel were the closest accommodation to the village of Rathloe, where her grandfather had once lived.

Outside, a straggle of old shops, all shut up tight except for Christmas decorations in the windows. Her footsteps were loud on the footpath. She pulled on a pair of leather gloves. Had everyone just skidaddled off, left town for the day? Some tragedy? Disaster? Something religious?

At last, the familiar smell of a pub – stale beer, cigarettes. From the front door she followed the sound of a loud television. Down an almost pitch-dark corridor towards a cloud of cigarette smoke, a shadowed room with a tiny bar, men staring up at a horse race on television.

'Come on, come on to fuck,' they screamed, echoed each other, jostled on their bar stools, one slapping his hip and buttocks as if he were riding a horse to a finish line.

'Are you all right there?' a barman with a beefy face asked her.

'Ah, bollix,' three of the men chorused.

'Are you all right?' the barman asked again rattily. The race over, the men's attention was now diverted to her, a strange woman.

'I . . . I'm fine, thanks,' she muttered. 'Just . . . looking for a friend.' She could hear the men sniggering.

On the corner of Main Street, the chip shop was closed, then she turned down a sloping street, High Street. Lights had come on in the houses; upstairs a chink of light between curtains; for which she felt relieved. This odd little town hadn't been deserted after all.

She turned into a grotty town park. It must have
rained a lot. The films, photographs, the documentaries
on Ireland – made you think of the place as some sodden
little hillock bracing for the next deluge. And true so
far. Two hours ago, her plane had descended out of
a dense, grey sky into an outpost of brown earth, a
religious basilica suddenly rising, appearing like an oil
rig from among the clouds and bog.

At the airport, the wind through the rental car office
door was bitter. All the way up here along those treacherous roads, the fields were frosted white, so that she
was glad she'd brought her old, sheepskin jacket and
beret.

A dog appeared out of the undergrowth – a golden
retriever pup who zoomed past her, its tail high, twitching. It turned, then came to trot around her.

'Hello there, little fellow.' She bent to pet its golden
head. 'You lost, then? Hmm? You wondering where
everyone in this town is, too?'

The pup reached to rest two muddy paws on her
jacket, hot doggy breath in her face.

'Down, Lovín. Leave the nice lady alone.' A stern
voice came from behind. She turned.

'Sorry,' the man said. 'She tends to get over-friendly.'

Distinguished-looking – incredible blue eyes, trim,
grey beard, a dog lead in his hand. Shoulders slightly
slouched the way tall men did. English accent. A fellow
tourist?

'It's all right.' She followed his gaze to the muddy
paw-prints on her suede jacket. 'Brushes off. Old anyway. Marvellous dog . . .'

'Yes, yes, she is.'

She'd never seen such blue eyes.

'Lovín!' he summoned the pup. To her he said, 'Well.
Enjoy your afternoon. Sorry again.' Then strode past
her. The dog, Love Dog, or something, chased madly

along the river, zigzagging in the long grass to follow scent.

Strange man. Strange name for a dog. Oh! damn, she should have asked him. He would have known somewhere to get some hot lunch or early dinner.

It was dark already, the frigid night sky dotted with stars. Had she walked back to a different place, a chameleon hotel? Music came from the lounge, a clatter of voices, glasses, throaty laughter. The lounge was packed. Two men in painted faces and scarecrow outfits – old coats, string around the waist, pyjama bottoms – were sitting on low stools, one playing an accordion, the other a fiddle. On a bar stool sat a woman, her face painted white, a high witch hat, black cape, playing a banjo. Up and down the lounge floor went two young dancers – children in clown costumes – faces painted white, round red noses, shoes painted in pink and purple. Everyplace around the tables were men and women, large family groups – mothers, fathers, children, grandmothers, a litter of orange, beer, sherry glasses, children munching on crisps. Every stool along the bar was full. A young barman in a white shirt pulling pints of beer, flipping the tops off tonic bottles, money being shoved at him, trays of drinks being passed out over the counter.

'Yow!' a man at the bar yelped, clapped his hands to the music. 'Another one now let ye,' he screamed to the young dancers who were curtseying and bowing to the crowd.

The fiddler started another tune. The children reeled up and down the lounge, feet high in the air, their white-painted faces laughing.

'D'you want to get in there?' a man at the counter asked her, shunting his bar stool aside. 'No joke trying to get a drink today so 'tisn't.' He eyed her, the beret, coat, well-cut trousers, laced-up winter boots. He picked up his cigarettes from the counter, offered her the packet. 'A fag while you're waiting, there?'

She shook her head, 'No.' Then added, 'But thank you.'

He roared down the bar, 'Oi, Gerry. Gerrín, there's a woman here what wants ya.' Instantly, the young barman came.

'Um . . . any chance of some lunch, dinner?'

He stared at her, a flicker of annoyance.

'I'll have to check in the back. I think they've soup. Oxtail. That's all we have and sandwiches. Toasted.' His eyes darted to left and right, to the waiting faces, hands raised signing for another round.

'Toasted ham and cheese, mustard. Bowl of oxtail.' He scribbled it on a dog-eared notebook from his shirt pocket.

'Right, it'll be a half an hour anyways. Busy day, like . . .' He went to walk away.

'Oh, and a gin and tonic,' she said, her voice pleading.

She stood to the side with her gin and tonic. Felt conspicuous, like someone who'd unwittingly walked onto a spotlit stage.

Someone pulled on her sleeve. 'Why don't you sit down?' A seventy-ish woman was smiling up at her, nodded to a lounge stool at a table. Susan sat obediently.

'Are you enjoying it?' the woman asked, nodding to the musicians and dancers.

'Yes, yes very much,' Susan said. All around their table was a huge, extended family: younger women, daughters with made-up faces, lipstick. Young husbands, sons who cracked jokes, drank beer, nodded curtly to her and then looked away. Children who swung their legs in time to the music.

'Home for the Christmas?' the woman asked. She had a wide, fleshy face, permed hair. She was sipping a steaming hot toddy, a lemony, clove smell that made Susan even hungrier.

'No, no. Just visiting actually,' Susan said.

'Grand to get the break all the same.'

'Yes.'

'Always nice to get the bit of a rest, isn't it?'

'Yes, yes it is,' Susan said, sipping her G & T. The woman flashed her a smile.

'Especially this time of year.'

'Yes.'

'Hard oul' going nowadays. Not like one time. 'Spose it's even worse in England?'

'Probably.'

'A pure rat race.'

'Perhaps.'

'Still, people'd be worse without a job.'

'Yes, I suppose they would.'

'That's th'only way to say it, isn't it?'

Susan eyed the woman discreetly. She had the feeling this conversation could go on all night, except that now everyone had stopped talking to clap wildly as the young dancers curtseyed to the crowd again. End of another tune. More yelps of 'Yow! Yow!' from the men at the bar.

The musicians started a slow, mournful tune while the children went from table to table, a hat held out to collect money.

'Buskers?' Susan asked the woman, but knew instantly she was wrong.

'Mummers. D'ye have them at all in England?

'Em . . . No.'

'I suppose ye don't. Big tradition here.'

'Perhaps somewhere up—'

'St Stephen's Day. Best day of the Christmas really.'

'Yes, yes. I suppose it is.'

'Grand to get out after all that cooking, isn't it?'

'Actually, I—'

'And the bit of a late sleep. No stir in any house until late.'

Susan nodded. St Stephen's Day. Boxing Day. *No stir in any house.* Was this where everyone'd been earlier then? The entire town hibernating until things started up at the pub?'

'You've them all home, Mrs T,' Gerry the barman said, delivering Susan's soup and sandwich and nodding around the table.

'I have. A pure madhouse, that's what it is. A pure madhouse. Want danger money to come into my house at the moment, so you would.' The older woman laughed.

The barman hurried back to a waiting bar, balancing his tray of empty glasses. Mrs T went to say something again, but stopped abruptly when she saw how hungrily Susan was eating.

It was half past nine, and the Hermitage lounge was really packed now. The young dancers had left, but the musicians stayed, set up formally on a little wooden stage to the left of the bar. Switched to an electric guitar and country music. Two or three couples shuffling, waltzing on a tiny space before the stage.

Faces came and went, visited the different groups gathered around the tables to shout hellos, welcome-homes. Mrs T's family was popular, well-known, and soon, strong, shirt-sleeved arms were being stretched in over Susan's head for handshakes, a playful punch on Mrs T's sons' shoulders, all the questions about where so-and-so was living now? What were they doing? How long were they staying around for the holidays?

'How did ye get over the Christmas?' most of them

asked. Curious, Susan thought, as if the holiday were a flu or a viral infection.

Hard to believe that only this morning, she'd woken in her flat at Railroad Place, stuffed some warm casuals in a suitcase and rung a taxi for Stansted Airport. Could it really be?

She'd had too much to drink. Her new friend, Mrs T – the woman finally introduced herself and each and every one of her entire clan – insisted on buying her a drink, a Christmas drink to welcome her to Ireland. And, of course, Susan had bought one back, and then suddenly she was included in this huge round of drinks.

She yawned.

'Sure you're not going already?' Mrs T asked.

'Been a very, very long day,' Susan said, stifling another yawn.

'But sure, the night's only starting. There's a dance on in the back in the ballroom, later on.'

'Really. I think I'll turn in. Thank you . . . for everything.' She touched Mrs T's shoulder, and the older woman stood to shake her hand solemnly.

'Oh! I hope now you enjoy your stay around here. Bad time of the year for travelling.' Mrs T seemed to be deliberating something. At last she said, 'Look . . . promise me that if you get stuck for anything, you'll ask Gerry the barman here or anyone for our house, take us as you find us, but you'd be very welcome, so you would.'

She lay there between the crisp, white sheets. She closed her eyes. She could hear some faint voices from somewhere down below. At last, her thoughts centred, came to rest until there was nothing but this high ceiling and a chink of streetlight through the curtain.

Chapter 17

Dismal little place. A road between ostentatious houses – balustrades and Italianate balconies, wide gateways with their landscaped gardens, double garages. Unfinished somehow, as if they'd just been plopped there at the edge of these tiny fields and were waiting for something.

Just as she slowed for a vicious turn and some faded 'Welcome to Rathloe' signs, there they were, just where the hotel manager said they would be: the high, elegant gates set between stone pillars.

She parked and got out. Stood staring through the gate's ornate railings at the frozen, churned-up fields beyond. Somewhere, a chainsaw raked across the frosted silence.

This was it. The gates, the driveway her grandfather had come through in another age. Pity. For the first time, she felt pity for the man she'd only really seen in dog-eared photos. Did he arrive here on a freezing morning like this? Like her, his solitary, tremulous steps through unwelcoming territory?

She crunched along the new, white gravel. Looking behind her as if waiting for someone to shout, 'Halt!'

At last the avenue curved under a scramble of briars and wild holly. Gratefully, she ducked under this arbour towards the clearing beyond.

'Ow!' A briar caught her cheek. Blood on her gloved

hand when she touched the scrape. It throbbed. Tears sprang to her eyes as she crossed the clearing before the house.

She sat on the stone front steps, a wad of tissues held to her cheek, turning to read the graffiti on the plywood doorway.

At last, the blood stopped. She blew her nose, got up to stride around the side of the house.

Disappointing. Very small for a country house. Nothing like the national registry mansions back home in England. And squarer, stolid stone with its thick ivy fissuring across the upper half. This, and the boarded-up doors, windows, gave it a shameful visage, a tramp with his patched, gouged-out eyes. Crows cawed in the shattered roof, the chimneys. The chainsaw had stopped.

Her feet were chilled by the long, wet grass in the rear gardens.

There was a stone urn – the only thing about this place still unharmed. She searched for a stone to break the film of ice that had formed on the green, slimy water. The urn was beautiful, the stone mottled yellow, but everything – the fluted edges, the carvings of grape leaves down the sides – was intact.

She crouched to peer through the windows at ground level – the only opening to the house. There was a fetid smell of drenched mud and animal dung. Chinks of light came through the stones, a wall at the front of the house. Her eyes adjusted to the dark. Were they fireplaces? Huge, high hearths – roasting hearths. She shivered. She was looking in the great kitchens, the place her own grandfather had once called for meals, bottles of claret; parish women probably stood scraping vegetables, mashing potatoes, kneading bread. Strange. All these years, yet here was this old kitchen, these blackened hearths – a mockery of all the people they had outlived.

'Oooh!' A dog lunged towards her. She toppled backward into the grass.

A tall man came striding around the house in an anorak, corduroys and wellingtons.

'This is private—' Recognising her, he stopped. 'This is private property,' he finished, but without the initial sharpness. He frowned at her face. 'What happened?'

She stood up, straightened the beret on her head. The man from the town park last night.

He came towards her, looked as if he might reach and touch the scrape, her throbbing cheek. He stopped.

'I caught it out there, in front.'

'Don't you think you need something? Antiseptic anyway. A Band-aid? There's a shop up in the village . . .'

'Look. I *am* sorry. About trespassing. I didn't know the house actually belonged . . .'

Something had softened in the features. He said, 'My dog Lovín seems quite keen on you.'

'What? Oh! Yes, in the town yesterday. Ballysh . . .' She petted Lovín's head, let her nuzzle against her. 'I'm staying in a hotel there.'

'The hotel.'

'Hmm?'

'The Hermitage. It's the only hotel. Run it in their own way, too.'

She laughed. 'Yes. Actually, I was looking about for food when I saw you yesterday. Thought the entire town had been abandoned.'

'Takes a while to get used to things around here.'

This accent . . . Vowels too round, soft for a native Irish, yet a burr of something. Cornwall? Wales?

'Where in England, then?' he asked.

'Cripton. North of London. You know it?'

He nodded.

'You?'

'Notting Hill.' She had the feeling he expected her to

113

contradict, to question it. 'Back home – or here – since October, but still keep business going over there. Foolish to give up . . .'

'Actually born here? Rathloe?'

'About forty miles away. A place called Carraig. Seaside. Went to London over thirty years ago.'

She tucked a stray lock of hair under her beret. 'First time in Ireland, actually. Yesterday . . . in that little park, I'd just arrived.'

'Look . . .' He hesitated, then something relented in the lean face, the blue eyes. 'Look, I've got some things to finish here, but I usually go for an afternoon pint in the village local. If my briars are going to almost tear your eye out the least I can do is buy you a drink. You can't miss the place. O'Neill's – bit odd, but cosy.'

She checked her watch. 'All right, then. Twelve-ish? Could do with some lunch first.'

He laughed – handsome. 'Depends on the landlady's mood, I'm afraid. But you could try.'

Going back up the garden steps, he caught her elbow. 'Careful. The place is a deathtrap.'

She turned for a last look at the house, the rear gardens, the orchard walls. 'Must've been a nice old place, though, don't you think?'

He stopped. 'Yes, I suppose it was. But now it's just . . . well, a liability. I put up No Trespassing signs, but they seem to disappear. Waiting for something worse than just a briar scratch to happen.'

They lingered on the avenue; she headed for the gateway; he ready to troop back across his frozen fields to his chainsaw. She shaded her eyes from the winter sunlight. 'Will you restore it, then?'

A frown passed across his features. Eyes hard, narrowed. 'Hardly.'

'I see.' She flashed him a tight smile, apologetic. For what?

'In the pub then,' he said, turning away.

'Great.' She'd been somehow dismissed. Pleasantries terminated.

'Wait!'

She stopped. He was a little out of breath when he caught up with her.

'Look, I don't know your name.'

'Susan. Susan Brown Whitaker.'

'John McHugh.' A practised, businessman's handshake. She watched as her name registered in the blue eyes. A flicker of possibility, curiosity.

'Twelve-ish then,' she said, turning again for the gates of Rathloe House.

Chapter 18

'Ah-hem.' Sweeney shuffled his feet on the rail of the bar stool.

Himself, Mannion, Walsh and O'Brien had been sitting with empty pint glasses for the last ten minutes. 'Ah . . . any chance of a pint, here, Kitty or are we supposed to order by computer now?'

She eyed the four men sourly, then crossed to the Guinness taps to start four pints.

She'd been discussing search engines, on-line trading and electronic travel magazines with Vinnie Mannion, Mannion's youngest son home for Christmas from the university in Dublin.

'Sent all the Christmas cards electronically this year, Kit,' Vinnie said, methodically peeling the label off his Budweiser bottle. 'All me girlfriends in Dublin, you know.' He winked at her, enjoying this torture of his father and the three codger friends.

'Oh! God yes,' Kitty said, watching the men's pints settle. 'Sure who could be writing and licking envelopes and stamps and the divil knows what in this day and age? Gone out with the flood . . .'

Finally, she delivered the pints to the four men. 'Now, men. Grand.' She stood there waiting as they mumbled and rooted in their trouser pockets for the money.

They'd been listening to her bragging to Vinnie about on-line trading, whatever that was, how a careful person can make money on that computer, and yet, not a sight of a Christmas drink on the house for them. Loyal customers. A lot more in her line than all this guff about computers that she got for free in the first place.

'Well, I'm off, Kit. Happy New Year if I don't see ya.' Vinnie, pulling on his leather jacket, was headed for the door.

'Lovely, Vin. I'll . . .' She mimicked someone typing at a keyboard. '. . . Send you all the news up there in Dublin. You have *my* e-mail, haven't you?' Kitty called after him, while the men counted out their money.

The door clicked behind them. McHugh. A bit early today.

But no, a woman in a beret and a suede coat, sheepskin collar pulled up around her neck as if she were in the Arctic. A big scratch on her cheek as if she'd just fallen in the ditch.

Kitty eyebrowed the men. They nodded knowingly.

Earlier, there'd been a phone call from Margaret that an Englishwoman had come in the shop looking for antiseptic ointment and a box of Band-aids. Said she'd sustained her minor injuries while taking a stroll around the big house. That very morning. Posh. Very posh.

'A wife,' Mannion had surmised when Kitty relayed the phone call from shop to pub. 'Deffo McHugh's ex-wife. And come for the pound of flesh. Ah, Jaysus, sure, didn't they know bloody well there had to be something fishy . . .'

Now, the Englishwoman seemed puzzled at the sight of Kitty behind the pub counter, arms folded, the lipsticked smile. 'Oh! Hello, again,' she said.

'Now,' Kitty said, waiting for the Englishwoman's drink order.

'Em . . . G & T, thanks,' the woman said. 'Lemon if you've got it.'

She turned to look around her, as if she'd come to investigate something, but now it was gone missing. 'And some lunch?'

'Hmm?' Kitty was great at playing innocent. Nothing nettled her more than having to make sandwiches in the winter. Not enough profit margin, phoning Margaret up in the shop for a few slices of ham, turkey, plugging in a sandwich toaster for a single sandwich.

'Some lunch,' the woman repeated. Oh, very posh indeed. Like something from a film or *Upstairs Downstairs.*

'What sort of lunch?' Kitty called over her shoulder as she pushed the spirits glass up under the Cork Gin bottle.

O'Brien kicked Walsh under the stool. A delighted smirk as they stared at the telly.

'Meat pie? Homemade soup? Green salad? Even a sandwich . . .'

'What kinda sandwich?' Kitty asked cagily.

The Englishwoman spread her hands, the voice apologetic. 'Whatever you've got on today?'

'I'd have to ring up to the shop, like. See what's available. This time of the year, the delivery men . . .' Kitty said, reaching reluctantly for the black phone that sat on a shelf.

'But you just came from . . .' the woman started to say.

The four men eyed each other. Brilliant. Oh! They loved when tourists got codded, thinking Kitty was Margaret and vice versa. Feckin' brilliant.

'A mistress,' Sweeney whispered, shifting the gabardine hat back on his head.

Mannion's eyes grew rounder.

Sweeney leaned in closer. 'Half a dozen of them he has. That's what I heard within in the town before

119

the Christmas. Not a skirt safe in London.' He nodded
sagely.

'Oh!' Kitty flinched. Moral outrage. 'But Mr McHugh
is really very nice . . . I mean, never an ounce of trouble.'

Sweeney took a long drink, eyed the television above
their heads.

They waited.

At last he whispered gravely, 'The quiet pig.'

'Hmm?' the others asked.

'That's what we heard ever, 'Tis the quiet pig that'll
root.' Sweeney nodded again.

The other three peered around to the fireplace where
McHugh and his mistress were sitting talking, heads
together; he with a suave, dazzling smile that they'd
never seen before.

O'Neill's was full by now, late afternoon. Families
home for the Christmas, daytrippers, locals who hadn't
gone back to work yet, bundled-up toddlers, children in
hats, scarves for a walk down the village, and then stop
to see friends at O'Neill's.

Out of her big coat and that beret, the men had to
admit she was a fine-looking woman. Refined features.

McHugh got up to the Gents'. On the way back,
stopped at the bar for another drink, th'oul grey jib
cocked in the air like a puck goat.

At the fireplace, that sissy oul' dog opened one eye,
got up, then rested its head in the mistress's lap.

Sweeney's little eyes were narrowed. He watched,
studied over all the heads, the Christmas-time smoke
and chatter. Something about this Englishwoman . . .
Worth a few enquiries for sure . . . And when was he,
Sweeney, ever wrong?

Chapter 19

'Em . . . you'll excuse me,' he said, almost stepping on Lovín's tail as he manoeuvred out past her, their pub table, the clusters of Christmas-time drinkers. Curtly he nodded to each group as he passed – young couples and children. Edel Quinn, Jarlath, Claire and Richie Sweeney, some others he didn't know. He walked down the corridor for the Gents'. Breathing room. Needed to take it all in.

The Gents' toilet reeked of bleach, disinfectant and old pee. He crossed to the basin to splash cold water on his sweating face.

'Yes,' she'd said when he'd finally asked her, tucked in at O'Neill's fireplace with drinks in hand. 'Yes. Right first time about the name. My grandfather died shortly after I was born, but my dad remembers being here . . .'

He leaned his forehead against the cold, white tiles. Strange day. Strange woman. And here she was now, back to find her roots, just like the Yanks did, only it was at Rathloe House – his house.

One thing for sure: he couldn't have her wandering around the village for the rest of her visit, get wind of the Preservation Committee. Edel Quinn and her yuppie friends. Right under their noses: the genuine article, true blood descendant of the big house. A bloody poster girl for their preservation nonsense.

121

'Em . . . are you all right there?' a young boy, headed for the urinal, asked him.

'Fine,' McHugh said quickly. 'Bit crowded out there today, what?'

He took a comb from a back pocket to tidy his hair. Blast it, what was it about this Brown woman? She was just his type, too – sophisticated, classy. He grinned at his reflection. Had to admit he liked the idea of British landed gentry – or the closest thing to it. And now, here she's come to look, beg for admission, apologise for trespassing on his land.

Cool. That was the way to handle this. Get her out of Rathloe before any of the preservation crowd got wind of her.

Waiting for his drinks at the counter he watched her. She was staring into the fire, cheeks flushed in the heat, the prim head sideways, sandy hair flattened from her beret. Something stricken about her chiselled face.

He watched the long, pale fingers stroking Lovín's head in her lap, scratching his dog's ears. He was wrong. Even he could admit that. Something about her besides the spoiled, English aristocrat. Even without that scratch down her cheek, she was . . .

She looked up. Smiled. He'd been caught gawking.

'Now. A G & T and a pint of beer.' Kitty plunked his drinks down. 'Got over the Christmas all right, did you, Mr McHugh?'

'What?'

'Did you get over the Christmas?'

'Um . . . Yes.' He handed her the money, but still she stood there.

'Your . . . ah . . . friend down there. Is she all right? Was her sandwich all right? She seemed kind of bothered or something there earlier on.' Kitty's sweetest smile, inquisitive little eyes fixed on him.

'She's fine.' McHugh shrugged.

He could feel Sweeney and the other men's gaze following him back down to the fireplace. Oh yes, tomorrow crack of dawn, he would get Ms Susan Brown out of Rathloe.

Chapter 20

People jostled against them on the pavement. Called, waved to each other from either side of the street: 'Howr'ya! Were you out yourself last night? You were? Any *craic*?'

Shoppers wandered off the pavement into the street, then back again, couples arm in arm, young men strutting in leather jackets, jeans, knitted hats.

Everywhere this buzz of chat and laughter on the Saturday afternoon air. She would remember Ireland this way: clusters of people laughing, smoking – all in on a private, nationwide joke.

A fiddle player stood in a doorway, wearing a stage-Irish tweed cap, blond hair, Scandinavian face. She stopped to listen, threw a pound in his box. McHugh doubled back to wait for her, stood slightly apart on the crowded pavement.

She was pleased, last night in the pub when he'd invited her. Shopping, a spot of dinner, perhaps jazz at his favourite hotel afterwards. Might as well see the best of the west while she was visiting. Not much around Rathloe. A date was it? She didn't know. Strange that. Not forty-eight hours in the country and Susan-Brown-Whitaker the almost divorcée was being taken out by a strange Irish–Englishman.

Christmas bulbs and tinsel lanterns criss-crossed over the main street. The smells – roasted coffee, a pastry shop, butchers with their strings of sausages, New Year's turkeys and geese. Here came the hopsy, smoky smell of pubs, windows steamed up from the chatting, laughing people packed inside.

Christmas. It was the first time she'd actually thought about it – like this, with twinkling lights, shops, something lit up and special. And if Galway City were anything to go by, the Irish did Christmas big.

'A few bob for the baby, missus.' A huge woman blocked their path. Moles grew from her chin, dirt in the fat crevices, a plaid shawl-blanket wrapped around her. Was there really a baby in there? A sour, unwashed smell. Susan reached in her shoulder bag. A five-pound note. Folded it into the woman's fat hand, watched the gleeful rheumy eyes. 'Ah, thanks, miss. And a Happy New Year to ye. I'll say a special prayer for ye. The dacentest of them all . . .'

McHugh tugged at her elbow. 'Come on,' he whispered, ushering her down the crowded pavement.

'What? I just—'

'She'll have half her friends and family trailing you around now; plus you've already supported every musician in Galway for the day.'

'I don't care . . .' Laughing, she waved away his vigilance – almost brotherly. Her tour guide in this bustling, giggling city. They walked on together. She almost reached to take his arm, but thought better of it. What did she know about this man, except that he'd bought the once temporary abode of her dead grandfather? A man with a purpose. And yes, a past. Steadfast yet skittish.

'Would you mind awfully?' She turned from a boutique window with hand-knitted, cotton sweaters. 'Won't be long . . .'

Inside it was narrow and intimate, pottery reading lamps, a huge, oval floor mirror in the middle. The

boutique woman commented on the chill afternoon
that was in it, like this for a week now, but better –
sure, anything better than the rain. Was she, Susan,
visiting or did she live here? A lot of people moving in
now, hadn't she noticed? Wherever they'd all live with
the way housing prices were. Shocking. Ferocious.

Susan fingered a cardigan on a mannequin – aqua-
green, with a low, scalloped neckline.

'You knitted this?' she asked the woman.

'That one, yeah,' the woman said. 'But some of the
plainer designs I contract out, like to a co-op. But the
designers I do myself. Would you like to try it?'

Susan stepped out of the tiny dressing room, the cardigan snug on her slim, willowy frame.

The woman fussed, straightened it on her shoulders,
then stood back, arms folded to admire. 'Oh! God, that
colour's only gorgeous on you . . . But here, let's get
the male point of view, what?' The woman turned to
where McHugh was waiting, his tall frame stooped in
the doorway. 'What does your husband think? Isn't it
fabulous on her? Belated Christmas present, I suppose.
Aww, now. Sleeping on the couch tonight if you forgot that, what?' Obliviously, the woman grinned from
Susan to a glowering McHugh.

Susan looked at him, made a 'sorry' face.

'Jesus! And you've the figure to wear it, too. Hasn't
she?' The woman accosted McHugh again, fixed him
with her saleswoman's eyes.

McHugh gestured to Susan that he'd be waiting out
on the pavement.

'I'll take it,' Susan said quickly. 'That and the pale
yellow polo in the window . . . could you giftwrap the
yellow? It's for a friend back in London.'

Outside, he said nothing. 'Sorry,' she said. 'I'm sure
she meant no harm . . .'

He shrugged. Looked away across the street to a large bookshop, then back again. They walked on in silence, he striding slightly ahead.

Darkness fell quickly, the street Christmas lights twinkling against the wintry sky.

The bistro had a bohemian air.

'Food's marvellous,' he said, a hint of defensiveness. 'Unless you'd prefer something . . .'

'It's fine.'

On each table, a stained, gingham tablecloth, a Chianti bottle with layers of hardened candle grease. The walls were painted deep red.

They took a small table inside the window.

'Wine or something to warm us up first?'

'Something hot would be nice. You choose.' She pulled her gloves off, holding her frozen fingertips above the candle flame.

Their Jamaican waiter brought mulled wine. She breathed in the cinnamon, nutmeg scents. It reminded her of Mrs T, the older woman that first night in the Hermitage Hotel with her hot whiskeys and huge family. Only the night before last.

He grinned at her above the rim of his glass. Leaned towards her across their table. 'You know, that awful boutique woman was right about one thing.' He paused. 'It did look marvellous on you.' He reached to touch her arm.

Ever since she'd met him yesterday in the gardens at Rathloe House he'd been like this – suspicion interspersed with these flashes of kindness, charm.

'Look, don't know about you, but I'm absolutely starving. Any suggestions?' she asked brightly, picking up the dog-eared menu.

'Look, let's stretch things out a bit, shall we? Sample some of this, bit of that? Take our time?' McHugh asked. 'Anyway, the jazz club doesn't get going till well after nine.'

The waiter brought two steaming bowls of chowder – enormous chunks of fish, potatoes, a whiff of onion, bacon, rich cream. The bread was nutty, still warm, a wheaty, gritty texture.

'Put the hairs on your chest,' he said, in an exaggerated Irish accent. He buttered her a thick chunk. 'Grew up on this stuff. My mother always made five, six . . .'

'Where is she, your mum?'

'She died. Five years ago. I was in London . . .'

'Sorry.'

'A long time ago now.'

'And your dad?'

'Died when we were kids. Cancer, I suspect, though of course, they didn't call it that back then. Quite a bit older than my mother. Rather common, back then, you know. At least in our part of the country. Sort of arranged marriages, really. Economic. Land arrangements, that sort of thing.' He poured them each a glass of white wine. Tucked the bottle back into an ice bucket by their table.

She had the feeling she shouldn't probe, ask too much about this man and his family or past.

'Were you . . . back home in London, then, this Christmas?' She asked it casually, though she knew she was really probing for details of grown-up or teenage kids, an ex – or even current – wife. His eyes met hers. He understood her unspoken query.

'No, not back in London. And no, nobody – or no Christmas duties – back there.' He cocked an eyebrow at her, teasing, as if they were dancing in some cat-and-mouse game. 'Never been married.'

'Oh.' She took a spoon of chowder. It tasted even better than it smelled.

'You?'

'Divorced. Or almost. Gerald – my ex – plans on finalising everything soon in the New Year.'

'Sorry.'

She flashed him a tight smile. 'Don't be.'

'Kids?'

She shook her head, then drank from her wine glass. 'Look . . . it's the oldest story in England, Ireland, everywhere, isn't it? You know it's not . . . well . . . not married bliss, but it's easier to just keep shunting along the tracks, isn't it? Until, of course, someone wants to get off the train. Finds someplace they'd much rather be.'

'And . . . that wasn't you?'

'No.' She swallowed.

'Sorry. There, I said it again.'

They laughed – light, self-conscious.

Outside, the passers-by and late shoppers had dwindled in the narrow street. Across from the bistro window, a man came to take in a sandwich board from outside a tiny art gallery, then pulled his heavy doors shut, locked things up for the night.

'Look, let's go back to Christmas, shall we? Where *did* you spend it, then?'

'My brother and his wife and their two boys. Still live at our old family place. North Mayo. On the sea.'

'Sounds absolutely lovely. Always wanted to spend Christmas on the beach. Had a friend moved to Australia once; and at Christmas she'd telephone us . . .'

He fingered the rim of his wine glass. 'It's always different when you've been away so long . . . almost worse now I've bought the land here. No' – he shrugged – 'belonging.'

In this hippie little bistro, she suddenly thought of Daddy's house at Hargrove, that day she'd gone to search for his extra clothes. Thought of her own new flat in Cripton, the spartan new rooms into which she'd stuffed her marital furniture – antiques, wedding

130

gifts, brocade and cherry wood. Yes, she understood belonging, or the lack of it. Eclipsed pasts.

He said, 'I always rather liked Christmas in London . . . used to spend Christmas Day up in Pinner with friends. And you? Friends? Brothers and sisters?'

She pushed her empty soup bowl away. Licked clean. 'My father . . . has been quite unwell for . . . well, over two years now. So, I spent Christmas Day with him in a nursing home. Hargrove. South Surrey. For Alzheimer's patients.'

The door clicked open. It was the gallery owner from across the street, a newspaper under his arm. He sat at the bar and ordered a glass of red wine.

'So . . . it sounds like *this* is our Christmas, then . . .' McHugh said. He refilled her wine glass, then held his up for a toast. 'Happy Christmas to us.'

His face was soft, the blue eyes kind.

He reached to touch the scratch along her cheek. 'Feel like a spot of jazz after this? Or we could just go . . . home – back to my cottage.'

'Home,' she said.

Chapter 21

'Look who's come to visit, Lovín! Your best new friend, eh? Oh! Poor doggie lonely all day? Have to go pee-pee now? Oh! Yes, licks from this dog, this *peata* of a dog.' He petted, laughed, frolicked with Lovín as she hurled herself on him again and again.

They were standing in a little pool of light from the back door.

He said, 'Look, she shouldn't be long. You can come with us or wait . . .' He nodded to the cramped living room inside – a fireplace, green-painted windows, white-washed walls, table, the floor cluttered with books, papers. She felt a stab of pity for him in this makeshift home.

They followed Lovín through a wooden gateway, then out across the back field. The light from the cottage fell behind them until it was pitch-black. Lovín took off into the night.

To the north, a whitish glow from the Ballyshee streetlights. She pulled up her sheepskin collar, hugged her elbows with her gloved hands.

They stood apart. He was looking at the star-dotted sky. 'Heavy frost again tonight. If January stays like this I'll never get the new grass seed in on my land.'

Somewhere, a lone calf bellowed.

'All right?' he asked, as if, even apart, he could feel her body tremble, shiver. His feet crunching across the frozen grass. She could smell him.

He reached for her. Drew her into his arms, her face buried in his chest, a hand cradling her head. The kiss was hard, insistent.

'Oh God, Susan,' he said. As involuntary as a sigh.

Part 2

Part 2

Chapter 22

The elderly man was slouched asleep on the red seat under the window. McHugh had often seen him here in the Hermitage lounge before; in fact, almost every time he came for lunchtime soup and sandwiches. The man had begun to snore – top dentures slipping and ready to clatter to the carpeted floor.

McHugh rustled his *Irish Times* loudly.

The Hermitage was a blasted hotel, wasn't it, not a dosshouse? McHugh sat to the left of the unlit fireplace. Gerry the barman sat on a high stool behind the counter, clutching a remote control and watching an afternoon film on BBC2.

McHugh checked the electric clock above the bar. Five more minutes. He'd arrived too early.

Outside, the sky was lightening above the roofs and chimneys of Ballyshee's main street, the pale February sun brightening the houses and shops. It had rained all morning – a cold, clinging mist over his fields. Again, he glanced across at the lounge window, watching for Edel Quinn's pert head to appear above the half curtains.

Why all this watching, this jitteriness?

Of course, he knew why Edel Quinn had arranged this meeting – some cocked-up rigmarole about Rathloe House and its preservation for the good of the village. Money. She thought that that public relations smile of hers would secure them, the Preservation Committee, a bargain, that he'd just hand over his big house and gardens at half the market value.

'Mr McHugh.' Suddenly, there she was, beaming down at him. Must have come in the back entrance. A pink, scoop-necked shirt under a dark trouser suit, a black leather briefcase.

He stood. 'Ms Quinn.'

She laughed, 'Edel, please.'

He said, 'Look, can I get you a drink? I was just thinking about some coffee . . .'

'Sparkling water'd be grand, thanks.' She sat, placing the briefcase at her feet.

At last Gerry brought their tray, plunked it down between them, then off back to his film. McHugh felt calmer now that she was actually here. He'd done this a hundred, two hundred times. Except this time, there *was* no deal, just a flat-out no. His property was not for sale. Even in these mad, yuppie Irish days, a man still had a right to keep what was his.

He flashed her a tight smile. 'No problem getting out of work, then?'

'They're fairly flexible. Traffic, of course. Never roadworks until you've someplace to be.'

She left a half-moon of pink lipstick on her water glass. 'Look, Mr McHugh, I have children to collect from the after-school programme in Rathloe Hall. And I notice you've been rather . . . occupied with work yourself. So why don't we get started here?'

He looked up from pouring cream in his coffee. 'I'm all ears.'

'Well, especially in a place like Rathloe – I'm sure you're not *unaware* of our Preservation Committee and the work we've been doing since last December.'

He smiled indulgently, like a father willing to hear out a child's outlandish request. 'It's come to my attention.'

'Yes. Well, I'll come straight to the point, then. We have been fortunate enough to raise some funds to date; in fact, people have been extraordinarily generous, so we have every expectation that, financially at least, and with the aid of some grants, the Rathloe Preservation initiatives can continue at the current pace.' She paused. Another sip of water. 'However, I'm sure you realise that finances are actually only a part of the equation.'

The man under the window had just woken up, stared around him with bleary eyes. McHugh watched him slug down the end of an abandoned glass of porter, the froth already stale and yellowed along the glass.

He said, 'And the rest of this – equation?'

'Mr McHugh, a project like this also rests on community support, ongoing enthusiasm among . . .' She took an overstuffed folder from the briefcase. Snapped off a thick rubber band. Handed him a thick sheaf of papers.

He leafed through them – pages of handwritten petitions. Messages, e-mails, dot-com, dot-org, ireland.com, hotmail.com, eircom.net. Chirpy, typed notes from the electronic message board: *'Keep up the good work'*, *'A marvellous thing for the area'*, *'Just what Rathloe needs'*, *'The last thing Ireland needs is to lose another architectural treasure'*.

'Very nice,' he said. 'I had no idea that Rathloe was such a . . . cohesive little community.'

Silence idled between them. The man had dozed off again, arms folded across his chest.

At last Edel said, 'Yes, well. All of this, of course, is to no end unless we have some kind of assurance that number one, the house and its gardens will actually be there for preservation. And number two, that as the original owner of the big house and the long-term operator of its abutting agricultural land, that we have your goodwill.'

He poured himself more coffee from the white, porcelain pot. Stirred his cup slowly, thoughtfully. 'Goodwill?'

She levelled her brown eyes on his. 'Given your property's historical significance and its very real potential for our parish, we had hoped for a philanthropic donation.'

He stared at her.

'Mr McHugh, there would – you would, of course, be invited to play a key role in the board of directors.' She eyed him. 'As a newcomer to the area, and as an entrepreneur, there could be some marvellous networking potential . . .'

He almost laughed out loud. 'And without this proposed level of . . . goodwill?'

Her dark eyebrows drew together. 'We'd be forced to entertain a reasonable purchase arrangement, but . . .'

He sipped his coffee. Winced as if it had suddenly turned bitter.

Snores from the man under the window again, lips pursed and vibrating.

'Look, have you and your committee entertained the notion that my property is neither for sale nor donation?'

Her dark eyes flashed. 'Yes we have and . . .' She hesitated. 'And to that end, we've explored . . . alternative routes.' She reached into her briefcase. Handed him a glossy brochure, a letter on embossed paper. 'StairEire,' the letterhead read. A Dublin address.

Dear Ms Quinn,

Thank you for your enquiry regarding grassroots preservation efforts and our part therein. From your initial description, it does indeed sound like the Rathloe preservation project would fall within the auspices of our national preservation work here at StairEire, which lobbies for and

supports preservation of historical sites and properties. We
have enclosed, for your review, our . . .
   Meanwhile, we would be happy to set up a meeting with
your committee to discuss possible . . .

He swallowed. Calm. His features still calm, polished.
Poker face. He handed her back the letter and brochure.
   'Interesting, I'm sure.'
   She flicked her long hair over her shoulder. 'If we
have reason to believe that a building demolition crew
is due any day in Rathloe . . . then it becomes not just a
local cause, but a larger, and very publicised issue. I'm
sure you can understand.'
   Methodically, he stacked his coffee cup, saucer, the
white porcelain pot and matching cream jug back onto
the silver tray that Gerry the barman had left. Slipped
a five-pound note under the tray, then picked up his
jacket and *Irish Times*.
   'Yes I understand,' he said. Deliberately pleasant. A
firm handshake. 'Look, have you a business card handy?
I'll let you know my thoughts – decisions – by the end of
this week. Prefer to be called at your home or on your
mobile?'
   'Em . . . home is fine.'
   He patted her on the shoulder. 'Cheerio, then. No,
don't get up. Sit and finish your drink.'

Chapter 23

Around each corner, he kept expecting to see Rita, his sister-in-law, in the family car or Seamus and Shep the dog driving a flock of sheep along the Carraig road. But the road was almost empty, the shadows across the mountain above him, new lambs dotted throughout the sloping fields.

Lovín sat perched in the passenger's seat, tongue lolling, eyes on the narrow road ahead. She was used to being brought everywhere now – pubs, shopping in Galway, the Hermitage Hotel for lunch. In Galway, McHugh had even found a dinnertime bistro where the waitress fussed over this golden retriever with the soulful eyes. She let Lovín sit under the table while McHugh dined and drank wine.

But this afternoon, she'd been left alone in the Volvo, the window left open while he'd sat in the Hermitage Hotel wrangling with Edel Quinn.

'Oh! Come on, now *girlín*,' he crooned to her. Reached over to scratch her ears. 'Thought I'd just be twenty minutes. How could I have known that . . .'

Lovín kept staring ahead, the eyes, ears alert. Oh, she was as steadfast as a woman when she was huffed.

At last he turned down the *bóithrín* to the beach, the Volvo swaying and bumping along the rain-washed road.

Lovín took off, tore down the path and onto the sandy beach.

McHugh opened up the rear hatchback for the wrapped-up bone he'd bought her at the butcher's in Ballyshee, a large Thermos of cold water for her, her dish and an old, plaid blanket.

He carried everything down onto the beach.

Since his Christmas visit, winter storms had blown the sand up high, scoured out holes in the dunes. He hobbled on one foot, then the other while he took off his socks, shoes, then left everything bundled up in the blanket.

The sand was cold under his feet.

He didn't know why he'd come here. Except that, an hour ago when he'd edged his Volvo down Ballyshee's main street, his mind was so seething that he could have driven on to Dublin, the Giant's Causeway, Cork or any anonymous, wide-open place with a salty breeze to unclench his teeth.

They'd cornered him. These preservation Nazis. Mad country. Crazy times.

Lovín came trotting back down the beach towards him. At last, he'd been forgiven. He stooped to throw a piece of driftwood for her. She splashed, bounded out into the waves.

Bullshit, not history. That was their game.

She came, dripping sea water onto his trousers. Dropped the stick at his feet. He threw it again.

He could picture Edel sitting across from him, dark, flashing eyes, smooth, confident voice: *Then it becomes not just a local cause, but a larger, and very publicised issue. I'm sure you can understand.*

The very thought of it was laughable, unthinkable. Dubliners and Rathloe blow-ins parading up and down outside his big house gates, placards, sit-ins, the six o'clock news, photos in every local rag newspaper.

He walked on. The sea was cold, ice-cold. His feet had grown numb and purple. Lovín came again, the face, eyes eager. This time, he arched his arm high, flung the driftwood viciously into the sea.

Of course he wouldn't *give* them his damn house. Even if he hated it, even if he'd already dug foundations elsewhere, near the crossroads, in Galway City or Dublin. Even if he moved lock, stock and barrel back to Notting Hill. Still, he wouldn't donate it to these vigilante, meddling yuppies.

Lovín came, drenched this time. Shook herself, sprayed him with water. She stared up at him, waiting for him to throw again.

What choice had he? He kept walking, Lovín trotting, panting behind. *As the owner of the abutting land, we depend on your goodwill.*

At the end of the beach, he crossed the stream. He zipped up his coat from the evening chill, shoulders hunched defiantly as he climbed the path through the dunes to the hermit spot where the writer's house stood.

A thin line of turf smoke came from the chimney. Crocuses under a hedge. In the back and side windows, the curtains had been hastily pulled. Somewhere inside, a dim ceiling light. The owner, this Dublin writer fellow, was visiting again. On one of his country-living spates, no doubt. McHugh stood staring at the weather-beaten house with its flaking paintwork, the cliffs above the sea. This miserable bastard had been let build, live in peace.

Somewhere a curlew cried.

He sat wrapped in the beach blanket. He shivered. His trouser legs still damp. The night was gathering in around them. The sea was leaden and still.

Lovín was lapping loudly at her water dish.

It reminded him of her. That night. Susan Brown Whitaker standing before his cottage fireplace. Each of them locked in some tacit waiting game.

Then she was gone.

When had it ever happened to him before? He, who had charmed his way into many a flat or luxury house in London. All the lazy Sunday mornings in Notting Hill when some classy woman had sat across his breakfast table from him, fresh-ground coffee, one of his dress shirts unbuttoned to show her breasts.

But this Susan Brown with the green eyes and the scrape across her cheek had bolted through his back door into the night, left him listening to the crunch of her feet under his window, then the sound of her car starting up outside.

It all seemed so long ago now and unreal. Watching the back of her head in the street in Galway, her eager, childish delight in that sweater boutique, her solemn face in the bistro candlelight.

Did she know, guess that he'd spent that entire December day imagining her up there in his loft bedroom, both of them tucked up together like children in a tree house? He had fantasised about that face beside him when he woke up next morning.

Chapter 24

Were his eyes codding him? No, there it was – perched at the roadside and teetering in the late-February wind and rain.

O'Neill's Traditional Irish Pub and Internet Café.

Sweeney shook his head and stumped back across the gravelled car park to the pub where he could already see the other three heads silhouetted in the window.

The door clicked open, but Kitty didn't turn from her spot under the back window. There, where a nest of lounge tables and padded stools used to be, was her pink raffle computer on a high contraption like a plant stand; one of the bar stools perched in front of it. A sign above the monitor, *£1 per minute. Please see proprietor.*

And there was Kitty, the back of the lacquered head, the slippered feet dangling above the stool rails.

She giggled like a simpleton at something on the monitor. 'Be with ye in one sec,' she said to the four thirsty men sitting along the counter.

'Jesus, Mary and Joseph,' Sweeney muttered and crossed himself.

'What in the name of shite?' Mannion said.

Walsh nodded to the *£1 per minute* sign and said, 'Her own best customer if you ask me.'

O'Brien elbowed him, for here came Kitty now, padding behind the counter, the face dreamy and pre-occupied.

She enquired how the men were, asked did any of them hear what kind of weather were they in for for the night; touch of spring already in the air yesterday, but sure wasn't it time for it, weren't they long overdue, and sure, wasn't that the way, if you hadn't the spring you'd hardly have the summer either, and if you hadn't the summer, there'd be no winter; one with the other, hah? Wasn't that the only way to say it, men?

They wouldn't please her to reply, just kept staring at the silent telly.

Since the New Year, the afternoon programming had been changed – a daily nature documentary instead of *Here's Lucy* now, and though Walsh enjoyed the baboons and koala bears peering down at them, the others missed poor oul' Lucy; at least, they said, she kept things cheerful.

Kitty didn't care if they froze her out. For the truth was, these four were the very reason that she'd decided to offer Internet access in O'Neill's pub, slapped out her sandwich board by the roadside.

This morning she'd put her sign out by the road, and already she'd had someone – a passing business-man who'd forgotten to e-mail a file from his office in Galway.

'A pure waste,' she'd said a week ago to Margaret over their nightly cocoa. Ever since Lent, it was costing her money, not making it, just to keep the lights on in the pub. And that was nothing to the price of coal, electricity, oil for the central heating, cleaning supplies for the Ladies' and Gents'. And all for what? Standing like Nelson's Pillar behind the counter waiting for those four to drag in whatever time of the day it suited them? Talking *seafóid* and grousing about every little happening for miles around.

'Might as well keep an eye on things on-line; make a few bob while I'm stuck down there,' she reasoned.

God, even Mr McHugh was missing in the afternoons now. And who could blame him the way those four gawked at him? But oh, divil a fear of those four staying away, giving her a bit of peace.

For Lent, Mannion had changed to drinking fizzy oranges – off the jar ever since the New Year and staying off now through Lent. O'Brien had taken to drinking red wine of all things, just the one glass a day, aping the Italian with that dyed black hair of his, claiming the doctor within in the town advised wine for his heart As for Sweeney and Walsh, every Lent they cut down to the one, half-glass of porter, nursing it and sipping at it the whole afternoon. Oh! 'Twas they that rose up in her head, gawking up at that telly that she had to pay a licence on, faces that'd stop a clock.

She plunked Mannion's bottle of orange in front of him. 'D'you want a straw?' she asked him cattily.

'No, but a glass,' Mannion said gallantly. 'And Kit,' he roared down the bar after her retreating back, 'throw a drop of water and a bit of ice in the bottom of the glass, would you? That orange's terrible sweet. Rot the teeth in your head.'

She turned to eye him viciously.

'And a bit of lemon, Kitty, good woman.' She shuffled the slippers, opened the fridge for a dish of three-day-old lemon slices.

'Maybe you'd like a paper umbrella too,' she muttered. 'Eat me out of house and home with your lemons and fal-dals.'

'Lovely, Nora,' Mannion said, rubbing his hands together when she came back with ice clinking in his glass. 'Now, how much?'

The same as the last ten evenings, you ignorant yob, Kitty wanted to hiss it at him so that he'd never, ever ask her the price of a drink again, not the longest day he lived, not even when they all went back on the drink – and she hoped to the living Jesus that was soon.

'Fifty-five pence there when you've time, Mr Mannion,' she said.

O'Brien took a slug of his wine and licked his lips like a cat.

Sweeney sipped fastidiously from his half-pint and then squinted up at the telly. They were showing rattle-snakes in the Arizona Desert or someplace boiling, roasting hot where you'd think Clint Eastwood would appear any minute.

Ping!

The four flinched at the electronic sound from under the window. Oh yes, that computer she won was the culprit – for all of this, the mood swings, the crankiness, slovenly service, the general air of rattiness around O'Neill's.

'Ye'll excuse me, men,' Kitty said, her face brightening at last. 'Have to see a man about a dog.'

And off with her, the slippers shuffling across to the computer again, a stupid sign on the screen, 'You've got mail.' They grimaced at that click, click, click of the mouse, nudged each other when she let out a high-pitched giggle at whatever she was reading on the screen.

'We heard ever 'twas only a halfwit that laughs at nothing,' Sweeney said, with a vindictive twitch of the head.

Ping!

They ignored it this time; the four sets of eyes fixed on the telly screen and the rattlesnakes.

This e-mail was from Edel Quinn, on behalf of the Preservation Committee. Please review attached before tonight's meeting. This, of course, the main agenda item – come prepared to discuss and suggest.

Kitty scraped her stool closer to read the scanned-in

letter with the name of some solicitor in Dublin at the top of the page. *Please be advised that my client . . . herewith known as the vendor, offers Rathloe House, herewith known as the property, to Rathloe Preservation Committee, herewith known as the buyer, for the sole purpose of a non-profit-making, historical and educational site, at the sum cited below.*

The four men squirmed on their bar stools as another rattler came slithering out from under a rock, th'oul fat, scaly body edging across the sand.

£162,325. Purchase agreement to be signed by 1 June, after which exclusive option to purchase Rathloe House and its rear garden becomes null and void.

'Sacred Jesus!' Kitty screeched, and leapt backwards, stool and all.

The four frowned at each other. Couldn't even watch the telly in peace. Didn't they know that computer yoke was nothing but trouble?

Mannion thumped the counter and said, 'Porr-un, I betcha 'tis porn! Some blackguard or latchigo with his clothes off.'

Walsh said, 'Naked as a baby's arse, well I never . . .'

'Jesus, Mary and Joseph, will ye shut up,' Sweeney said. He was off his bar stool and already halfway across the floor towards Kitty and her computer station.

'Look!' Kitty whispered, her finger quivering as she pointed at the monitor.

Sweeney leaned over her shoulder to read. Let out a loud whistle.

'What? What?' Mannion called impatiently.

O'Brien, who had joined Sweeney and Kitty at the computer, said, 'Ah, bollix.'

'Cursed Jesus; will you tell us,' Mannion screamed.

O'Brien turned back to the counter and announced, 'The pup, the returned Paddy, Mr McHugh is asking

£162,325 for his oul' rambling rookery, the big house below.'

Suddenly, Kitty switched everything off and jumped down from her stool. The computer monitor went dark.

She shuffled behind the bar, picked up a pint glass and started polishing it with a linen tea towel.

'Are you all right, Kit?' Mannion asked at last.

But Kitty just kept bunching the white linen down into the glass and swirling until it squeaked.

No tourists. No big, CIÉ tour buses pulled up outside in the car park, winter and summer. Special tours, that's what Edel Quinn and that Claire Sweeney had talked about; outreach galore to historical societies, royal Hibernians, history departments, archaeology students, Yanks, hill walkers. . . Hot lunches; she'd been studying menus at kitchen.com; food.com; she'd been exchanging e-mails with a chef at an Irish restaurant in Paris and one in Atlanta, Georgia. Mighty profit margin on boxed lunches for picnicking tourists. She'd even been looking up barbecues.

At last Walsh said, 'Arrah. A blessing in disguise . . . Didn't I say from the start that 'twas no good resurrecting things nobody wants resurrected? My father, God rest him, used to say, "Man proposes but God disposes."'

O'Brien finished his red wine, tipping the glass for the last drop. 'Sure, maybe you're right, Walsh. You're seldom right, but maybe . . . Anyways, the wife wants me home early for the tea; she's rushing off to this preservation meeting tonight. Sure, I'll let her go, the creature, no point telling bad news until she finds out herself.' He fumbled in his jacket pocket for bicycle clips.

Walsh said to him, 'Throw th'oul bike in the boot and I'll drop you down.'

The two headed out of the door. 'Good night to ye, Kitty, good luck,' they called. Nobody answered them.

'No way they'll raise that kind of money,' Mannion said.

'They might and they mightn't,' Sweeney replied.

'Done for now, anyways. No tourists and the devil knows what for the big house below,' Mannion said.

For a long time Sweeney didn't answer, but kept staring up at a fella with a snake draped around his neck like a scarf, th'oul tail twirling and curling.

A sly little smile was forming, twitching at the edges of Sweeeney's mouth.

God, he thought, I haven't lost it yet, my uncanny nose for knowing what's what.

He swivelled around to sit staring at the pub fireplace, where Kitty had let the turf and coal burn down to cinders. For a long time, he just gawked, wordless.

He could picture them there, last Christmas, McHugh and that swanky Englishwoman of his with the scraped face.

Mistress. An avenging wife; they'd all had their theories, but didn't he, Sweeney, know better? Had his suspicions from the start. Aha! Wasn't that the advantage of having lived in England? Not as innocent or as ignorant as the rest of the yahoos around here. Ah yes, fair play to me, he thought.

In the weeks after Christmas, he'd made discreet enquiries to Margaret O'Neill above in the shop. More in the Hermitage Hotel in the town.

At last he turned back to the counter. Said to Mannion, 'We'll have another. A pint this time? On me, go on . . .'

Chapter 25

The grandfather clock chimed through the cottage. Four in the morning, and Johnny Monahan tiptoed across the darkened front hallway to the parlour.

He closed the door behind him, switched on a lamp and bent to stoke the last of the coals in the grate. A tiny flame came at last. He tongsed extra coal on – quietly so as not to waken his brother, Micheál.

The lamplight cast a soft glow around the wall-papered walls, the velvet couches with their starched antimacassars, the ferns in the front windowsill.

Little hisses of flame as the fire caught, then flickered, shimmered against the diamond-paned windows, the hanging portraits and photographs around the walls: a watercolour of the seaside in Sligo, a portrait of Gretta, their dead mother, in a long evening dress, Johnny's parents' wedding photo, a snapshot of Johnny in his cap and gown when he received his library degree in Dublin, another of Micheál and him as young boys, all dressed up in suits with short trousers and knitted knee socks.

Against the far wall, his mother's piano, dusted every Friday; a man summoned every year from Galway to tune it.

Johnny always said that he himself had none of his mother's musical talent, except the few popular songs he'd learned by ear.

Now, he lifted the cover, tightened the belt on his dressing gown and began to play.

On these sleepless nights – ever since the Rathloe Preservation Committee with its flyers and fundraising appeal letters shoved through his front door – it soothed him to play the old songs, always in the same order: 'Banks of My Own Lovely Lee', 'Slievenamon', 'Love Letters in the Sand', 'Rose of Mooncoyne'.

The notes filled the room. He hummed along, an old man's voice rising, falling, barely audible above the music.

He hadn't attended the last few preservation meetings in the hall. Couldn't. Wouldn't. Respect for his dead mother. The Monahan brothers weren't people to shun a parish event, but well . . . this was different.

He played on. A second verse, then the refrain with its high notes at the end, 'On the banks of my own lovely . . .' His racing thoughts, fears, settled now, came to rest over the ivory piano keys.

Some nights, the dreams that woke him were cast in a gauzy light – a young girl kneeling before a fireplace blackening a grate, cleaning out ashes, a young head inside a white servant's cap. And in the shadows, standing under framed portraits of men, hunting dogs, horses, there was a dark figure prowling, waiting.

'Slievenamon.' He picked out the notes, his voice floating to the window and the black night outside.

Tonight, a different dream. Swirling, lurid colours, faces, people he knew from the parish – children, mothers, Mrs O'Brien, Mr O'Brien, Sadie Sweeney, Claire Sweeney, dogs gambolling across the green lawns, women in bright dresses, cameras dangling from their wrists, straw summer hats, men in sunglasses. All talking, milling around, swarming like Technicolor insects around the big house, its windows and doors open to the sunshine, painted signs for 'Visitors' Entrance', 'Café', 'Gifts'.

The parlour door creaked open. Micheál. The grey hair flat against his head. His face pink and bruised from sleep, a dreamy little smile on his face. He cocked his head, listened to Johnny's playing, then hummed, swayed to the music like a child. Always like a child.

'Your dressing gown, Micheál,' Johnny said, frowning at his brother's pyjamas and bare feet. 'And slippers.'

'Don't forget the vanilla,' Micheál called from his bedroom off the kitchen. Johnny watched the blue flame of the gas cooker, removed the hot milk just before it boiled over. His brother always liked hot milk sweetened with vanilla essence.

'Johnneeee,' Micheál called pettishly.

Stepping up to his brother's room, Johnny glanced at the red Sacred Heart lamp under the picture of Christ with the tilted head, the storybook face. Finger pointing to his heart.

'Coming,' he called out to Micheál, and muttered a prayer that their days and nights, would one day become peaceful again.

Chapter 26

Anna stuffed the remainder of her sandwich back into its brown paper bag, looked around in vain for a rubbish bin, and then lit a cigarette.

Since Christmas, she had switched to a French brand. Weedy, stronger than usual. Georges' influence, of course. Always the same with each of Anna's new romances: borrowed gestures, changes in dress, phrases and intonations. Then one day . . . all gone, dropped like hot cakes along with the accompanying lover. And there would be Anna – Panny – back to her old, blunt self.

Susan shaded her eyes from the sudden, lunchtime sun in the courtyard. She studied her friend's profile on the outdoor bench beside her: boyish, spiked hairstyle amidst the glint of sunlight on windows, swatches of sky and cloud reflected in the two rows of glassy offices. Anna even held her cigarette differently now – petulantly, as if posing for a 1940s film.

All around the Vernon Place courtyard, women and men sat in smart suits, winter coats draped around their shoulders, eating takeaway lunches or smoking. Conversations rose and drifted – last night's wine bar, a concert someone wanted tickets for, a bothersome client finally told to stuff it via telephone.

Susan took a bite from her cheese sandwich. Sip from her water bottle. Waited. She knew why Anna had interrupted the day's mayhem of telephone calls, meetings and to-do lists to invite her out here for this, their first lunch together since Anna and Georges had returned from a skiing trip to Vermont.

'Any word, then?' Anna asked, gesturing her spiked head towards the street, a noisy trafficked world that existed somewhere out there beyond this courtyard and office suites.

'Nothing. Yet. But I thought it was the right thing for Stephen, don't you think? Give him the damn Farnsworth account and see what he does with it.'

Anna eyed her. 'You know very well that's not what I'm asking.' Exhaled a long stream of smoke that drifted Susan's way.

It reminded her of late autumn. A bonfire of raked weeds, twigs, old leaves in their rear garden at Cripton Mews. Gerald on one of his reluctant spates of gardening.

Susan took another bite of sandwich, then shoved the rest back in her paper bag. 'Can never eat a full one of these.'

Anna was waiting. A sly but determined look.

Susan wasn't sure she liked this. Like boarding school again. Giggle coyly, work up to that very moment of telling, of secrets divulged in a darkened dormitory: 'Look, I met a boy.'

At last Susan said, 'No. No word from our Mr McHugh in Ireland.'

Anna asked, 'Good in bed, then, these Irishmen?'

'Wouldn't know, Pan.' Susan looked away – to the courtyard fountain with its choreographed water. A line of international flags above a glassy corporate entrance, revolving glass doors.

Had that other place ever existed? Impossible to imagine here. Now. A freezing, black night in an Irish field. A star-filled sky. A calf bellowing. A man's breath in her hair. His mouth . . .

Anna grabbed her elbow to swivel her back into their conversation. 'You mean you didn't . . . ?'

Susan nodded. Bit her lower lip.

'Some kind of Catholic Irish virgin, this chap, or what? Keeping himself for marriage and all that? Or all those Irish tweeds and welly boots constrict the old libido?'

His face came – drifting suddenly across the glass office windows. Subtle changes, mutations. Questionable items, details. Had his eyebrows been dark or grey like his hair?

Anna poked her. 'Come on, then. Tell!'

'Look, it was just shopping and dinner. Galway. Marvellous city. You'd like it. You and Georges. Edinburgh, but livelier. Even had a Boots on the main street.'

'And after this dinner you . . . ?' Anna made a hand-twirling, let's-hear-it-all motion.

'Didn't stay around, actually. Thought it better not to.'

'Stay,' McHugh had said, but not turning from the fireplace to look at her. His dog, Lovín, in a corner lapping water from a dish.

He'd turned at last, the eyes a heavenly blue in the firelight. 'Susan. I'd really like you to stay.'

Anna lit another cigarette and said, 'Didn't he think that odd, this fellow? That you just left? A touch . . . prim and proper, Miss Brown?'

Susan said, 'Look, I *did* have that career expo the next day . . . our exhibit being delivered . . .'

Anna slipped her arm through Susan's and said, 'Look, Suze. I think it's bloody marvellous. You know . . . Well, you needed this. I mean, after . . . everything. But look, weren't you curious if this Irish fellow was the breakfast bacon-and-eggs or organic-muesli type?'

She had stumbled in the dark up McHugh's gravelled path to where her rental car waited by a glittering, country road. All the way into Ballyshee, her headlights had picked out stone walls, ghostly silhouettes of trees, then finally streetlights in that odd little town. She ran, pounded up the night-lit stairs of the Hermitage Hotel, her room key at the ready.

She'd run from something – oh, not him, but what she herself would have done in that cramped, loft bedroom. Cry, scream into the night wantonly, greedily. Cling to his long, tall body, bite down on him to devour, to beg.

Anna got up, dusted off her trouser suit. They strolled together across the courtyard to the iTemps entrance.

Anna entered first, Susan followed.

'Good-looking at least?' Anna called over her shoulder.

Chapter 27

She stood inside the window, listened to the nurse rattling around behind the bathroom door – wastepaper emptied, things wiped, cleaned, replaced.

Slats of daylight came through the openings in the window blinds. His room had two white walls, two deep green. Depth perception. She remembered now, another Alzheimer's memory aid. Last June, when she and Gerald had delivered Daddy here, the matron had explained. Another state-of-the-art feature – like a garage man selling a new-model car.

A Friday then. Just like today. Two Fridays. One June, one March. Almost a year. Mad thoughts. Nothing but mad, silly things on the drive down here, things jettisoning about in her head, racing, escaping.

Not a nurse. A care assistant. At last he came from the bathroom, nodded deferentially to her, then started to tidy the magazines under the TV. A rat-faced little man, green scrubs with elastic-leg trousers. Face familiar; she'd seen him in the corridors, the drawing room, shunting patients across the courtyards.

Susan said, 'Look, shouldn't someone have telephoned me last night?'

Together they studied Daddy propped up asleep in bed. The assistant gave her a disapproving look. Obediently, she dropped her voice to a whisper. 'It's just . . . I would have liked to have been informed sooner.'

Briskly the assistant flicked a duster around the TV, the high, wooden table. 'Just a touch of flu, we're sure . . . but the doctor will see him . . . but Friday afternoons are always . . .' He smiled, almost winked at her, as if they were both hapless but resigned victims of fickle GPs.

He padded around the bed, straightening, tucking – pick up this, discard that – like a hotel housekeeper on his rounds.

Daddy was like a child in a pram, swaddled and propped against the layers of pillows. His chin slumped forward on his chest, the face somehow shrunken. Not snoring but a rolling of the lips like a child playing with toy cars or lorries. Under the sheets, the adult nappy well out of sight, a little reservoir of shit and piss. Above the top pyjama button, the chest flaccid, flesh like the underside of a fish.

Susan snapped the blind up.

A drizzling afternoon. Dripping from the trees and hedges. Islands of tulip beds. A litter of yellow, crimson petals in the grass. The driveway glistened wet.

The assistant hovered in the open doorway. Susan could hear faraway voices down the corridor.

She asked, 'Look, what time did you say that doctor will be here?'

He shrugged. 'Hour at the most. Does his rounds like . . . Look, I can have a cup of tea sent . . .'

Susan shook her head. No.

'Well, if you change your mind . . .' He shut the door behind him.

In Daddy's ten months here she had almost avoided his room with its depth-perception walls, the furniture she and Gerald had brought from the house at Hargrove – a mahogany and green damask armchair, the television table, a bedside table that had once held a plant under Daddy's dining-room windows. Just the ticket. She could hear the matron's trilling voice. Try to provide a home away from home.

Through the window she watched a woman dashing from the front portico, a little canter across to the car park, a newspaper over her head from the rain.

Twenty to four. The digital figures on the bedside clock glowed red.

He stirred, the eyes staring unseeing at her.

She started from her place at the window. 'Daddy.'

The head sagged back against the pillow. Eyelids fluttering, then asleep again.

His breath deepened. Wheezing, a whistle in his chest.

Chapter 28

Edel Quinn pulled the sides of her coat together and looked out of the doorway. Sleet was falling. Nobody walking up the village street. Curtains drawn in front windows, smoke from the chimneys.

'Not a bloody soul,' she said, ducking back into the hall cloakroom. Claire Sweeney was reading a glossy magazine in the ticket booth.

'They'll come,' Claire said, without looking up from the quiz she was reading – *Do you take time just for you?* 'Honest, Edel. This is the way. Nobody will abandon their bar stools below in O'Neill's until this shower of sleet is over or Kitty kicks them out, whichever comes first.'

Edel raised her eyes to heaven. 'Country people,' she almost said, but caught herself in time. The longer she and Jarlath lived down here, the less she got used to these maddening things, like nothing ever starting until after pub closing, or this Arctic weather on the weekend before St Patrick's Day.

She took her coat off and shook it dry. 'A pure dead loss,' she said, hanging it inside the door, a lone coat on a row of wall hooks. She wore an emerald-green shirt over black trousers – green not her best colour, but suitable for a St Patrick's preservation fundraiser dance.

Inside the hall, metallic green shamrocks dangled from the ceiling. A disco ball sent pips of light across the empty dance floor. There was a huge, green and white banner over the stage, '*Erin go Bragh*; St Paddy's Day, Rathloe.'

Édel did another round of the hall to check everything one more time: the chairs lined up along the walls, a food buffet in the corner, the beer and wine bar set up on tables with green paper cloths.

Hail ticked against the windows.

An hour ago, the three band members had arrived, carried instruments, a sound system up on stage, complained about treacherous road conditions and visibility.

Now, they sat around the bar. The lead singer, a plump woman in a black, sequinned jumpsuit, was slumped in a chair reading the *Sunday Independent*. The guitarist, with day-old beard and bloodshot eyes, was straddling his chair, arms folded along the back rail. He had nodded asleep. The fiddle player sat cross-legged on the floor, his back against the back wall, a lager can at his feet.

'Hail glorious St Patrick, huh?' Claire nodded towards the high windows that were being battered by weather. Édel, back out at the office again, scowled at her. No time for jokes.

Ah, here came a car, headlights turning in the car park between church and village hall, the beams arching against the outside walls. Things perking up at last.

But it was only Babs Mannion's brown Ford, the wipers thwacking furiously. She pulled up as close to the door as possible, and here came Sadie Sweeney and Babs, puffing, balancing trays of food under their chins.

'Desperate night!' Sadie panted to her daughter-in-law, then the two older women picked their way across the tiles, their high heels skidding in the sludge.

This was their last food trip, ferrying trays of sandwiches

and cocktail sausages and sausage rolls from house to buffet. Each trip, praying for a full or half-full car park and music and chatter from inside the hall.

Babs straightened a tablecloth on the buffet table. She wore a rose-pink dress with a bright-green necklace cascading over her huge chest. Sadie, in a lime-green dress and best pearls, muttered, 'Jesus, everything'll be dry as a board.'

Hearing steps and commotion, Father Briscoe appeared from behind the red stage curtains. He was wearing a striped, vaudeville suit, a bowler hat and oversized green bow tie. He was on his mobile phone.

'Kitty? Father, here. Listen, have you many, Kitty? Uh-huh. Yeah. I see.' He glanced out over the hall, the bar, the empty dance floor and chairs. Sighed. 'All right. Sure, a horse to the water . . . right, Kitty, hah?'

'Oh!' Claire started at the man peering at her through the ticket-office window.

'Is this where the card drive is?'

'Huh?' Claire blinked at him.

'A card drive. Twenty-five. Poker. In aid of the rugby team . . . Brutal shaggin' roads down this way. Only came out 'cos the brother's on the rugger team. Saw the light and thought it might be . . .'

Claire said, 'Oh, I think that's in Ballyshee. Probably the hotel or the Christian Brothers' hall. You could ask. It's only three miles . . .'

The man was already headed out the door.

Babs nudged the guitarist awake. 'A cocktail sausage? Shame to waste them. Grand with a drop of beer. Or would you sooner a sandwich? There's plenty.'

It was ten past twelve. Nobody had arrived except for Sweeney, Mannion, O'Brien and Walsh, who were sitting on the chairs along the back wall, lined up as if before a firing squad.

A half an hour ago, each had been summoned via

mobile phone from their warm living rooms and tellies.

'Just for Edel's sake, the poor creature,' Sadie had wheedled down her phone to Sweeney, who, in fact, was just getting ready for bed. 'And each of ye bring your own car. If people see cars outside, it might encourage . . .'

Babs Mannion offered her sandwiches and sausages to the other band members. His bow tie dangling, Father Briscoe sat at the bar drinking red wine from a pint glass. Babs said, 'Father, what about yourself? And the four musketeers. Men. Don't be shy. Eat up. Ham, ham and cheese, sardine.'

'A scourge,' Sweeney muttered to the other three. 'A pure scourge.' He munched on a sandwich, then took an aggrieved swig of lager from a can. Bad enough they had to come to an oul' dance that never was, but there was no draft stout.

The guitarist dusted sandwich crumbs off his waistcoat. Looked at his watch and said, 'Ah, look, ladies, *Padre*, if it's all the same to youse. It's heading for one and . . . look, we'll just get our gear . . .'

The women, Father and Edel listened to them thumping around behind the red stage curtain, instruments and portable sound system being unplugged and loaded onto a trolley.

The lead singer poked her head around the red curtain. 'Look, do yez want the radio on back here or something?'

'That'd be lovely,' Babs, undaunted, called back to them. 'No point in sitting here feeling sorry . . .'

'Thanks anyway, folks,' Father called after the three musicians as they trailed out through the doorway.

'Well?' Sadie and Babs Mannion stood before the four men.

A sizzle of radio static came from the stage, then the RTÉ announcer's voice: 'For all you night owls out there, here's an old bedtime favourite . . .'

'Ah, come on.' Babs tugged at her husband's sleeve. 'Sure, no point in letting the night be a dead loss altogether.'

'Moonlight Serenade.' The tune filled the hall. Sweeney eyebrowed his wife, then whispered, 'Stop. For the love of Christ, will you stop making a fool of yourself before the seven parishes.'

'Weeell?' Babs, one hand on her hip, twirled her green necklace.

'What about yourself?' Sadie poked Walsh in the arm. 'Exercise never killed anyone. Ladies' choice, so it is. Bring Edel out dancing there. And Father, shake a leg.'

Sweeney thought he might cry. Drink taken. His wife had drink taken. Claire, his daughter-in-law, and that Edel Quinn and the Preservation Committee. Nothing but daft ideas in the woman's head.

'Come on so.' By the elbow he herded Sadie out before him onto the dance floor. Anything was better than her standing there with that cracked Babs Mannion and the priest and everyone laughing at them.

Half past two in the morning, and the sleet had lodged against the outside doorway, along the village street, and whitened the straggle of cars in the car park. O'Neill's pub had long been shut up for the night; the village houses were all in darkness. But light still came from the high, narrow windows of the village hall.

Inside, the five men and four women were still dancing, shuffling around under the dangling shamrocks, their faces dappled in the light from a disco ball.

Another radio tune came to an end. Walsh went to escape Babs Mannion's clutches, but she drew him back again.

'Just one more, lads,' Father Briscoe said tipsily. Several empty wine bottles were lined up along the bar. Unsteadily, he climbed the stage stairs to fiddle with the radio again.

'Brilliant. Intimate,' Edel said, her voice throaty and slurring. 'No money for the Rathloe Preservation but . . . an intimate night.' She giggled.

'In the Mood' came from the radio. Here came Father across the floor, a cigarette dangling from his lips, his bow tie missing altogether, sidling his hips to the music. Babs, Sadie, Claire and Edel clapped loudly.

'Brilliant choice, Father,' Sadie screeched, as if the priest had somehow finagled the Dublin radio DJ to play their favourite late-night tunes.

Chapter 29

'A Mr McHugh to see you?' Savita, the receptionist's voice came over the speaker phone.

Susan sat staring at her black desk phone as if this voice, this news were something lunging and horrid.

'Em . . . Susan?' Savita's voice again.

Susan snatched the receiver. 'Have him wait downstairs. I'll . . . I'll come down.'

She hunted for the shoes she'd kicked off under the desk. Yanked open the top left drawer for a comb, lipstick, a mirror. Paperclips spilled, scattered across the floor.

'Shit,' she said it aloud. 'Shit.'

The lift pinged shut behind her. He was sitting under the windows to the right of the entrance reading *Time* magazine. Taller than she remembered. A denim, Levi's shirt, khaki chinos, long legs crossed. He hadn't seen her yet.

'John,' she said, her heels clicking across the marbled foyer.

'Susan.'

Handshakes. Their bodies pitched, leaning towards each other like saplings in a breeze. A kiss? The suggestion came then went away.

'What brings you . . . ?'

'Flew over last night . . . liquidating a property . . . not far from here . . .'

They stood facing each other. Behind her, the purr and trill of the telephone. Savita's singsong voice, polished. 'Good afternoon. iTemps, may I *help* you?'

'Tea? Coffee? Water?' she asked. 'It's no trouble; I can . . .'

He shook his head. The face seemed thinner, paler.

He said, 'Look, I really was just *in the neighbourhood*, as they say. If I've come at an inconvenient—'

'No. No.' She held up a hand to shush him.

'Things going well, then?' he asked, glancing around the pale, marble foyer with its fluorescent lighting, coffee tables and chairs, unnecessary reading lamps, an elaborate floral display at the horseshoe-shaped reception desk.

'Things have been great,' she said. 'Bring any of those clever Irish network engineers over with you? We could do with at least two dozen more – and that's just this branch.' She gave a forced laugh.

'Wouldn't know where to find one.'

She could smell him. Hair gel, a briny, male smell that made her blush.

'And how is your dog? Lovey?'

'Lovín.'

'Sorry.'

'Growing like a bullrush. Eating me out of house and home.'

'And your place – farm?'

'Excellent. Grass came in earlier than I expected. This mild weather.'

'Good.'

Savita's voice, cutting across the trilling phone lines. 'Still holding? Yes, I'm afraid he's still on the other line. Would you like his voicemail?'

The sounds, the fluorescent lights, the streaks of sunlight through the vertical blinds – suddenly, she found them exasperating. Like trying to chat at an airport.

'Look I—' she began.

'I should have telephoned,' he said.

'It's all right. Look, what are your plans for this evening or have you . . . ?'

He shook his head, 'No.'

'Why don't you come see my new flat, then? Well, not that new any more, but . . .' She tucked a lock of hair behind her ear. 'Sevenish? Give me time to get home, cook something. Italian all right?'

'Fine.' He smiled. He touched her arm, 'Look, I really didn't mean to . . .'

'Sevenish, then. Are you driving?' She peered past him, through the front glass, as if he might miraculously have edged his Volvo up along the courtyard between the tulip beds and the fountain.

'Taxis. Easier.'

At the reception desk, she signalled Savita for a pen and message pad. Scribbled her address down, her mobile number.

'All right, then,' she said briskly. 'Number eleven, Railroad Place.'

'Right,' he said, and turned around to take a tweedy jacket from the back of the chair.

Chapter 30

Wisps of hair had come undone from where she'd pinned it up at the back. She wore a white shirt over jeans, a coloured tea towel slung over her right shoulder. From the couch he watched her move from cooker to sink, then back to the cooker again, stirring, sampling, seasoning things in saucepans. A smell of garlic and fresh basil through the house.

He liked this woman better than the sealed-up, career-suit creature who had fidgeted and squirmed in that glassy office building.

Yes, he had missed this. The delicious air of expectation, a woman's steps back and forth across a kitchen, the face flushed, smell of cooking. Tantalising, like some drawn-out mating dance.

She turned from the cooker, leaned across the red breakfast counter between kitchen and lounge – a bridge between the two of them. She refilled her red wine, gestured with the bottle if he, too, was ready for a refill.

'Hope you're not absolutely ravenous. I think there's some pâté in the fridge . . . Too chilly to take our wine outside. She nodded towards the glass kitchen door that opened onto a small, high balcony.

He longed to spring from his white couch and take her hot face between his hands and kiss her.

'I do like your place,' he said. 'Really.'

She had turned back to her cooking again. The oven

door cranked open, then banged shut. Her voice vying
with an extractor fan. 'Everything you see is new. I
moved all my – our – old things in here, but then one
Saturday, I woke up and just . . . Rang three charity
shops and told each the first ones here could have it
all – antiques, old wedding presents, family heirlooms,
the lot.'

'You gave away your antiques?'

'Yes. All those Queen Anne legs and brocade cushions . . .' She turned, twirled her wooden spoon to take
in the lounge and dining area. 'All wrong for this place,
don't you think? A new start and all that.'

Another wisp of hair had come loose.

'A marriage of minimalist and retro,' she'd called it
when he'd arrived on the dot of seven at her intercommed
door. Open-plan with high, white walls. White couch
and armchairs with tapered chrome legs. She'd poured
them wine from a coffee-table-cum-wine-rack with a
large, glass top balanced on welded chrome cylinders.

Inside a bay window was a glass dining table with stout,
pewter legs, matching pewter chairs. They reminded him
of giant cutlery pieces. The whole effect was industrial,
almost vicious.

He set his wine glass on the coffee table and edged
towards the other end of the couch. Leaned over the
arm to peer up through her black, spiral staircase. Lights
were on up there, track lighting in a white ceiling. He
leaned further, craned his neck for a glimpse of . . .

'Ready then?' She came clunking across the pale,
wooden floors, a casserole between oven-glove hands.
Gave him a puzzled look.

He stood abruptly. A little boy caught peeping.

She leaned across the table to light three candles. Her
top button undone. He eyed the rise of her breasts,
cleavage between white lace.

His mouth went dry.

He topped up their water glasses. She spooned pasta onto their plates.

'Smashing,' he said. 'A real treat. 'Fraid I've been playing the bachelor since moving back to Ireland.'

She gave a high, deliberate laugh. 'Don't tell me you're on beans and toast?'

'We lunch at the Hermitage Hotel every day; then Lovín and I fend for ourselves in the evenings. But the Hermitage is hardly haute cuisine.'

'How *are* things at the Hermitage these days?'

'Same. They can have all the Celtic Tigers they want. Places like Ballyshee and the Hermitage Hotel will never change.'

'Odd little place, but you know, I really rather liked it.'

'Oh, it's got its charm.'

'And that pub in Rathloe? O'Malley's? O'Brien's?'

'O'Neill's.'

'Still that inquisitive little landlady?'

He was growing impatient. They were like two people who'd met on a foreign holiday, and now – back in neutral lives – avidly hanging onto familiar, shared things.

'Don't really go there any more.'

'Because . . . ?'

He swirled a piece of tortellini in the marinara sauce, popped it in his mouth. 'This is incredible pasta.'

'So you've stopped going to the village pub altogether, then?'

He refilled his wine, surveyed her features. Did she know something? Somehow got wind of this preservation nonsense – Edel Quinn and her blasted websites and newspaper articles? Impossible. Paranoia. Here's what those blasted busybodies had reduced him to.

'Em . . . things have been busy, you know; that and the country village thing can get tiresome . . . More wine, then?'

Across a car park, there were more flats just like hers – red-brick frontages, steps to hall doors, lights in kitchen windows.

High above the roofs and chimneys of Cripton, a radio mast flashed red against the amber-lit night sky.

He pictured himself down there, years and years ago, among London rooftops, high-rises, scaffoldings. Then home on the Tube to his bedsit flat in Shepherd's Bush, avoiding people's eyes. Ashamed before women like Susan. And where had she been then? Reciting French verbs in some fancy boarding school with high windows. Or trailing around an ivy-walled university with her indolent, wayward friends.

'Why did you leave my house that night?' There it was, sooner, more petulant than he'd intended.

'I had to drive to Dublin next morning – that career expo.' She was sitting erect, the chin jutted defiantly.

He shifted in his chair. 'But there was . . . And since then. Back here, you could have . . .'

Her green eyes narrowed at him. 'Could I?'

He sat alone at her dining table. Reprimanded. From the kitchen he heard dishes rattling, water from a tap, cupboards yanked open and banged shut.

It felt good to be back – even here, in this flat with a woman who was annoyed with him.

Yesterday he'd felt it, in Jimmy his manager's car coming from Stansted Airport, the easy, unguarded chatter, wheeling up to Jimmy's driveway to where Phyllis was already waiting with hugs, kisses, a lunch table set inside.

And last night in his own flat in Notting Hill, he'd felt a sudden, childish delight at being home among his own things, his furniture. He took a late-night stroll through the streets that had once intimidated him. He was a missionary on city leave from the bush country, a

180

reprieve from the self-inflicted loneliness of his County Mayo existence.

Why had he come here? The question shimmied along her white walls, skittered and slithered over her weird furniture.

She was loading the dishwasher. Hair fallen across her face. He could see the line of her backbone through her shirt. She had grown thinner since Christmas. Worry? He hadn't even asked after her sick father.

He reached and trailed a finger down the curve of her back, the nubs of her vertebrae. 'Susan, I'm sorry. So sorry.'

Because you wouldn't leave. In his head, the answer to his own question about why he'd come, why he'd hunted her down, accepted her invitation to dinner. Since that frozen December night, the damn woman wouldn't clear out of his head. Walking through his Rathloe fields, sitting on his lumpy couch before the cottage fireplace, waking in the dark in his loft bedroom – there she was, a spectre. Longing.

She shut the dishwasher door. A hiss and torrent of hot water as she turned into his arms.

'Stay,' she whispered, taking his hand to lead him up her spiral, black stairs.

Chapter 31

Sweeney had chosen Thursday, cattle-mart day, when Ballyshee and the Hermitage Hotel were abuzz with cars, men and trailers, the whiff of cowdung and the burr of the auctioneer's voice.

Countrymen had arrived in town, as they did every Thursday.

Sweeney, his gabardine hat shoved back on his head, sat at the corner of the Hermitage bar, not invited into the rounds and company of the other men, who, over ham sandwiches, soup and whiskey, were arguing about Irish divorce and the dangers of going to hospital for tests.

Under the front window, the old man was asleep, a half-drunk glass of stout in front of him, Adam's apple bobbing in the scrawny neck.

The mart men were growing louder, who was right, who was wrong, who spoke the truest word ever spoken. The government? The TDs? Sure what did those shaggers care about divorce or families with their Mercedes cars and hotel dinners, farmers' subsidies always the first to get the chop, and half of them divorced or separated themselves.

On and on it went, growing raucous, louder, until the debate switched to a competition for whose parish, village, had sunk to the most wanton, torrid behaviour in this immoral age.

Sweeney caught Gerry the barman's eye, then shook his head gravely.

'What?' Gerry asked. He was picking his teeth with a matchstick.

'You're a better man than me, Gerry McTigue,' Sweeney said.

Gerry leaned over the counter. 'How d'you mean?'

'Don't know how the dickens you do it, so I don't. I do be always saying the same to poor Kitty O'Neill abroad.'

'Do what?'

Sweeney gestured his head towards the other men along the counter. 'Listening to this kind of *seafóid* and nonsensical chat day in and day out. The patience of Job, Gerry. They must train ye in special patience at hotel management or whatever school you went to.'

Gerry plucked strands of the mangled match from between his teeth. He dropped his voice. 'To tell you the honest to God truth, Mr Sweeney, it's the deaf ear I do give them half the time.'

Sweeney said, 'Nerves of steel you must have. Now, what hour of the evening will the likes of them go home?'

'Ah, could be closing time. Longer if you left them in it.' Gerry's voice had warmed; flattered by Sweeney's empathy.

Sweeney shook his head. 'Jesus Christ and his sacred mother. Sitting in a pub all day. An awful waste of a life, though, hah?'

''Spose,' Gerry said, and rummaged in an open box for a fresh match.

Sweeney winked conspiratorially. Dropped his voice again. 'Come 'ere, *a mac* . . .'

Gerry leaned out over the counter.

'While I think of it, now I'll ask you. The wife has me tormented every time I come into the town, but I

184

keep forgetting. There was a neighbour of the wife's cousin beyond in England – London – came there at the Christmas; came and had the cup of tea with us, but she was staying in a room here, like. Anyways, a grand woman, nicer never stepped in shoe leather, and if she didn't send us the huge box of chocolates with a ribbon and a big thank-you card when she arrived beyond again.' Sweeney stopped to take a sip of his porter.

Gerry waited, the face expressionless. Countrymen and their rambling stories. No punchline. 'Yah, yah, so what about this woman, a cousin, whatever?'

'Oh! Where was I? Oh yes, what's knocking the story out of me, is . . . Anyways, the wife wanted to send her a nice Easter card; actually, I'm glad you reminded me, 'cos that's another thing she wanted me to buy . . . Anyways, between the Christmas fuss and all the hopping and trotting abroad at the house, didn't we lose this woman's address.'

Gerry frowned at him.

'So, the wife warned me today to drop in and ask you so she did; ye must have some kind of hotel ledger, a book of some sort, with addresses of people that stayed . . .'

'But . . . like, wouldn't she have the same address as your cousin, only one number up or down?'

Sweeney's smile froze. The eyes startled. Then a loud, theatrical laugh. 'Ah, ha, ha, ha, ha, that's a good wan all right, Gerry. A damn good wan. God, you're too good to be pulling pints behind that bar, so you are. Ha, ha, ha. No, she's a *neighbour*, in the same housing estate but across the way, a different avenue from the wife's cousin, but . . . the same parish, like.'

'Here! Young lad!' one of the mart men growled at Gerry. 'Any chance of a bit of bread with this soup?'

'Back in a sec,' Gerry said to Sweeney.

Sweeney smiled sweetly at him. Fatherly.

The men were debating the European parliament when Gerry came out around the counter, beckoned to Sweeney to follow him out across the front hall to the reception desk.

Sweeney jabbed a finger towards the computer. 'The twenty-sixth or twenty-seventh of December . . . no, the twenty-seventh. I'm sure of it; day after St Stephen's Day. Remember it well.'

Gerry looked over his shoulder in case the manageress came back early from lunch.

'Brown?' Sweeney said, an elbow on the desk, the voice deliberately casual. 'Try Brown. Good man yourself.'

Gerry said, 'Ah, Brown Whitaker, Susan. Ms. Checked in and pre-paid her bill the twenty-sixth of December; left her key with the night porter on the morning of the twenty-ninth.'

'Th'address, th'address beyond in England?'

Gerry clicked again. A raking back and forth sound of a computer printer. He tore the paper along its perforated edges. Shoved it at Sweeney. 'Here. Look, if anyone found out . . .'

'Fair play to you. You're a mighty young lad, so you are. A drink? Something to wet your whistle and give you strength for that shower within?'

One of the mart men was coming up the corridor from the Gents', zipping up his fly. He glowered at Gerry. 'We were wonderin' where you went to. A sad show when a man is thirsty and there's no . . .'

'Can't you see the poor lad is busy?' Sweeney snapped, then tucked Gerry's paper into his top jacket pocket.

Chapter 32

The train swayed, then picked up speed as it headed out of Cripton Station. She grimaced at the twittering headphones on the girl's head beside her. She'd seen this girl at the station for the past few weeks – always with an *A–Z* map of London, mismatched jackets and skirts, tanned legs above knee-high, spike-heeled boots, always oblivious and lost in this tinny music.

Susan eyed the large, brown envelope with the Irish postal stamp sticking up from her briefcase pocket.

The morning post had arrived just as she left for work – the usual bills, catalogues, a postcard from Anna from the south of France. But immediately she'd pounced on this one, stuffed it in her bag to read on the train.

A red postal mark, *Rath Luach, Co. Mhaigh Eo.* Even she could understand this piece of Gaelic Irish. Had to be from him, McHugh. But why? And what? Another invitation to go back over there? It would have to be after – this week, more, a fortnight at least. When Daddy was more stable. Out of hospital now, all those drips and intravenous feeds, convalescing at the Manor with enough penicillin to either preserve or kill a horse.

Or McHugh coming to visit her again. But why the big, business envelope? A holiday brochure? Check it out. *Go on, then, let your hair down and let's go for it. You and me.*

From the envelope she took two newsletters, one with

a charcoal drawing of a country house – Rathloe House – on the front page. On the other, dated last November, she recognised the photo of the little landlady in the Rathloe pub: 'Kitty Takes Home Raffle Booty.' There was a letter on embossed paper, with a smaller replica of the house drawing in the top left-hand corner.

She angled it towards the train window, one elbow on the ledge.

Dear Miss Brown,

I'm writing to you today from Rathloe, County Mayo, Ireland. First, I should introduce myself, I suppose. I'm Mr Patrick Sweeney, native of this parish, as was my father and his father before him. Me and my wife are now semi-retired at my residence outside the village. However, I spent a mighty time in England at the start of my structural engineering career, where I learned many a thing or two.

Indeed, though retired as I said, I'm finding my career more useful than ever these days as we in the parish of Rathloe have formed a working committee to preserve and rebuild Rathloe House, our local history treasure.

The other great thing about retirement is I've time now to follow my always keen interest in local history. Now, me and the Preservation Committee have researched the families who have occupied the big house here in Rathloe – and I am inclined to think that your good self, Miss Brown, may have some connection to a Mr Richard Brown, last land agent, R.I.P., and a very highly regarded man in our parish.

I gather that you have been lucky enough to have visited our lovely village and our local taverna or pub. Unfortunate it was that our paths didn't cross at that time. Me and the wife would have loved to have you for the cup of tea. However, what with historical research and my other studies plus the odd bit of horticultural work, one doesn't get to visit the village's meeting spots as much as one would like. I'm sure you know how it is.

*Anyways, our Preservation Committee has been extremely
busy raising funds and support for the purchase of Rathloe
House. As you can see from enclosed, people near and far
have written in support of us keeping and rebuilding this
lovely residence as a historical and tourist attraction.*

*However, we have been recently disappointed to find out
that the selling price of the property at said location is higher
than we'd expected. But that's the way it goes I suppose. No
way to predict how the winds will blow, is there?*

*Anyways, I won't keep you. Except to say that if you saw
your way to supporting our project out of respect for your
dead ancestors and the preservation of both of our histories,
we would all be very delighted. Also, we were thinking, maybe
you even have some artifacts or old antiques from the era when
your grandfather was here. Except for the records in the town
library here near us, I'm afraid we've little to go on.*

*I'm enclosing our lovely preservation newsletters, and
copies of our signatures of support. Also, as I spend a lot of
my time looking up things in the town library, a photocopy
of what we hope is the right person, the last land agent of
Rathloe House, Mr Richard Brown, R.I.P. A lovely man, my
father and grandfather always said.*

She skipped down through the rest of these rambling,
handwritten lines about weather, *We won't feel it now
until the summer, thank God, lovely around Rathloe and
County Mayo in the summer, maybe you'd like to come over
and take a look for yourself? You and your husband would
be heartily welcome . . .*

The train raced into morning sunlight, then out again,
the buildings, the city pale, diaphanous against the
sky.

The girl beside her had turned the volume up. A
witch-like wailing song above thudding drum sounds.
A man opposite looked up painfully from his newspaper. A woman on her mobile phone put a finger

189

in one ear. *Please, please switch off that music. And stop jigging your knee against mine.* She wanted to scream it into the girl's face.

She stuffed the letter back into its envelope.

It came seeping up, this flood, the wake of sudden knowing, of secrets finally told.

He'd kept it from her. In her upstairs bedroom at Railroad Place, back there in those wild, frosted gardens at Rathloe House, in that village pub, in the city. His voice, the face came back to her now, *I don't really go there any more*, he'd said about the little village pub. Then mumbled excuses about being busy.

His features, the set of his lean jaw came back, that evening in her flat, then the rest of it, clicking along, the scenes, snapshots transmogrified against the backs of the houses, allotments, fences, trees that were flashing past the train window. Rathloe House. O'Neill's pub. The Galway City streets. The bistro with the red walls. His kitchen. Her dining room. Her bedroom. Where were the clues? Lurking here? No, no, what about there? Let's look at the next, then. Where was it, the devious deception? Where were this Mr Sweeney and all these preservation people who somehow seemed to know more about her and her grandfather than she knew herself?

They were stopped at another train station – tubular benches, advertisements on the wall.

Doors swooshed shut as the train shunted off again. New footsteps down the carriage, feet, trouser legs, hands clutching briefcases, a newspaper stuffed in a pocket.

A long spate of sunlight. Then a shadowed tunnel of houses, bricks, garden walls. It rose higher inside her, sour as bile. She had been duped, shepherded this way and that, shielded from what McHugh thought she shouldn't see or know.

First Gerald and now John McHugh. Clever men. Flitting about, arranging their little schemes like the jester in a children's pantomime. And there she was, Suze, the unsuspecting idiot.

The girl beside her had slouched further down in the seat, the tanned legs, the whole body jigging, gyrating to the music. Susan tapped her on the knee.

Nothing.

Susan stood to pluck the earphones off her head.

'Whaaa— ?' The girl's eyes flew open, terror at this mad, middle-aged woman in the Lady Di suit.

'Turn it bloody off!' Susan shouted at her, jabbing a finger furiously between them.

The man with the newspaper, the woman on the telephone stared, waited, then started a slow, steady applause.

Chapter 33

It was hot and dusty. She'd never even been here before. By the looks of things, the shed was beyond Mr and Mrs Lawson's jurisdiction of cleaning, trimming and checking.

Inside the door was an old wardrobe, suitcases stacked on top, footstools with missing legs, chairs with stuffing escaping from faded, velvet seats. Opposite were two old tables, one inverted on the other, the legs sticking up into the air.

She coughed in the dust.

God, she felt guilty. Weeks, months of avoiding Daddy's house except to write a monthly cheque for Mrs Lawson and now, here she was: a hovering scavenger.

Artifacts, that's what that Mr Sweeney had asked for in his letter two days ago. And that night, lying in the bed that she'd once foolishly shared with Mr John McHugh, she had remembered. Christmas. Daddy's last spate of lucidity. *There were things from then, down at the house.*

She pulled down a suitcase, hauled it across into the window light. Inside were old university notebooks with Daddy's name on the inside cover in his pointed, high script: Richard J. Brown. Each page covered with faded handwriting, diagrams, notes crammed in the margins.

She stuffed them back in, clicked the rusted locks shut, then swung the suitcase back up on the wardrobe.

She pulled at the two tables until they budged to the left, then squeezed between them and the wardrobe to a mahogany cabinet in the back. The top table wobbled. A leg almost caught her eye.

She pulled the cabinet drawers open. In the first, old buttons, a crumpled, ten-shilling note, a sewing bobbin, a packet of rusted drawing pins. Next, a winter cap with its bobble chewed off.

The middle, biggest drawer stuck. She pulled again. It yanked open, crashed crookedly to the floor. The edge caught her toe.

'Oh, shit!' Tears caught in her throat. More papers and notebooks littered across the floor.

She wriggled her big toe. Not broken. Oh, she should just abandon the entire thing, leave the documents until some mice came and chewed them.

But she crouched, careful to avoid being jabbed by more stray furniture. She gathered up as many papers as she could, stuffed them back into the drawer.

She opened the old ledger, the pages edged with brown as if dipped in tea. In the flyleaf, *Richard T. Brown, Crown Agent, Rathloe House, Townland of Rathloe, Barony of Ballyshee, County Mayo, 1916–1922.*

She traced the handwritten names down the page, tried to pronounce the Irish – Gaelic Irish – words.

Walsh, M. Baile na hAbhann: £2
Joyce, J. Cregmore: £1
Moran, S. Seanbhaile: 8s
Joyce, K. Creagh: 9s/2d
Sweeney, R. Sruth: 8s/4d
Murphy, J. Deochuisce: 6s/2d

She mangled them. Impossible damn language. Far too many vowels.

Pages and pages of lists. On some, lines drawn

through the names – delinquent accounts? Reminded her of their bookkeeping, back in the early days when iTemps was a small, secretarial agency with typists who appeared for interviews in stockings and flared skirts.

Question marks appeared after other names, some in red. Most surnames were repeated three, four times, only the first initial different – sometimes even that was the same. How did they – or her grandfather – tell them all apart?

In the back of the ledger was a hand-drawn map, the same place names handwritten, lines marking what she assumed were fields, roads, and a rectangular area marked 'Rathloe House'.

Here was a letter dated 4 December, 1916, verifying that Mr Richard Brown would oversee 408 statute acres at Rathloe Estate in the townland of Rathloe, under the request of a Lord John Biltmore for a stipend of fifty pounds per annum.

She held the watermark up to the shed window: 'Commissioners of His Majesty's Woods, Forests, Land, Revenues, Works and Buildings.'

Her toe still throbbed. She leafed through the ledger again: name after name, rows and rows of people.

She would send it to them over there. Why not?

Since his letter, she'd pictured this Mr Patrick Sweeney: a studious little man, the country cottage type, fussing over his perennial gardens, committee chair of every library and church committee, he and his wife walking their Pekinese through the village every evening. She had to admit that she hadn't seen anyone like that in Rathloe, during her short visit to the pub there, only some old men who had peered at her, reminded her of peasants from a Thomas Hardy novel.

A crazy paving path led up through the garden and around the south side of the house. A dazzling forsythia in full bloom against the conservatory wall.

She stood watching the chimneys, the tiled roof against the brooding, thunder sky. The rent book reeked of mildew, dust, things crawling between the pages.

It was as if Daddy would come out that back door any minute, look to the sky and the weather, cross to the iron patio table with drink in hand, a magazine or book under his arm.

It had always pleased her that her father had aged handsomely, elegantly – craggy features, white hair, a tennis player's body.

Then she pictured the other houses: Rathloe with its ramshackle gardens and graffitied doors; her and Gerald's semi at Cripton Mews, and her new spot at Railroad Place with its layers of lookalike doors and balconies, like roosts in a chicken factory.

In this sultry afternoon they blurred in her mind, not as stalwart structures, but as rather pitiful things – four walls, gardens, bolted-up doorways. Useless, weren't they? Mortar, timber, rafters. All useless in the face of death, madness, divorce or foolishness. One the same as the next, interchangeable.

The Sweeney man's letter came back to her: *at that time we had not realised your historic and significant connection with Rathloe House and demesne.*

At the top of Daddy's lane, she turned left for Hargrove village instead of right for the motorway. She should have put the old rent book in the boot. She could still smell the mildewed pages from the back seat.

The car clock said a quarter to five. She came to a Give Way sign before the main village street. What harm could it do? A brief chat with the local estate agent. What's best? How quickly?

Her idea buzzed in her head like an advertising jingle. A house for a house. An eye for an eye.

Chapter 34

Damn. McHugh leaned on the horn as another car stopped dead in front of him. It pulled off the road onto the grass. Already, a line of cars along the Rathloe road where the crossroads forked right for the village school.

A young man hopped out, waved at McHugh cheerily, while Mother and two little boys came around the other side to the boot.

Lovín tensed in the passenger seat, ears, face alert against the windscreen. She growled. From the boot they took an animal cage, two cats' eyes looking through the wire door. McHugh watched the family troop down the side road towards the school sports field. Up ahead were other families, toddlers being wheeled in buggies, more pet cages, mothers in cotton sunhats.

Around town and on the roadside electricity poles he'd seen them, fluorescent posters for Rathloe Sports Day, all funds for the Rathloe Preservation Committee.

He manoeuvred the Volvo past the lines of parked cars towards the village and Rathloe House.

Through the open car window, the tinny, megaphone voice: 'Would all contestants now for the pet show please take their places near the . . .'

At last, Lovín had calmed down beside him. McHugh smirked at his dog, to himself. Kitties and white rabbits on parade for history. Laughable.

'Oh, come on!' He slammed on his brakes again, leaned on his horn to scatter a group of teenagers pedalling along the middle of the road on their bicycles.

Lovín ran ahead. McHugh followed her up the avenue. Now that his cattle, his cattle crushes, water and feeding troughs were installed – plus new gates in the stone-wall gaps, he itched to get on with his other work – clear the shrubbery before the house, prepare the site for the demolition crew, then get the builders started on the foundations.

He'd already been sketching plans, blueprints, was researching architects in Galway. Now . . . it would be all waiting. He sighed. All he'd done since he'd moved back here – wait. For workmen to clear his fields, his new grass to grow, for all these yuppies to stop playing high jinks with this damn preservation nonsense.

And Susan Brown to call him back. Two nights ago, he'd left a message on her answering machine. 'Lovely time over there . . . Look, give us a ring sometime – soon.'

But nothing – yet.

Today was Sunday. He didn't even know what she did on Sundays. Probably visit that father of hers or outings with that friend she talked about. Or maybe she was away on business again.

Stop. Stop. Better to think of other things. His house started, and all would be different. Just a month. Less.

Lovín was barking – high, delighted yaps. Voices came from the front of the house.

He stopped in the archway, peered through the lilac bushes. Four men and two women, walking around the clearing, pointing up at the big house windows, the chimneys. Tourists. Their voices twittered like birds.

They turned at his footstep.

'Hi there,' a man called out in an American accent, a

wide grin as if McHugh were the long-awaited arrival to their party.

'This is private property,' McHugh said. A Japanese man was petting Lovín, the tail wagging blissfully.

'Ah, we are not allowed?' a second Japanese man asked.

'Not open to the public,' McHugh enunciated stiffly, waved a hand around him to take in the roof, rafters, the walls with their fringe of ivy. 'This is a working farm. My farm.'

'Ah,' a Frenchman said. 'But we have come to see this house, this Rathloe House.'

'Yeah,' the American wife said. 'We were just talking with your two young ladies down at the church fête or county fair or whatever you got going here, and this wonderful historical cause of yours . . .'

'Decided to take a look for ourselves,' her husband finished for her, the grin back on his face.

'Private.' McHugh walked closer to them.

'But the house . . . on this website . . . here,' the Frenchman produced a printed page from his shoulder bag, a manicured fingernail pointing to a digital photo of the big house.

'And the Irish girls, they ask for donation . . . so, *naturellement* we come to see . . .' his wife said.

McHugh held up a hand as if to hush some clamouring children. 'Look, I understand. But the *Irish girls*, as you call them, misled you. This is not a tourist attraction.'

They exchanged puzzled looks. 'But the girls, in the tent, they say . . .' the Frenchman tried again.

'Never will be,' McHugh said with a dismissive smile. *This was one unfriendly Irishman*, the looks, the faces said.

'We can take photo of old house?' Lovín's Japanese friend asked.

McHugh shook his head.

'How 'bout your beautiful farm?' the American woman asked with a determined smile. 'With Shep or Spot here, or whatever you call this little fella?'

McHugh shrugged. 'Yes. If you like. Just the fields. And just the dog.'

They trooped across the clearing, ducked through the briars and the lilacs onto the avenue, Lovín, the ambassador dog leading. McHugh followed them, as if somehow they might hoodwink him, double-back another way.

'Here. This is *vraiment* beautiful, yes?' the French wife gestured to take in the fields, the walls, the shiny new gates in their gaps. In this near field, two black and white heifers lay in the shade of the high wall chewing their cuds, lazily swishing their tails at flies. Everywhere was the sweet smell of new pollen and fresh cowdung.

'This farm,' the French husband asked. 'In your family for many . . .' He foraged for the word – 'generations? And the *maison*, this chateau? That, too, of your family?'

McHugh scowled at him.

The Japanese man patted his thigh for Lovín to come and be photographed.

They giggled, said 'smile' and 'pepperoni' as the cameras clicked.

At last they turned down the avenue towards the gates. He watched them crunch along, a swish of nylon backpacks, sportswear. Off for their lunch and pints of Irish Guinness at the genuine Irish O'Neill's.

Beyond his fields, his walls, he heard the tinny voice on the megaphone again. 'Would all our footballers for the over-sixties versus Rathloe Senior Team please report to . . .'

He turned for the house and the old stables where he'd erected a makeshift, tarpaulin roof for his cattle troughs, feeding buckets, syringes, cattle doses.

It would never happen, would it? Three-legged races and cat shows and tour buses couldn't raise enough money for their purchase deposit by 1 June?

He sank his hands deep into his pockets and whistled for Lovín. No. A week. It would all be over. Plain sailing and digging a foundation after that.

Chapter 35

'Ah, cottage cheese there on mine whenever the comedy show is over,' the young man said rattily. He was standing at the top of a long queue, all waiting at the potato booth in the middle of the school sports field.

'Oh, pardon us, but we were just laughing because, well you see, my friend Bridgie here put a statue of the Child of Prague in her front window last night – for a fine day today, for the sports day here today like – you know, like we used to the night before a wedding long 'go . . .'

'Look, are you getting my spud or not?' the man interrupted. Behind him, people in the queue shuffled their feet.

Babs said, 'Ah, sure, you're too young to remember all that, I suppose. Cottage cheese for this poor *ladín* there, Bridgie; he's starved, the creature.'

Their potato booth was a makeshift wooden counter that two days ago, Mannion had been commissioned to hammer together from boards and a shed door. Bridgie had painted a sign on a sheet and strung it across over the counter between two poles, 'Spuds O'Bridgit.'

Mannion mocked that the whole thing looked like a hacienda on a cowboy film, but Bridgie and Babs had been steadfast: this is the kind of malarkey that people liked, tourists especially – daft oul' names like you saw on pubs in Killarney.

Charcoal smoke billowed from the two huge barbecues behind them as the women, in matching striped aprons, tongsed roasted spuds onto paper plates and scooped fillings for the waiting punters.

'Now. Three pounds fifty please. Salt and pepper?' Babs handed the man his steaming spud with cottage cheese.

'For a bloody potato? Three-fifty for a shaggin' spud?'

'That's right.' Babs' jaw jutted defiantly. 'It's for the preservation of Rathloe House, a good cause so it is.'

'Preservation and good cause my arse,' the man said. 'It's bleedin' extortion. I can get three bags of chips for that. Is there no chip van here today . . . ?'

The two women smirked at each other. Certainly not. The committee made blinkin' sure there were no competing vendors.

Bridgie said, 'Chips are bad for your heart, your ulcers. Now, give the money to Babs there when you're ready. Yes, next please.'

A woman with three waiting children recited: 'One with broccoli and cheese, two cottage cheese, one curried beans.'

'Grand. Fourteen pounds please and if you step over there, now, my friend, we'll look after you *in a jif*. Here, you'll need a tray for all them. Now, next. Yes, love.'

'One with curried beans, please.'

People in T-shirts, jeans, cotton palazzo pants were still coming through the school turnstiles, where Richie Sweeney and Father Briscoe were collecting entrance fees, tearing off tickets, marking people's hands who wanted to come back in later. People arrived with dogs on leads, cats in carrying boxes, young boys with guinea pigs in cages. Father directed them to the animal pen halfway down the field, where the lovely Mrs Sweeney would sign them all up for the pet show, plenty of time, for it didn't start until three o'clock.

Halfway down on the right side of the field, youngsters clamoured around Sadie Sweeney and Mrs O'Brien, who were busily taking registrations and entry fees for the three-legged race, the egg and spoon, tiny tots, mothers' and sack races.

At the far end, a shrill whistle came from the parish football pitch, where a white leather ball went up in the air. The kick-off for the under-twenty-one football between Rathloe and Ballyshee.

Mannion and Walsh came stumping across the school tarmac, through the gates to the field, both weighed down with basins of washed potatoes.

'Where do you want them?' Walsh growled at Bridgie.

'On top of the blinkin' school chimney! Where d'you think we want them but here, where we're baking and selling them?' Bridgie eyed a waiting customer and looked to heaven. Men!

'But the football . . .' Walsh said, nodding towards the end of the field.

'Football later. Feed these poor people first,' Bridgie said.

Obediently, the two men plopped down in the grass, where they began to prod the spuds with a fork, then wrap each one in tin foil for baking.

Up in the village of Rathloe, Margaret O'Neill was edgy with these hordes of youngsters from the town, locals, and those from surrounding parishes.

'Let's get a move on,' she said with a tight smile as they hovered in over her ice-cream fridge. 'Have to make a decision. Other people besides yerselves . . .'

Next door, Kitty had dragged three picnic tables into the car park, resurrected some free, beer-company umbrellas. No need for her roadside sandwich board to draw people in today, for by two o'clock, the picnic tables, the bar, the lounge tables inside were packed with people.

They'd left the city for a lovely drive out in the country, been surprised and delighted at having happened on such a lively little spot as this Rathloe. Never pegged it for such a happening place. All great *craic*.

Kitty rushed from bar to tables and back again; a white tea towel slung over her shoulder, a notebook in her apron pocket, delivering pints, minerals, G&Ts, and telling each group they'd just have to hold their horses. 'Only two hands,' she told one Dublin couple. Only two hands on any human being.

Vinnie Mannion, home for the weekend, had been whisked from his bar stool and his quiet bottle of Budweiser to deliver trays of sandwiches and drinks.

'This isn't Galway, Dublin or Limerick,' Kitty told one extra-loud family with chirping, demanding children. If they wanted the country, well, this was how it was.

Deep breaths, she told herself as she stood topping off a row of Guinness pints. Deep, deep breaths. Count to ten. For after all, wasn't this what she'd been craving? People on the premises. Money in her till. Deep breaths and just keep running. Make hay while the sun shone.

When the tour bus arrived, Edel Quinn caught Claire Sweeney's eye and winked triumphantly. 'Told you,' Edel said.

The two younger women were hosting the Rathloe Preservation tent just inside the admission gates. The tour company was a main advertiser on the tourism website Edel managed, so it had been no bother to persuade the driver towards Rathloe for a taste of the unspoiled Ireland.

The bus backed into the school gateway, then pulled forward, then backed up again to park along the front school walls, its smoked-glass windows and metal glinting in the afternoon sun.

'Jesus, Edel Quinn, you're something,' Claire said. In the field, people turned to watch as tourists descended the bus steps, came through the turnstiles where Richie Sweeney collected their money.

The foreign women grinned, nudged their husbands, and then pointed towards the 'Spuds O'Bridgit' potato booth and its homemade sign. They strolled down through the field, heads swivelling right and left, pointing, rummaging in their shoulder bags for cameras – the pet show was about to begin, and oh, look at those adorable, freckled children with their dogs and rabbits. And the shouting. Everyone at the end of the field shouting, screaming, cursing so excitedly as a leather football came lobbing through the blue sky.

'Please. Please. We take your photograph.' Two Japanese men stopped at the Spuds O'Bridgit booth, nodding apologetically to the queue of waiting customers. Babs and Bridgie fluffed out their hair, straightened their aprons, and held a pair of tongs each in the air to pose coquettishly.

'A little to left, please,' one Japanese man said.

'And please, with potato,' the other insisted.

Behind them, Mannion nodded at Walsh. At last a chance to escape.

Off the two men went down the field, glancing nervously over their shoulders, sneaked down behind the pet pen, lost themselves in the hordes of children and parents and animals, never stopped until they were safely installed on the sidelines of the football pitch where the over-sixties football match was about to start.

Sweeney and O'Brien stepped out of the boys' outdoor toilets. Sweeney cursing as he tried to tuck his football jersey into his trousers. It was his old football jersey from his heyday on the main Rathloe team. But look at it now: shrunk to the devil in that new washing machine of Sadie's.

'Haw, haw, haw.' He stopped tugging and puffing to point and snigger at O'Brien in his football shorts. 'Sure you're not going out before the seven parishes with those oul' white legs on you? Like some old fella you'd see in a morgue or a hospital.'

O'Brien, his dyed hair glistening in the sun, scowled at him and headed off down towards the football match. 'D'yeh think 'tis on holidays in Spain y'are?' Sweeney roared down after him. 'Pleurisy, that's what you'll get in them yokes. Nothing but pleurisy.'

Last night, as she aired his football jersey in front of the sitting-room fire, Sadie had babbled on as usual, hoping the nine o'clock weatherman had been right, hoping there'd be a turnout for the sports. A tragedy, pure tragedy if it flopped like the St Patrick's dance. The only time she had stopped talking was to answer the mobile phone in her apron pocket.

Oh, how he'd been tempted to blurt it out! No need for half, nor quarter of this fuss and pet rabbits and baked spuds and football matches. Just a matter of waiting for her nibs, Miss Brown, to come through with the readies.

Nearly two weeks since he'd posted his letter. And a mighty letter too, though he said so himself. Wasn't it time for some answer? Some word. A cheque? A postal order?

Every morning at the house he'd waited for the post; every afternoon pestered Kitty O'Neill if there was any sign or tidings of an e-mail for him on the pub computer.

The megaphone again, 'Ladies and Gentlemen, the over-sixties versus Rathloe senior team will soon be starting. All footballers should please . . .'

'Are you coming or not?' O' Brien stopped to wait for him, the legs glinting in the sun.

'Soon, Micheál, soon.' Johnny tried to calm his brother as they sat in their striped deck chairs, coordinating shade umbrellas held over their heads. Micheál, in immaculate football jersey and pressed white slacks, looked more like a cricket player than a footballer.

For over an hour now, he'd been jigging and fidgeting, standing up and then sitting back down again, waiting for the starting whistle and the referee to throw in the ball for the over-sixties football game.

Johnny handed his brother a bottle of spring water. 'Important to stay hydrated,' he told him.

Oh! The whole thing was growing more and more distressing.

Of course, it was wrong to take pleasure in another's misfortune, but Johnny had felt a great relief when he'd heard McHugh's asking price for the big house and with the ensuing lull around the village. But now this sudden upsurge again, this ranting, greedy buzz, rising anew like wasps after their winter hibernation.

But how could he have refused his brother when all this and the week before, every afternoon down in O'Neill's shop, there'd been nothing but *good man yourself, Micheál. Counting on you for the over-sixties,* just like the old days, blocking those balls from going in the back of the net.

It was like pedalling a bicycle down a very steep hill, the wheels going faster than his feet could keep up. Impossible now to stop, to turn around now and say, 'We, the Monahan brothers, have had enough, thank you all the same. Enough of dances, sales of work, newsletters and garish appeal letters through our letterbox – and all to rake up the past.'

'Now, Johnny, now,' Micheál said again, jumping up

again to peer over everyone's heads to where the two teams – grey-haired, elderly gentlemen and prancing young men – were gathering around the referee.

'Yes. Now,' Johnny said, then sent his brother off onto the field.

Chapter 36

They were sitting on Susan's tiny balcony, with glasses of white wine, smoke from Anna's cigarette billowing between them. Anna, just back from the south of France, reminded Susan of a forest gnome – the brown eyes in a bronze, tanned face, eagerly relaying holiday stories, interjections, wondering if Georges wasn't getting carried away these days, too serious about her, declarations of undying love with the Mediterranean sunsets and all that. She crossed her tanned legs, flash of turquoise thong sandals, and held the Gauloises aloft.

What did she, Suze, think? Anna's voice, face were mischievous. Loved a romantic intrigue – especially when it was hers.

They'd had this conversation a hundred times through the years. Only the men, the lovers had changed. Her friend Panny, always in fear of getting trapped into the net of commitment.

Inside, Susan's kitchen phone rang.

'Ms Brown? Susan Brown, is it?'

'Yes?'

'It's Jenny. Jenny Paige of Paige and Lunt Estate Agents? Down here in Hargrove?'

'Em . . . yes.'

'Look, sorry to bother you on a Saturday afternoon but we have an offer on . . . your – your father's house.'

'Oh.'

211

'We know it's not the most ideal but, of course, we're not London. Lovely young couple. Renting at the moment; he's been here a year as a senior registrar at Hargrove General Hospital. Has even heard of your dad . . .'

'What is it – their offer?'

'Three-twenty-five-nine. But look, don't give us an answer now. We've got the weekend. But get back to us Monday first thing . . . or we could wait for a few others, but you did say you're in rather a hurry . . .'

Susan watched the back of Anna's head through the glass door.

'Ms Brown?'

'Yes.'

'Monday, then. I wouldn't leave them waiting any . . .'

Susan chewed on her lower lip. 'I'll take it.'

Silence. Then an indrawn breath. 'Look, we can certainly . . .'

Susan drummed a finger into the kitchen counter's red surface. 'No. No. Look, I really have some deadlines here . . . another property venture of mine . . . Look, fax me the forms, would you? Here at my flat . . .'

'If it's what you . . .'

Outside, Anna had propped her feet up on the balcony railing. Scarlet-painted toenails pointing towards the flats across the courtyard.

'Yes, Jenny. Yes, it's what I want.'

Chapter 37

It had grown chilly in the parlour where Sadie Sweeney, Babs Mannion, Bridgie Walsh, Mrs O'Brien, Edel, Claire, and Father Briscoe were gathered around the priest's table. Behind them, a window was pulled open, the night breeze ballooning the sheer, white curtains in and out. But each of them was too busy counting money and scribbling down numbers and amounts on pieces of paper to get up and close it.

Father Briscoe lit a cigarette. Took a drag and left it smoking in the ashtray. Edel's lips moved as she counted. Babs' tongue jutting between her teeth as she swished fivers, tenners, twenties apart and then stacked them. Bridgie clinked coins – one pound, fifty-pence, and ten-pence – divided and lined them into the piles in front of her.

On the mantel, a shiny gold clock ticked, gold pendulums rotating. Right, then left, then right again. A present for the tenth anniversary of Father's ordination.

Mrs O'Brien wondered if she shouldn't offer to get up and wet a hot drop of tea in the priest's kitchen. God knows, they could all do with a perk-up. She could wash out these mugs that were already scattered around the table.

Edel flicked back her hair. Nobody had spoken for over a half an hour. Sadie and Babs looked up and smiled at her, expecting some word, some update, an end to this night.

The mantel clock chimed midnight.

'All right,' Edel said. 'Where are we all?'

'Nearly there,' Father said.

Babs and Bridgie had been sitting waiting, their eyes growing heavy and sleepy, hands flopped in their laps.

'Reports?' Edel said, arching her back. Claire stretched her arms high above her head, fingers laced together.

'Admissions?' Edel asked.

'Fifteen hundred and twenty-three pounds, fifty pence.'

Edel raised her eyebrows in a question mark. They'd charged three pounds per person, expressly so there would be no uneven numbers or coinage.

Father shrugged helplessly. 'Some maintained it should be half price for children.'

Edel sighed heavily. 'Jesus! All right. No pleasing some . . . . Let's move on. Concessions? Babs, don't tell me they wanted half-potatoes?'

Defiantly, Babs folded her arms across her huge chest. 'No, but we've reason to believe there were thefts.'

'Oh, sacred Jesus . . .' Mrs O'Brien crossed herself.

'Final amount from concessions?' Edel's voice impatient.

'Four hundred and twenty-four pounds, thirty-six pence,' Babs said.

'Great job, ladies,' Father Briscoe said, exhaling cigarette smoke and beaming down the table. 'I saw ye down from me there roasting and selling like a Turkish marketplace.'

'Ah, thanks, Father. I was only saying to Mrs O'Brien there a while ago. The secret, really you see is—'

'Moving on,' Edel interrupted. 'Entrance fees for sporting events. Sadie! Mrs O'! Got anything for us?'

'A hundred and fifty-two pounds from sporting events. Twenty-seven-fifty from the pet show.'

214

Edel flung her biro against the table. She enunciated it slowly. 'It – was – two pounds – *per – pet – entered*? So, how did we end up with . . . ?'

'Ah, one of the young Cartys came with a white mouse. Ah sure, the *creaturín*, we couldn't charge him full . . . 'twouldn't have been . . .'

'And some came with kittens, not fully grown cats . . .'

Edel put up a hand. 'OK, OK. Fine. Claire, do you want to report from the preservation tent?' She passed a slip of paper to her friend.

'Two hundred and ten people joined our mailing list. We received . . .' Claire frowned, brought Edel's paper closer as if she'd gone short-sighted, 'sixty-two pounds, twenty-five pence?' She looked wildly around. 'Edel, are you sure this is . . . ?'

Sadie said, 'But that busload of tourists . . . they seemed very keen.'

Edel sat poker-straight in her chair. 'Six of them – the Japanese, an American and a French couple, our heaviest hitters – went off rambling around the big house. Met the man – McHugh – himself, and he assured them Rathloe House was not and never would be a visitors' attraction. That they had been hoodwinked. Back they came to us saying they'd changed their minds; they'd be donating nothing, and they spread the word among their fellow bus bums, and . . .'

Babs said, 'But I thought . . .'

Edel continued, 'So those who *had* already donated came wailing around the tent asking for their money back.'

The parlour was dead silent.

Everyone adding up numbers in their heads. Babs, Mrs O'Brien, Sadie and Bridgie thinking about miracles, special, last-ditch novenas, another collection outside mass.

Claire, exhausted, dialled Richie, who was home on

babysitting duty, to see if the kids had finally gone off to sleep.

Father lit another cigarette.

Yes, they were finished. Done for. The Rathloe Preservation Committee and all its dreams.

Chapter 38

'Isn't it true for me?' O'Brien said with a dip of the head. 'Get tired of anything, so you would.'

Sweeney sipped from his pint and went back to watching the afternoon nature programme. Today it was bats in a Tasmanian cave.

O'Brien held his fist just under his chin. Tapped it like an imaginary microphone. 'Hello! Testing, testing. Anyone hear me out there on planet Earth?'

Sweeney muttered, 'We'd hear you a damn sight better if there was one spark of sense in what you were saying.'

'Look it, I was only saying that people from them hot countries; sure they must get tired of the sun sometime, beatin' down on top of them, day in day out, like we had here last week.'

Mannion's head whipped left and right, the eyes delighted. Oh, there'd be sport yet between these two.

'There's plenty of sense in it, like at least we get the few soft days like this, but in Africa and Portugal and them places . . .' O'Brien nodded towards the pub window where rain was streaming down the glass.

Sweeney's face was red, then purplish. 'Sure, when the hell would the likes of you meet anyone from Africa or Portugal or d'you even know where they are? Yeh big eejit?'

'And you would, I suppose?' O'Brien countered, relentless as a terrier.

'Yes,' Sweeney thumped the counter. 'You're right there, Mr O'Brien, sir. As a matter of fact, I would.'

'Ah, la-ads . . .' Kitty drawled over her shoulder from her computer stool under the window.

'What? I was only saying . . .' O'Brien said.

'You were only saying nothing, nothing, like you're always saying, talking about things you know nothing about,' Sweeney said.

'But—' O'Brien started.

'Didn't I work with many's the Spaniard beyond in England, didn't I? And no, they never got tired of the bit of sun, but spent their whole time up on top of buildings, teeth chattering with the cold, with three even four *geansaí* on them because they couldn't get used to the English weather?'

'Look, I was only—' O'Brien tried again.

'So there's the horse's mouth, so why in the name of Jesus don't you stick to things you know something about like turnips and sheep and the price of shaggin' diesel?'

'Language, lads . . .' Kitty drawled again as she clicked away.

Mannion nudged O'Brien to stop.

For the past week, Sweeney had grown rattier by the day. Who knew when he'd turn on you like a dog?

The four were back watching the telly where a lad was prowling with a big torch into a cave with a thousand bats hanging, like mice stuck upside down with Sellotape.

Rain battered against the pub window, the sandwich board – O'Neill's Traditional Irish Pub and Internet Café – by the roadside.

Silence. Just the click, click, click of Kitty's keyboard.

Ping! The four didn't look around.

Never bothered now, for they were as used to that computer as they were the polished pint glasses on the shelves. Hardly even bothered to peer at the young people or the passing commercial travellers in suits who sometimes swerved in the car park, forking over good money just to perch up on that computer stool.

'Mr Sweeeeney,' Kitty called in a strange, fluting voice, as if summoning a favourite poodle.

Sweeney, his face set in a jowl of disgust, pretended not to hear her. Probably more guff about conducting himself in a licensed premises. She'd been raging with him yesterday when, on his way back from the Gents', Sweeney had told some web-surfing youngster that a good kick up the arse would soon cure him and his likes of this Internet crackedness.

'Mr Sweeney, *Esquire*,' Kitty called again, louder this time. 'An e-mail for you here. Would you like me to print it up or would you like to read it on-line? I'm sure you'll want your privacy.'

The other three men nudged and gawked. Sweeney getting messages sent to him at the pub?

Kitty came behind the counter. 'Now, men? Three more pints, is it?'

'Hey!' Sweeney growled from the computer. 'Sure, how can a person read an oul' picture?' He sat blinking at the screensaver, a photo of a Florida beach and waving palm trees.

'Ah, for the love of . . . Jesus, a child wouldn't be as helpless!' Kitty's slippers slapping across the floor, where, leaning over Sweeney's shoulder, she clicked on things until the printed letter appeared before him.

'But there's only half—' Sweeney started to say. Sighing, Kitty scrolled down the screen for him, her head averted towards the fireplace, making a big show of not reading a man's private letters.

Sweeney's body tensed, then the shoulders, head seeming to quiver under the gabardine hat.

'Oh, Jesus, Mary and Joseph,' he whispered. Sacred hour. The ship come in at last. But whoa! Easy, easy does it, he told himself. Cool as a shaggin' cucumber, that was the way to go. He read the letter again:

Dear Mr Sweeney:

Thank you for your letter. Apologies for not getting in contact sooner, but as a researcher, I'm sure you agree that it's always best to wait until one has gathered all the actual facts and information.

I am, of course, interested in your preservation project, and you are correct in your assumptions as to my family connections with Rathloe House. In fact, I have since unearthed a rent book which may be of interest as you add to your artifacts and historical collections.

Most urgent, at this point, is your request for funds towards the purchase. I am attaching a copy of an affidavit certifying that, upon closure of another family property sale here in the UK (May 27), the required ten per cent purchase deposit for Rathloe House will immediately be transferred to your preservation account.

After that, the remaining funds from the UK property at Hargrove village will be put in escrow – an educational endowment for when Rathloe is actually restored, open to the public and functioning as a non-profit-making historical home.

At that point, or as soon as your renovations are under way, I would be interested in some measure of involvement – perhaps at the board or volunteer level. This we can discuss at a later date. I am certainly willing to attend one of your planning sessions.

By reply, please let me know your telephone number, plus the Preservation Committee banking information for the timely transfer of funds.

*Again, I fully support your heroic endeavours to preserve
this delightful house. Also, please accept my congratulations
on your own, personal commitment to this worthy endeav-
our. Between now and May 27, the affidavit should allow
you and the committee to proceed with the purchase.*

*Meanwhile, I'll await your contact and financial details.
Please let me know if you need anything further.*

Best regards, Susan R. Brown

Sweeney shoved his hands in his pockets to stop them
shaking. He'd won. All his little hunches, enquiries, his
discretion had paid off.

Wasn't he always saying to Sadie up at the house?
There were them that knew how to do things and them
that didn't.

Now he, Mr Sweeney, had the last bloody laugh.

Chapter 39

'Here! Here! Plenty more where this came from,' Kitty said, reaching around with the second bottle of champagne. 'All for our loyal friend Mr Sweeney here. Saved the day for us all and Rathloe.'

Sadie screeched when the bubbles went up her nose. They clinked glasses.

Father Briscoe wiped his mouth. 'Lovely drop of champers, Kit.'

They had come from the village hall, where Edel, Claire and Father had sheepishly hosted a final, dismal preservation meeting. Bad news: except for St Jude or a miracle, and despite everyone's wonderful work, the funds for the purchase of the big house just weren't there.

Father, puffing on a cigarette, had been waffling on about how other parish projects would soon be under way; all not lost, funds never wasted, never fear . . .

Edel's mobile phone pealed through the village hall.

Kitty, in a high, shrieking voice. *Dismiss the meeting. Immediately. To O'Neill's pub. Pronto. Or better yet, bring everyone down here. She had a marvellous surprise for them all . . .*

Now, Father turned to Sweeney, who was perched like a king on his high stool. 'But, were you not nervous, like, asking her, this woman. A complete stranger or almost?'

'Hah? Oh, divil a bit,' Sweeney said, and took another swig of champagne. 'Sure, Father, what are friends for, really?'

'And tell us again how you got to know this woman, the genuine article, descendant of the big house?' Edel asked.

Sweeney shrugged, the voice deliberately casual. 'Oh, 'twas nothing really. Just a mate of mine beyond in England is a great mate of hers, like. We all knew each other from the dancing days long 'go around Camden Town and Kilburn. Always kept up the friendship, like.' He paused. He was going to make them wait, enjoy every last minute of this.

'And . . . ?' Claire asked.

'Well, sure, when I saw things *weren't going too well*, the odd thing backfiring, you could say, with the big house . . . I knew 'twas time to put in the word.'

Sadie, her face flushed from drinks and the delightful shock of the news, reached an arm around Sweeney's shoulder. She sang, 'This little man of mine. He's gonna make us shine . . . This little man of mine, he's gonna . . .'

He grunted at her to have sense in public.

'Well, it's nothing short of a miracle,' Father said, saluting Sweeney with his champagne glass.

Sweeney gave a smug little laugh, 'Ah, all due respect, there, Father. But miracle me arse. More a question of who you know. Right mate, right person, right time.' He beckoned them all in closer to him – Father, Edel, Claire, Sadie and Kitty – 'But the left hand can't know what the right hand is doing, capeesh?'

'Capeesh?' Father looked befuddled. 'What the dickens does that . . . ?'

Sweeney tapped the side of his nose, just like he'd seen once in a Mafia film on the telly.

'Capeesh,' he whispered again.

Chapter 40

The stranger's crotch was level with Johnny's face as the man leaned upward, grunting as he pushed a huge bag into the overhead luggage bin.

At last, he sagged into the seat opposite Johnny and Micheál Monahan. Johnny, his hands in his lap and his thumbs twirling nervously around and around, thought he should at least say hello, comment on the morning's weather. Surely it was rude to sit this close to someone and not bid them the hour of the day?

'Not a bad day now at all,' Johnny said, nodding to the little aeroplane window and the pale morning sky beyond the airport terminal.

The man frowned across the aisle at Johnny, then unfolded an *Irish Times*.

'Seatbelts.' The girl with the powdered face and pink lipstick came parading down the aisle, her head swivelling left and right.

'Pardon?' Johnny said.

'You have to fasten your seatbelts; the both of yez,' the girl said again, and bent to reach for someplace near Johnny's private parts.

'Oh,' Johnny yelped. 'Oooh!'

'Is there a problem here?' Her pink lips drawn acidly together.

'Em . . . em, I can take care of it myself, thank you.'

'And yer friend . . .' the air hostess nodded at Micheál,

225

who was staring out of the tiny window, watching every truck, every trolley, the airport men in their boiler suits and the loads of luggage being wheeled into the bowels of the aeroplane.

'Sir, your friend will have to . . .'

'Micheál, it's time to . . .' Johnny tapped his brother on the shoulder.

At last, Micheál turned, grinned at the air hostess. 'Hello, I'm Micheál Monahan. What's your name?' He held out his hand for a handshake.

Realisation, then disgust across the girl's face. A retarded man. That's all she bloody needed on the early morning flight to Heathrow.

'I'll see to my brother, miss,' Johnny said, the voice quavering. Oh, he wished to heaven they'd stayed in their little cottage outside Rathloe. He'd been a fool to come. An impetuous fool.

Yet he had to. All that buzz of news around Rathloe, all the screeching, excited chatter among the women around O'Neill's supermarket checkout. Everyone congratulating Sadie, saying, oh, they hoped she wouldn't take offence, now, but deffo, that husband of hers was a dark horse. Never thought Sweeney had it in him to save the day for the big house. The women had accosted him. Surely he, Johnny, had heard the mighty news? Powerful, wasn't it? Who would have thought? Darkest hour before the dawn.

The past few nights he'd spent pacing between the bedroom and their parlour, his mind decided, then changed, then decided again. Back and forth his thoughts went, back and forth like a shuttlecock. Wasn't it better to just live and let live? Let them celebrate, toast this new windfall, and proceed with the big house? What harm?

Yet, as dawn stole across the Monahans' flower gardens, Johnny, bleary-eyed, would look out across the beds of sweet williams, the borders of purple and white alyssum, the trim hedges, and know that in a year, maybe less, when the village was a-buzz with all these tour buses and historical guides and interpreters, that things would have changed drastically for the Monahan brothers. That he would never again be able to drive past the big house gates in his yellow Mini Minor without waiting for something to pounce, like a cross dog lurking inside a garden wall. For this was the way, wasn't it, with festering, untold secrets?

Johnny clicked Micheál's seatbelt shut, then tightened his own and leaned his head back against the aeroplane seat. His throat was tight and dry.

He hoped Sadie Sweeney hadn't smelled a rat when, two days ago, he'd telephoned her looking for Susan Brown's address. Muttered excuses about his old library contacts, a book he'd found, with reprints of big house documents . . . Needed to verify his research.

A relation of their own. A strange thought. No, hardly a relation like his uncle Charlie in Blackrock, Dublin. Or his great uncle James, Gretta's uncle who was long dead. Or a cousin of Johnny's dead father whom they always visited on the way to their annual holiday in Sligo. No, this was different, a tangled, frayed kind of thing.

It came back to him, what those mart men had said in the Hermitage Hotel lounge, that awful day four years ago. *A man like a horse; there's them with breeding and them without. Purebreds and mongrels.*

They were off. Johnny's thumbs twirled faster, round and around furiously. He closed his eyes and prayed, for here they were rumbling down the runway. A rolling barrel, a loud roar. Louder still. His head bursting with the noise, but here they were off the ground. Everything slanted – windows, seats, backs of heads in front of him. The lump in his throat painful.

Then suddenly, flat again. A low, humming noise, a ping and the lit-up seatbelt sign above his head.

He opened his eyes. Longed to loosen his top shirt button, to unclasp his bow tie, but a person leaving Ireland for the first time should look his best. First impressions, that's what his mother always said. Courage, she'd said, too. Courage, that's what her two *menín*, Johnny and Micheál would have. The courage to do the right thing.

Micheál screeched loudly, pulled at Johnny's sleeve. Quick, look out of the window at the bog falling away beneath them, the white religious basilica, a street with houses, then the distant shadow of hills, mountains, more houses, rooftops, tiny cars on a road.

A big secret, Johnny had warned his brother. Ever since they'd bought the tickets at the travel agent's in Ballyshee. Not a word to the nice ladies in O'Neill's shop. No, not even the barman in the Hermitage when they stopped for their weekly tea. Just their secret, the Monahan brothers', a secret little holiday to London to visit a friend, a nice lady.

'Drinks?' The girl with the pink lipstick was back, this time with a rattling trolley.

'I like Fanta orange,' Micheál told her, giggling.

'Juice, tea or coffee,' the girl snapped, not looking at them.

'Tea for me; juice for my brother.'

'Put down your trays,' she commanded.

Johnny thought he might cry. What tray?

Impatiently, she reached across him to clack down a small, plastic thing on Micheál's side, and nodded to Johnny to do the same.

This wasn't a tray, Johnny thought. Not a proper tray with an embroidered cloth and doilies.

*   *   *

'Mr Kenneth Trent, please pick up the nearest information telephone. Mr Kenneth Trent . . .'

Johnny felt his legs buckle; sure they wouldn't even
carry him across this huge, fluorescent room of voices,
noises, lines of people rushing past them, wheeling
bags, some in brightly coloured shorts and blouses,
straw sunhats. People didn't turn around to apologise
when they pushed against him and his brother, standing there petrified, matching overnight shoulder bags,
two little men in outdated suits and bow ties.

What should he do? The travel agent had said there
were several ways to travel from the airport to the Brown
woman's office. A coach, or the Heathrow Express, or the
Tube – a stop, in fact, straight across from Vernon Place,
where this Brown woman worked. Very convenient.
That'd be easiest of all.

And it had seemed easy, two days ago, in a tiny, Main
Street travel agent's in Ballyshee. But now, stranded in
the middle of this horrid place, with strange people,
dark faces, turbans, everyone with luggage wheels,
mobile phones and glazed eyes . . .

'Flight 101 to Glasgow now boarding at . . .'

'Would all passengers for flight 205 to Madrid now
go to gate . . .' The voices went on. It was a very bad
nightmare.

A silent prayer to God and his blessed mother to
help them.

At last, tugging at Micheál's elbow, he started walking, the two of them weaving between the queues of
people, the wheeling suitcases, babies in buggies.

'Hello,' Micheál said to this one and that. 'My name
is Micheál Monahan. What's yours?'

'Please pardon us,' Johnny said as he ushered his
brother onward. People frowned at them, then walked
blithely on.

*　　*　　*

'Now. Seven pounds and fifty each,' the man said, shoving two tickets under the glass window and waiting for his money. 'Take the lift downstairs, and your Tube is there.'

'Are you sure?' Johnny asked. A desperate whisper. 'It's just that we have to . . .'

The man frowned through the glass at him, then looked past Johnny's shoulder. 'Next please.'

Chapter 41

Their tails were caked in dung, hairy bodies sashaying towards the gap. McHugh sprinted behind his herd of cattle, darted to left or right when one balked before the open gate. Their eyes were limpid and ghostly in the pre-dawn light, an army of rumps and heads trooping into the summer meadows.

'Hup!' McHugh's voice carried in the stillness. Again: 'Hup there.' He lashed his stick through the air, not so much to drive his cattle, but to punctuate, finalise this act.

It had rained in the night – harmless, light showers. But now, a thin stripe of pink light had appeared at the edge of his fields. In an hour it would be daylight.

Last night, after the solicitor's phone call and news, he'd ranted, paced, even snapped at Lovín when she scratched at the cottage door to go out.

They had won. The preservation fools. Ready and waiting, affidavit in hand, cash transferred just in time for tomorrow, when he lost the big house. A charity donation from England.

'Who?' he'd shouted down the phone at Terence, the Dublin solicitor. Word for word, date, time, signatures, exact amount. But he'd already guessed, dreaded the benefactor's name.

They'd beaten him. She'd beaten him. Of course she hadn't returned his phone calls. Too busy plotting to ruin him, too busy cosying up to the rest of the silver-spoon brigade, Edel Quinn and Claire Sweeney. Probably half of London's charity circle chipped in: tea and cucumber sandwiches and ladies' fashion shows. A worthy cause. What was money when it came to saving history? *Oh, do pass the mint tea.* Dig deeper in their blue-blood pockets to ruin him.

Tomorrow, he and Lovín would walk into Ballyshee to the solicitor's office, a poker face as he accepted the Preservation Committee's deposit cheque, shake Edel Quinn's and all their hands. Wish the committee the very best.

After his first, ranting fit last night, he'd poured himself a large Scotch, drank it seething and gazing into his empty fireplace until he fell asleep on the couch where he dozed fitfully.

He woke with it throbbing at his temples, like the tail end of a vivid dream. Sell up. Get out. To hell or to Connaught. To hell with Connaught. With Ireland.

Today, in four, five hours' time, when those old Rathloe men stirred, finished their boiled eggs and tea and went shuffling off to their fields, they would notice this. Afterwards, reports around the counter at O'Neill's how Mr McHugh's cattle were sighted in his meadow, no hay left to cut this summer, no bailer arriving, nothing for winter fodder. Oh! They would relish the rich possibilities.

The last of the cattle ambled through the gap, hoofs thucking in the still-damp mud. McHugh went to swing the gate shut, but he stood there watching the beasts gambol across the high meadow, some already wandering towards the next gap into his second meadow.

Lovín stopped to sniff at a young, roan bullock, but yelped away when the beast ejected a stream of piss.

She had lost her puppy look now, but he felt more protective than ever towards her. How would she

weather the move back to London? Would she adapt
to life back there in Notting Hill? The surety of his
question pleased him, and he did a mental inventory
of the streets around his flat, tried to remember if he'd
seen owners walking their dogs.

They could, of course, buy something bigger, a little
less luxury inside, but with a big back garden for
Lovín. Not like he couldn't afford it after he sold these
twenty-five pristine, restored acres. A housing estate,
offices, county council flats. He'd sell his fields to a
bloody nuclear plant for all he cared. In fact, the nuclear
plant idea was delightful.

But not now. He'd wait until September when he
could recover his investment in the cattle. After all
these years, John McHugh's first bad investment. In
County bloody Mayo.

Turning, he followed the path the cattle had trampled
through the grass. He whistled for Lovín though he
knew it was useless. She would come hurtling past him
just when it suited her.

Nearer the house, the copper beeches were a lumpy,
dark silhouette against the paling sky.

The possibilities whipped through his mind. Buy
the rental cottage and add on? Live in Galway City,
drive the twenty-odd miles and widen his agricultural
entranceway from the crossroads end? Teach himself
to ignore the idling tour buses, the twitter of tourists'
voices carrying across his fields?

No. Come September, he'd be back where he'd come
from. Affirmation of some grudge against the country
that, years ago, had sent him away, and now couldn't
take him back.

He bent to pull a wisp, a *tráithnín*, to chew on,
just like his brother Seamus liked to do, like they
always did as boys at Carraig. He'd have to tell Seamus
about his impending move. Not now. Perhaps in July

when he had to attend Lorcan and Tomas's graduation party.

The invitation had come in the post last week. *Mr John McHugh and guest are cordially invited . . .*

It would please Seamus to see his brother go back to England. Seamus, like their dead mother, liked things, events to remain tidy; everything come full circle.

McHugh slashed his stick against a clump of high grass and laughed out loud. Oh yes, Mrs McHugh the widow had been right, hadn't she? At least about her younger son. Paddy-come-marching-home, now Paddy go toddling back.

Bees hummed in the wild roses in the archway before the clearing. There was a deafening twitter of dawn birds.

The walls of the house, the chimneys were growing sharper in this gauzy light.

In the rear garden, two birds pecked at the edge of the stone urn. He wondered if it was a sign of something; One for sorrow, two for . . .

No. No. He must stop this. No more old-wives' proverbs and superstitions.

In the bushes, the roof, the birds grew louder.

He should leave now. Tea and hot toast back at the cottage. Then get on with his day.

Yet he stood in the garden, hands stuck deep in his pockets, staring up at the back of the house and vowing to drive it away – this little-boy hurt, this disappointment inside him. Susan Brown, the woman he'd made love to in her warehouse flat, had ruined him. How had they found her, the preservation sharks? Now, he could and would bury this hurt in some secret place, push it down deep like a thousand other hurts.

Across these ramshackle walls, boarded-up windows, here she came, a vision of her, that Christmas morning – this very spot, the beret askew on her head, sprawled in the grass with Lovín licking her face. Longing. He despised, mocked it as a thing apart. But uncontrollable, like a facial tick.

From the stables came a frantic, high-pitched barking. Lovín. A rat. She'd cornered them in there before, growled and strutted before retreating sheepishly to his side.

He waited. She didn't come. The barking grew louder. He tensed for something deathly and vicious. The grind of teeth against bone.

Chapter 42

She watched Johnny Monahan's small, white thumbs twirling frantically around each other. His whole body was sprung, tensile like something inside a clock.

He was getting to the worst part of his tale – the part about an Irish servant girl in a tryst with none other than Susan's own grandfather. How did she know this before he even told it? You always knew, didn't you? Policemen, ambulance drivers ringing on your front door in the dead of night. Never had to tell you the actual news because you already knew.

Susan forced her attention back into the iTemps conference room, the old man's threadbare suit, the mouth and lips, moving, producing words.

The other brother sat at the end of the big conference table, noisily turning the pages in the women's magazines she'd given him. He stared at each glossy photo – Paris fashions, perfume, Dunhill cigarettes.

Across from her, the halting Irish voice went on, lilting, yet oddly genteel.

'Of course . . .' Suddenly, the thumbs stopped twirling. 'Of course, Miss Brown, I wouldn't dream to insinuate how a person like yourself should spend your own money, but . . .' The old face puckered.

Oh, please don't let him cry, she thought. Now that really would be the absolute pits.

'But we thought – my brother and I thought – came

here to . . . well, let you know the whole story, so that you might . . . for all our sakes . . . reconsider . . .'

Another magazine page swishing. She could smell a perfume sample from a glossy advertisement.

Through the vertical blinds, she saw the day had brightened outside, patches of pale sky mirrored in the glassy suites across the fountain. People crossed the courtyard to lunch, lighting up a fag, gossiping about normal things – last night's nightclub, if they'd choose a kebab or a green salad today. Not new-found, bastard relatives.

Her fists clenched under the table. This blitz of news. Now her morning – the train, a teleconference, coffee with Peter, the iTemps marketing director – it all seemed frivolous.

And it was all because of these two little men who'd just turned up at Savita's reception desk. Tricked. The word clicked like dominos inside her head.

Micheál – or whatever that mad, Irish version of his name was – had stopped turning magazine pages. He glanced from Johnny to Susan and back again. What? The childish face seemed to say. What is happening in this room between my brother and the nice English lady who gave me magazines?

She'd seen a poster once – a charity appeal from the RSPCA, a pyramid of unneutered dogs. Layer upon layer of the hapless little animals – all sired by the two dogs on top. Feckless procreation. Wasn't this how it was with her and these two Irishmen? Here she was, Dr Brown's daughter, and there they were, Richard Brown, the land agent's grandsons. Laughable.

Micheál grinned nervously, eyes flitting from one to the other, waiting for it to pass, this horrid thing in this strange room. 'Johnny, I'm hungry,' he said shyly.

She stood suddenly. Clapped her hands together as if

rallying a group of boy scouts or children in a nursery school. Said briskly, 'Yes, yes, of course. Both of you must be famished from your morning flight, your journey here.' Savita – our receptionist – can book us a table someplace. My treat.'

'We wouldn't dream of imposing; it's bad enough that we've . . .' Johnny began. But Micheál had already closed his magazine and was studiously placing it on top of the others, all the covers facing upwards, all the edges lined up perfectly.

He carried the magazine pile down to where Susan stood. Handed them to her and said, 'Me and Johnny have our tea at the Hermitage Hotel on Thursdays.'

'Johnny *and I,*' Johnny corrected.

Micheál said, 'Do you like the Hermitage Hotel, Susan Brown?'

'Yes, Michael,' Susan said. 'I too had lunch at the Hermitage Hotel once and it was very, very nice.'

'*Micheál*; that's my name,' Micheál corrected.

Susan and Johnny stood waiting in the courtyard. At last, here came Micheál now. He'd made a detour to the Gents' toilet. He stepped into the glass revolving door, came around, then went around again. Laughing, waving at them madly.

From the benches, the fountain, people stopped to stare at the little man in the bow tie, bouncing in delight. He waved when he came around to the front again.

'Micheál!' Johnny called firmly. 'Micheál Ignatius Monahan! Miss Brown and I are waiting.'

Round Micheál went again, the face through the glass, shrieks of delight.

Susan clicked her mobile phone open. 'Jonathan?' she said, pacing across the courtyard. 'Oh, when will he be back? Lovely. Well, could you have him call me immediately? Yes, going to lunch myself now, but I can be reached on my mobile. Yes, rather urgent. I need to stop a transfer of funds . . . Today.'

Chapter 43

Sadie scraped the last of the chocolate icing from the bowl and licked the wooden spoon clean. She'd already set the kitchen table, and though the evening was mild, she'd lit a fire in the inside sitting room. Above the cooker, she had a plate of uncooked rashers, sausages, pudding, mushrooms, and two brown eggs ready to crack into a sizzling frying pan.

She carried her cake to the fridge behind the door, cautious, deliberate, as if waiting for either the cake to topple from its plate or for the mobile phone in her apron pocket to ring.

She wished now that Claire the poor creature had never bought the bloody phone for her at all, but then corrected herself. Of course it wasn't the phone – in the hall or in her apron pocket; it was the fierce disappointment of this morning's news. And it was worse now, waiting for Sweeney's car in the yard, the cock-a-hoop face behind the windscreen. Oblivious to what awaited him.

She sat back down at her kitchen table, started unfolding and folding the white paper serviettes.

Three times she'd taken the phone from her pocket to ring Edel. As the chair of the Preservation Committee, she, Edel, should be first to hear the news. But three times she'd clicked it off again. No. Her own husband should be the first to know. Like informing the relatives of the dead.

Like every piece of sudden, bad news that had come whirling through that kitchen door, she couldn't even recall her conversation with the Englishwoman now. Just the posh voice, the halting words, asking Sadie to be sure to let Patrick Sweeney know. She'd follow up with a letter from London; yes, of course she would. But felt he – plus the Preservation Committee – should know immediately. Before tomorrow and the proposed purchase of Rathloe House. There'd been . . . a change of plans. Sorry about that. But couldn't be helped. No funds for Rathloe House after all. Really, truly, she was sorry for the sudden change but . . .

When those other pieces of bad news had come – Eileen knocked from her bicycle at college; Richie in a car accident, Sweeney attacked by a bull – disbelief at first, then airy, giggling humour. Blissful forgetfulness, the news drifting away for hours at a time. Then returning when you least expected it. A sickening thud in the guts.

Sadie reached in the table drawer for her bread knife to slice up the cake of freshly baked soda bread on the table. She held the knife towards the window and the sheds outside. Oh yes, she could kill this Brown woman with the English accent if, this minute, she came strutting across the Sweeneys' tarmac yard. No, not for what she'd done to the Preservation Committee, to Rathloe House, to their parish, but to Sadie's husband.

Often over the years, she, Sadie, had wondered about that. *Would* she kill someone, like in a pinch, for the right reasons? Now she knew. A quick, deep thrust into the *crá* or chest, like killing a Christmas goose.

Ah, here he came now, the car rattling in the gate, gabardine hat cocked back on his head.

Herself? Disappointed? Strange, here was this relief, as if they could all go back to being themselves now, the way each January you're delighted to strip the house of Christmas decorations at last – just as you were excited to put them up in December. But without their meetings, phone calls, planning, newsletters, the days stretched on ahead of her now. For the first time in months, Sadie Sweeney felt very old.

Sweeney peered suspiciously at the set table.

He hadn't had his tea ready and waiting for him since . . . Since his wife had gone off making a fool of herself with those yuppie women and the Preservation Committee.

'Now. You're here,' she said, crossing to the cooker and clattering the pan over the hotplate. The rashers sizzled in the hot grease. Sweeney sniffed like a badger at the whiff of fresh baking and a fry.

From the cooker, she could smell his familiar scent – fresh porter, and a mild whiff of cowdung on the boots that she begged him to take off at the back door, but just to defy her, he never did.

'It'll be ready in one sec,' she said over her shoulder as she cracked the eggs into the grease, burst the yolk just the way he liked it.

At the table he eyed her over his mug, the hat hung behind him on the chair rail as usual. He cocked one eyebrow at her. *I know your game,* he seemed to say. *It's me, Sweeney, your husband of forty-five years; know every thought in your head before you know it yourself, so why don't you spit it out, whatever it is.* Probably angling for a lift to town or Galway City for a new frock. A hairdo. Spring shoes. Get her eyebrows tinted or some other ridiculous excursion. So just spit it out so I can make a great compliment out of it, mutter that I've jobs for doing in the vegetable garden, but then, cave in at the last minute as if it were the greatest sacrifice since the crucifixion.

'Nothing new or strange?'

She hesitated. Said nothing.

With his fork he folded a rasher of bacon in two, then crammed it into his mouth, washed it down with a loud slug of tea. Blast her if she was taking the good out of it, ruining his appetite, when she knew he adored a fry in the evening. His favourite thing.

She left her fork down. 'There was a phone call for you.'

He grunted, 'Oh aye,' and forked a piece of sausage into his mouth.

But something in her voice made him stop in mid-chew. He looked across at her, where the evening light from the window caught her grey, permed hair, the furrow of her aged brow.

'What time?' he asked gruffly, as if this were a crucial detail.

'Just before lunch.' She added, 'You were only just pulled out the yard.'

He slugged at his tea loudly. 'Richie said he'd give me a few hours Saturday with that roof on the back shed. He hasn't changed his mind, has he?' The voice was tinged with his usual mockery at the frivolity of his son's life, Richie and Claire's yearly holidays in the sun, trips to leisure lands and water-slide parks for the children.

'No . . . it was a bit of bad news, so it was.'

She watched the flicker of panic across his features.

'One of the children?' he asked.

'No.' A quick, relieved smile. She reached for his hand but then stopped midway across their Formica table. 'No. Nothing as bad as that. It's just . . . your friend, that Brown woman, the woman who's sending us the big house money.'

He sat with his knife and fork aloft, like, she thought, a cartoon of a squirrel with his feast of nuts.

'She's . . . she's not transferring any money. Changed her mind.'

She watched the old Sweeney bravado deflating. She knew this sag of his old shoulders that said, *Ah, yes, sure I should have known all along that misfortune would eventually come, sideswipe me, send me off on a path other than the one I'd planned on. But I know it now, don't I? Better, even at this late date, eleventh hour, to know the worst rather than being made a fool of.*

She took a sip of her tea and added, 'I didn't tell anyone else yet.'

He was pale. Deadly pale. His eyes took in the kitchen, the table, the cooker, the transistor radio and old cookbooks on a shelf. Around the walls were framed snapshots of his family: Richie and Eileen's college graduations with Sweeney and Sadie standing each side, Richie and Claire's wedding outside a grey church in Meath where Claire was from, the grandchildren's baptisms, first communions, birthday parties, Sadie and his fortieth wedding anniversary, and a recent snapshot of Sweeney and Richie, father and son in Rathloe football jerseys at the Preservation Sports Day.

Pity rose in her. The weight, she thought, the sheer burden of living a life like his, vexing himself with all this to-ing and fro-ing inside his head, dwelling on un-righted wrongs, torturing himself with all this resentment over life's disappointments. And Sadie knew that all his disappointments could be traced back to that original one: in his early twenties, her husband's reluctant return back home from England.

Through the years, each fresh misfortune – death of cattle, newborn lambs, a bad year in the turf bog, sheepdogs who died of fits – to him, they were all mutants of that first one.

She knew he'd had a girlfriend over there in England – found a photograph of her once in an old suitcase.

She knew, too, that he had probably been a different man with that red-headed, smiling nurse. If they were together now, forty-five years later, this redhead and him, would Sweeney be the same, growling old man?

And the big house . . . just his way of regaining that lost ground, of getting his own back – not so much on Mr John McHugh himself, but on what he represented, an image of what he, Sweeney, had been diddled out of.

Ever since that woman's promise of funds, Sadie had let her husband strut like a peacock around Rathloe, stay late at O'Neill's while people shook his hand and bought drinks for him, tolerated his old lies and talk that this Brown woman was a friend from the old days.

Now, he had crossed to their side kitchen window. He stood with his back to her, blocking out the evening light. His shoulders heaving furtively. Crying.

Oh, she thought, the vexations of that man's mind, forever torturing himself with daft questions.

She longed to go over to him now, press his old head into her bosom, hold it like those dome ornaments with the shaken snow, hold it until everything stopped rattling and jigging around.

'Pity all the same,' she said. And started to scrape the greasy plates, piling them one by one, then the saucers, on top of each other.

Chapter 44

She eyed first her left, then her right ankle. Left foot. Right foot. Black, low-heeled shoes set together on the wooden floor. Should have gone a shade darker with the stockings – match her dress. I hate this dress, she thought, fingering the charcoal-grey material with the lighter pinstripe. Bought it in a hurry yesterday. Like a man's suit. An unfashionable man.

The sun through the stained-glass window tinted the air between her and the minister. Green and purple. Dust motes glistening.

She took a tissue from her patent black bag – not to blow her nose or to dab at tears, but for something to do.

The vicar's words came and went. Like a bee. Buzzed in closer around her head then off someplace else, then back again, barging across her thoughts. The voice echoed in this small church with its dribble of sympathisers, a smell of furniture wax. 'Dr Brown . . . respected physician . . . active member . . . great lover of our unspoiled little corner of the world down here . . .'

And then the voice drifted away again, like a radio being carried to the far end of the house.

Anna sat across the aisle – spiky hennaed hair, still tanned. A smart black trouser suit.

Good old Panny. She had arrived at Susan's flat yesterday – no, it was the day before yesterday, Thursday –

as soon as she got the news, car keys jingling, a takeaway bag of steaming coffee in paper cups, bagels, a fruit salad.

Made Susan sit, centre herself at the kitchen counter – important to get some food in; here, is there enough? Got any milk that's not soured? Look, had the Manor telephoned her immediately? The very instant? Well, thank goodness for that, eh? Good they didn't wake her up in the middle of the night. I mean, what good? Things always harder, weirder in the middle of the night . . . And they've been good, efficient with . . . the cremation and everything? You never knew with these country people, did you? Look, could Georges be of any help? He specifically wanted Susan to know he was available. Really, just say the word. Maybe go down there and collect things – people, flowers, Daddy's . . . effects. He had made friends at the Manor, her father?

After coffee, Susan had telephoned the local Hargrove newspaper to place an obituary. Then unearthed Daddy's black leather address book – salvaged with his other personal things before the house sale at Hargrove. She read out likely names, telephone numbers while Anna, puffing on her Gauloises, compiled two handwritten lists: 1. Call immediately/definite. 2. Call just in case.

Then Susan made telephone calls. The burr-burr in an unknown house, in a doctor's office somewhere, hospital intercom voices twittering while she left messages with crisp secretaries.

There was a cousin of his in Kent. A little woman she remembered. At last someone answered, mystified, sleepy. No, that woman didn't live here any more; never heard the name.

Women's names in her father's small, pointed writing. Janes, Dianas, Priscillas. Margerys. One or two voices she, Susan, thought she recognised.

Really appreciate her calling. Yes, yes, of course they'd

come to the service. 'And look here . . .' one woman with a brisk voice asked, 'look, will *you* be all right, dear?'

And Gerald. Wasn't there some etiquette, protocol in these things? Not that there'd been any love lost between the two men, but it seemed only right. In the end, she rang. A female voice on an answering machine. She left a message, hearing her own, stilted voice: 'Just thought you should know that Daddy . . . my father passed away last night.'

Discreetly, she edged the pinstriped sleeve up over her wrist to check her watch. Twenty past eleven. An old trick from boarding school days. Count time – everything portioned out into hours, half-hours, half-terms, Christmas holidays. Better when you knew exactly. An hour at the most and this would all be over, handshakes and goodbyes with sympathising strangers, plans to stay in touch more. Promises to call if there was anything she needed.

People shaded their eyes from the sudden sunlight between the yew trees. She'd promised herself she wouldn't do it, but here she was scanning the heads, each little cluster of people for Gerald.

The last time she'd stepped out into a waiting churchyard had been on his arm at a friend's wedding. And before that, in her own flouncy white dress and wide-brimmed wedding hat.

The faces came and went. Firm handshakes, murmured words, like people identifying themselves at a business conference. *We worked with your dad at Hargrove . . . Lectured together at Edinburgh . . . Brilliant man . . .*

'Susan?' A tall woman with grey hair in a navy-blue suit. She had been hovering, waiting at the edges. She introduced herself, an American twang. 'I was . . .

a good friend of your father's; if there's anything I can . . .'

Susan recognised her from the travel snapshots on Daddy's bookshelves at Hargrove. Older now, but the eyes lively in the lined face.

'Thank you for coming,' she said to the woman. 'I know he'd have liked . . .'

The woman's voice quavered. Grief. 'Susan, he worshipped you . . . Always felt he should have . . .' Embarrassed, the woman glanced away to where a man was waiting for her, holding the door of a navy-blue Mercedes.

Chapter 45

Sadie searched for a footing in the high orchard wall. 'Blast it to hell,' she cursed aloud in the morning air. Things like this always happened when you were in a hurry. She tried a different spot, a dimple between the symmetrical stones. She should have worn shoes with ridged soles – an old pair of trainers her daughter, Eileen, had left behind or even winter boots. This time, her sandalled foot didn't slip, and she reached for a high, vertical stone to lever her old body up on top.

Her housecoat, her skirt bunched up around her buttocks, then her waist. The crotch of her tights, the flash of white, cotton knickers visible to anyone who passed along the road. But nobody was coming. Nobody on foot or in a car appearing through the morning mist. Too early. All the young people had driven off to work already, and the Rathloe natives wouldn't be out and about, mooching up through the village towards O'Neill's shop for another hour or so.

Last night, around O'Neill's checkout counter, she'd heard the news. Today would be the day. Yesterday, yellow plastic fencing along the tops of the big house walls, a sign on the high gates: *Keep Out; Demolition Exclusion Zone*. While the women were standing talking around the checkout, a young fella calling himself a demolition operative came to buy milk and cigarettes. At it hammer and tongs since dawn, he'd said, removing slates, the inside stairs, two old mantelpieces, casings, cast-iron ovens. For sale, if Margaret O'Neill or the women knew anyone interested . . . Oh, but that stone urn in the garden. The McHugh bloke wanted that for himself.

No joke, that fella. No flies . . . Some slave master. Took them ages and six men to get th'oul urn safely away and onto a truck. And tomorrow: D-day, when a thirty-ton machine and pulverisers would tear th'oul place down.

'Will we go?' Babs Mannion had asked, rubbing her hands together as if proposing an outing to a dirty film.

'No.' The women flinched. Mrs Walsh and Mrs O'Brien said they didn't think they could stomach it; it'd take a lot out of them to watch a thing like that. Even if there hadn't been this bitter disappointment and last-minute shock of her English nibs withdrawing the funds . . . it was just, well, hadn't it always been there, its roof and high windows among the trees, for their childhoods, their courting years, their young married lives? Yes, for better or worse, there it had always been, a backdrop for their comings and their goings, their fortunes and misfortunes.

Margaret O'Neill had vigorously agreed. What's done is done. McHugh could have his oul' house now; nothing but consternation since the day that fella stepped in this parish.

Now Sadie felt with her foot for a ledge on the inside of the wall. Missed. She jumped, landed in a flurry of white underwear and her cotton print skirt.

Her face flushed, she shifted the scarf on her head. Picked herself up.

Along the second orchard wall near the house, another web of plastic fencing, another sign: *Keep Out.* And there it was – a yellow, hydraulic arm dangling like a broken limb above the trees near the house.

The old apple trees crouched like hunchbacks in the mist. Branches grazed her head as she ducked among them, her feet soaked already in the summer grass.

Surely it was imagination? The unseen but certain presence of another person or persons among the trees. Something skittered through the grass in front of her. She tensed, arms folded and ready. Something pink moving up ahead. Distant voices. Men or women?

She ducked lower down, veered left and around two old pear trees and peered through their branches. Two men, not young demolition men like the lad in the shop yesterday, but elderly, shuffling along through the grass, one in a pink rainhat; the other in a matching powder-blue, white rain capes fanning out around them.

Johnny and Micheál Monahan!

Strange, she thought. The Monahan brothers of all people, when they hadn't chipped in with all the Preservation Committee's efforts. And yet here they were, trudging through the grass, circling, doubling back, searching for a safe spot with a bird's eye view.

Beach chairs! Just like the Monahan brothers not to forego their comforts. There was Johnny unfolding the striped chairs in a clearing between trees.

The two brothers sat rigid, motionless, staring up at the back walls of the ivy-clad old house with its stripped roof, as if waiting for the lion and the MGM sign to appear on the cinema screen.

She tiptoed towards the side wall and its thicket of gooseberry bushes.

She remembered these bushes well – from years ago, when she and her school friends had come to fill their pockets with the sweet, green fruit. They'd always selected Babs, the tallest and the cheekiest, as the lookout in case old Cronin would suddenly appear, lashing his stick and threatening to tan their backsides for them if he caught them near his orchard again.

Good days, them, she thought. If they'd only known then, any one of them, what lay ahead. The years of loneliness, love, friendship, bitterness. The disaffection and affection of their own children. And husbands.

Now, she hurried towards the bushes, installed herself under an arch of greenery where the gooseberry bushes and the other undergrowth tangled to form a roof. Underneath, the grass was almost dry, and she plopped down gratefully, her knees gathered to her chin.

The tractor revved and trundled over the rise at the far end of the field.

For days now, the men were used to its persistent rattle and the sight of Sweeney's hatted head inside the glassed-in cab, a *tráithnín* between his teeth, glancing over his shoulder at the attached machinery that spun the summer hay high in the air.

It turned at the top, then grew louder as it headed towards them again.

Walsh stopped forking hay to cough in the silvery-grey dust. Hack, hack, hack. He rummaged in a trouser pocket for a big, cotton hanky into which he deposited a thick, throaty mucous.

'Desperate,' he said, just as he'd said fifty times already this morning, and a thousand times all day yesterday, though none of them bothered to ask what was so desperate.

The early morning mist had cleared. O'Brien shaded his eyes to look at the sky, shook his head disgustedly at the clouds like dirty cotton wool. They could do with another fine spell. Even the one fine, sunny day itself would make the hay so much easier.

'Are we right?' Mannion screamed above the approaching tractor at the coughing Walsh and the sky-gazing O'Brien. 'Or is it a feckin' nursing home we're running here?'

The two scowled at him. They were working Mannion's field of hay today. Two days ago, when it was Sweeney's hay, and last week, when it was O'Brien's, there wasn't a hurry in the world on Mannion. O'Brien held up two fingers to Mannion's back. Walsh sniggered.

The three settled back into it again, the rhythm of their day: hayforks rising, turning, Mannion, his tweed cap cocked back on his head, raking between the rows of just-turned hay. Walsh's bald spot was covered in hayseed already, the sweep of cover-up hair had come undone and was cascading down like a Hare Krishna's ponytail.

Sweeney saluted the other men as he passed. The red tractor turned at the gap near the road, then rattled back up the rutted field.

It was Walsh, the slowest worker, and therefore still nearest the road, who heard it first. He stopped as if stung, shoulders tensed, then stuck the two prongs of his hayfork deep into the ground. Mannion and O'Brien, about fifty feet further up, frowned at him, baffled, then followed his gaze and pointing finger to the high, metallic arm angling above the distant trees towards the big house roof.

Mannion, from habit, removed his tweed cap and hastily crossed himself. O'Brien and Walsh leaned on their fork handles and waited. The yellow arm rose higher. Closer, closer, a little game with a Meccano set, it swung high and wide, then the huge, metal claw crashed deep into the roof rafters.

In her leafy bower, Sadie Sweeney sank her head

between her knees. Stuck her fingers in her ears. But still she heard the crack of timber, the clatter of stone upon stone.

In their beach chairs, Micheál grinned wordlessly at Johnny, and Johnny reached for his brother's hand.

Blackbirds, crows, rooks rose like black confetti from the tumbling house.

In the hayfield, the men strained for more sounds. Nothing. Only that first crash. Too far away to hear or see the rest, though each of them imagined in his mind's eye.

The tractor became a distant hum again as Sweeney, oblivious to the big house wreckage, nudged the big front wheels back up over the rise.

Part 3

Chapter 46

Her red rental car skidded, swung to the left and stopped just before the stone wall.

She shoved the car into neutral, turned off the ignition.

Gingerly, she opened the driver's door, squeezed out between the car and the wall to find whatever animal she'd killed. Under the front wheel – a mangled body of a rabbit, dog, a cat? – who knew what was out here in this wild place, where, for the last mile or two, she'd convinced herself there was absolutely no holiday home.

Nothing. No dead animal, just the green stripe of wild grass down the middle of the narrow road, the blood-red fuchsia that drooped over the walls. But there had been something, hadn't there? She was certain of it – a quick dart of white, but whatever it was, it was gone.

She stood in the middle of the road. An unnerving silence. Just a screech of seagulls. Behind her, a mountain loomed, its hillside fields dappled in sunlight and dotted with grazing sheep. Down along this road, more tiny fields, some with lines of haycocks, sloping between her car and the sea. This morning, the Atlantic was pale and glassy.

A house. She squinted towards the horizon as if somehow it might appear – a chimney, a tiled roof

– above these meadows and stone walls. She folded her arms and walked a short way down the little road towards a sharp turn and a wide gap where she could climb on the farmer's gate for a good look for this fantasy holiday rental by the sea.

Otherwise, she would just drive to the gateway, try to turn the car around and . . . what? She didn't know. Her hands were still shaking from the sudden stop, the suspicion that she'd been led down a garden path by yet another Irishman.

A crunch of wheels on gravel behind her. Step up on the ditch. She watched her red car rolling towards her, bumping along over grass and pebbles. The handbrake. She'd forgotten. She reached hopelessly as it trundled past. But it picked up speed near the turn, the gap.

A crash, splinter of glass, clunk of metal and stone. She opened her eyes. There it was, its rooftop bright in the sunlight, the front end buried in the stone wall.

Her steps quickened going down the hill.

On the ground, splinters of glass from the headlight. The right wing bashed in over the wheel. A crack down the bottom right of the windscreen.

She slid her body over the gear stick into the driver's seat. The engine turned over instantly. Good. This is good. She shoved the car into reverse. A deafening sound as the front wing disentangled, and then, here she was, facing down the hill again.

The car laboured downwards, the metal scraping against the front tyre. Please, she pleaded inside her head, please let me just make it to this house – if it exists – a public telephone, a beach shop.

Suddenly, there it was, a widening of the road, and a sandy pathway leading to a bungalow that squatted on a cliff.

Chapter 47

'Hellooo!' she called, though the Dublin owner had said on the phone that he wouldn't be here – he'd leave a key under a window box. 'Hello!' she called again, the front door slamming behind her.

She was standing in a huge living room with mismatched furniture that looked as if it had been randomly dropped around the green, shag carpet. She shivered in the room's sudden chill and a smell of old, wet soot from the wide fireplace.

Everywhere were books and papers – piles of typescript pages, books piled into corners, magazines, a huge dictionary left face down on a coffee table, newspapers peeping from under the cushions of an orange armchair.

The room had the widest window she'd ever seen. Outside, the colours were deepening, the sea blue and glittering in the sunlight.

Next to the hearth, a door led to a narrow, dark corridor. A musty, damp smell followed her from room to room. A bathroom and master bedroom to the left, two bedrooms to the right, a bicycle propped against a bedroom wall.

The master bedroom was large, floral curtains, cream walls, the bed hastily made.

In the corner was a cheap, brown wardrobe, a mirrored door that hung open. Inside, a man's cardigan – in those Irish, fisherman stitches, once creamish or white but now filthy and reeking of old fish – two shirts, and a woman's dressing gown.

She banged the wardrobe shut, saw her own reflection in the mottled mirror.

Her eyes had purple shadows from the early-morning flight from Stansted. Her cheekbones had grown more chiselled to give her a severe appearance.

She looked, she thought, like some insipid old maid, the type of woman she often saw on the Cripton train or wheeling a shopping trolley along the footpath – colourless, stiff, fearful eyes.

Her clothes were far too big. She could buy some smaller sizes while she was here – perhaps drive to Galway City one day and shop in those boutiques for jeans, trousers, shirts – whenever she got a replacement rental car.

Grief, her doctor in Cripton had said. Often had this effect. Six months, a year, sometimes eighteen months, before life became normal. A kind of deadening feeling.

But he was wrong. For ever since Daddy's funeral, she'd felt something growing, not dying inside her – a burgeoning dissatisfaction, a gnawing exhaustion that kept her sleepy during the day and awake and roaming around the flat at night.

She'd become an expert on late-night BBC television, the exact time her neighbours across the Railroad Place courtyard came, went, banged out of their front doors each morning. It was as if she were watching somebody else fumble through these summer days in London: forgot to collect her summer suits at the dry-cleaners'; last week missed a luncheon appointment with a possible client. Every morning and evening she nodded off on the train to and from Liverpool Street Station.

She'd been mad to come here, to this desolate spot,

and now with a crashed car, a holiday house that needed a good cleaning, some crazy writer's abandoned, smelly house.

'At least give this chap a ring.' She and Anna were sitting in a wine bar after work one Friday. Panny read the advertisement aloud from a newspaper:

Glorious, ocean vistas from this three-bedroom house on West of Ireland coast. Immaculate. All mod cons. Very reasonable rates. Private beach. Weekly or monthly. Close to village and all amenities.

With their next glass of Cabernet, Panny had grown relentless. 'You need something. Suze, can't keep going on like . . .' She'd waved a hand non-committally.

Look, Georges and she would even come visit if it got lonely. Neither of them had ever been . . . Perfect really. Just what Suze needed. Time to . . . Well, read some juicy novels, the bit of sea air, that wholesome Irish food, and look, wasn't she at least curious about how things . . . ?

Anna paused, then said archly, 'Well, how *certain Irishmen* have fared in the end?'

One of the world's special gems, the Dublin writer fellow had said on the telephone, a haven for body and soul – available for the rest of the summer if she wanted it. He'd be there himself except he was working on an important film script in Dublin.

Now she looked around the bedroom again: not even a chair, a proper dressing table – nothing like her and Panny's vision of a glittering little seaside cottage, quaint seafood restaurants, pottery shops.

And those funny little Monahan brothers. The nights she roamed around her flat at three and four o'clock in the morning, a guilty voice had nagged inside her head. She should tell them about Daddy's death, shouldn't she? Ring them up and politely, respectfully let them know that their half-relative had passed on.

In the end, she'd decided to tell them in person, invite them for a visit to her idyllic Atlantic cottage.

It was almost twelve o'clock. She was hungry and exhausted. She went back up the dank corridor to the living room again.

Off the living room was a kitchenette with a black vinyl wall phone. She searched in her shoulder bag, her jeans pockets for the number of the rental car company, and then lifted the receiver. Nothing. She clicked furiously on the round buttons where the receiver rested. Dead.

She slammed the phone down. All mod cons my foot. Did this writer chap take her for a complete fool? She would telephone him in Dublin immediately, scream and rant down her mobile phone, demand that something be done.

'You'll receive the bill for a cleaning person. I absolutely *must* have a working telephone. And fresh bedlinen. Oh, and there's some sort of abandoned, untamed animal, Mr Parkinson. I want it all taken care of . . . I'll leave you my mobile phone number. It's 044 . . .' She shouted above the seagulls as they wheeled and dipped along the edge of the cliff and the front garden.

Next, she called the rental car company to report her accident – another answering machine to say the office hours were nine to six, with an hour for lunch from one to two. But it was only seven minutes to one o'clock now. She repeated her mobile phone number again to be called back as soon as possible.

She tucked the phone into her top shirt pocket and headed down the cliff path.

Chapter 48

She woke feeling rested, happy, and lay with one arm shading her eyes. She was on holiday; that was good. No work today, just unpack in her holiday cottage by the sea.

It came stealing back then, a rolling car, clunk of metal, scrape and thup, thup, thup of tyres. Oh, God, and that grotty little house. Her chest tingled.

She sat up, reached for her shirt in the sand. Her chest, breasts, were sunburned, the skin pink and throbbing. Stupid. She of all people who always lathered on Factor 15 every year in the Mediterranean, Barbados, the Greek Islands.

She checked her mobile for a text message, a voicemail from Mr Parkinson the slumlord or the rental car company. Nothing. Just her batteries running low. She'd recharge the minute she got to the house. It was just gone four o'clock.

Distant voices from a public beach, way beyond these rocks. Children bathing, screeching. A distant hum of traffic.

She buttoned her shirt, stuffed her bra in the pocket, and started back up the cliff path. From here the house looked almost magical, perched above her on the edge of the cliff, windows glinting in the sun. A tang of salt, seaweed and, just before the front door, the smell of lavender from a rock garden.

She'd passed a little grocery shop up there on the main road, in that village, slotted in between the painted two-storeys and white bungalows. But how far back up the grassy side road? The car wouldn't make it, she was certain of that.

The sun had warmed the house. She opened the front window, then unplugged a lamp to recharge her phone.

No, no, couldn't be. Surely not.

She flipped on a light switch inside the door.

Nothing.

She tried a Transistor radio on the mantelpiece. But there'd been a line of telegraph poles, hadn't there? A house like this had to have electricity.

On the mantel, stuffed between an empty Chianti bottle and a cigar box, were old letters, envelopes, bills. She flopped into the orange armchair to read:

Dear Mr Parkinson,

Despite our ongoing efforts to collect the outstanding amount for residential supply at 'Súil na Mara', Cnoc Road, Carraig, County Mayo, you are in arrears to the amount of £1,500. If we do not receive payment by Tuesday, May 3, we will be forced to discontinue supply until payment has been received. Please contact our office immediately at . . .

She read the others, all on official letterhead.

Dear Mr Parkinson,

On January 3 you were sent final notice for nonpayment of your residential telephone bill at the residence . . .

Court summonses. Speeding tickets. Groceries delivered by the village shop. A car on hire purchase.

Oh, God. Here it came again, that thing rising, ballooning up inside her. Panic.

Outside, the late afternoon light was mellowing, the sea striped turquoise and green. High, wispy clouds gathered at the horizon. She would leave, of course, first thing tomorrow when the rental car company came. Or a bus? A train? Surely this godforsaken spot had some kind of taxi service.

Half past four. She could make it up to the village to phone the rental car place again. Demand an answer. And tomorrow . . . Back to London, phone the travel agent on Cripton's High Street for someplace warm and luxurious. Never set foot in this country again. Rancid place, with nothing but people and places full of treachery. Yes, she thought, brushing sand from her jeans. The word cheered her, goaded her to action. Treachery. Ireland a nation of tricksters.

She hadn't cycled on anything since God knew when, but the old bicycle with the Mary Poppins basket was definitely better than walking.

She strained against the hill. Her foot slipped, pedals hit her shin, but then suddenly she got the hang of it, a forgotten rhythm returning, leg muscles stretching, cheeks blazing as she puffed up the side road between the overgrown fuchsia.

Chapter 49

The village phone box smelled of stale pee. The last coin clinked down, then a voice answered. 'Hello? Is that Economy Rental? Yes, yes, I've been trying . . .'

The rental car woman put her on hold to some awful Spice Girl song, and Susan watched as the digital numbers on the phone changed. Fifty, thirty, then twenty pence. Please, she prayed. Don't let my change run out. No more catastrophes today.

'Right. We should have something for you by Thursday, Friday the latest,' the woman said.

'But . . . that's three – four – days from now.'

'High season,' the woman said. 'Hardly any cars in stock . . . We could try for tomorrow, but can't promise . . . high pilgrimage season, like.'

'All right,' Susan said wearily. 'You have the address . . .'

'Yeah—' the woman started to say, but then there was a click and she was gone. Susan leaned her forehead against the metal phone box. She'd forgotten about 'pilgrimage season' and that airport religious grotto. Trust Ireland not to have a normal airport with a Boots, a McDonald's and a Eurocar.

The faces at the glass startled her. Two young boys.

One stuck his head in the door. 'Will you soon be ready there?'

The other giggled. She would like to punch them,

269

both of their freckled little faces, like something off those tacky postcards at the airport. Hilarious grins that all the Irish seemed to be born with.

'Down below y'are, is it?' the shop fellow said with a cheery tilt of the head towards the road.

'Yes. But not for long. Place a bit of a disappointment, I'm afraid.'

'One of the guesthouses?'

'No. A house. *Su . . .*' She abandoned any hope of pronouncing the house's Irish name.

'*Súil na Mara.* Parkinson's place?' The shop man looked perplexed.

She nodded yes.

'No chance he left any cash down there for us, is there? That bastard owes . . .'

'I know. Owes you money.'

He grinned over the top of the meat slicer, shouted above its electric hum. 'I suppose I'm only one of many?'

'Looks like it. No electricity, phone. And I had a bit of an accident, I'm afraid . . .'

He slapped her packet of sliced turkey breast on the counter in front of her. 'Nobody should ever have built anything down there. One more bad storm and they'll be fishing the slates and rafters of that place out of the sea beyond in Newfoundland. Though he probably owes money over there, too.'

She shrugged. 'I suppose we're all in the same boat, then. But once they come and replace my car I'll be . . .'

The man was forty-something, prematurely grey, balding at the temples – had twinkling blue eyes that reminded her of John McHugh. She met his gaze, then glanced away. Embarrassed by the kind smile, the way he was leaning over the counter towards her in his nylon shop coat.

'Ah, sure, what's your hurry? Promised a great spell of weather for the week, anyways.'

'But the house is . . .' she started. 'Even my mobile phone battery's gone dead.'

He frowned, puzzled, as if her protestations were outlandish, the most fastidious holiday requirements. 'Sure what d'you need a phone for? Isn't it on holidays y'are? And as for th'oul electricity. He's a gas cooker, hasn't he? And can't I drop you down a cylinder of gas once we close up here. Sure you'll be on the beach the whole time anyways. And if you're that badly off for phoning people, leave th'oul mobile phone here, I'll charge it up for you and either myself or the wife'll drop it down with the gas cylinder.'

Was this fellow just the kindest man in the world or yet another treacherous Irish man with some rip-off scheme? 'But . . .'

He leaned across the counter again. 'Look, Miss . . .'

'Brown. Susan Brown.'

'You're not the first tourist that bastard has hood-winked, and you probably won't be the last. But even I'll admit the bugger has the nicest spot in the West of Ireland down there. And once you get th'oul phone going, you can ring us up here if you want groceries or anything . . .'

'Oh, I couldn't. I just couldn't . . . It's all been just . . .' Her voice grew high, frantic.

'Look, what about a drink?' He grasped at this solution to the difficult, demented customer before him. He followed her gaze to the gold ring on his left finger. He blushed, a flush of crimson to the receding temples. 'Oh, I mean, next door, like in the bar. The wife's in there and a few of the regulars. I do the grocery and she does the bar. Stick to what you're good at, hah? Listen, go in and say hello anyways, like, and . . .' He hesitated. 'A drink might do you good . . .'

Before she could protest, he took her plastic bag of groceries and headed past her, to a brown door at the back of the shop.

'This is . . . sorry—' He'd forgotten her name.

'Susan.'

'My wife, Nuala.' The woman was petite, brown eyes, a high ponytail in a silvery clip. She smiled, shook Susan's hand warmly.

The grocer said, 'Susan's staying down below.'

There were three men sitting at the bar. The one in the middle had a mud-smeared vest and a red bandana around his neck. He said, 'And our Mr Parkinson had the red carpet out for you, I suppose?' The three all laughed.

The one to his left had sunburned arms, a blue T-shirt flecked with hayseed. 'And the kettle down?' More laughter.

A young fellow with a baseball cap chortled into his pint glass of lager. 'And all the tablecloths freshly starched and ironed?'

'Any dealings with that lad and you'd want a strong drink,' the red bandana said, shunted his bar stool to make room for her among them. 'Nuala a *ghrá, ban*, give this poor woman whatever she wants. On me.'

Nuala grinned at her. 'Listen, Susan, just ignore these lads. Easy for them to be the great comedians. Mr Parkinson doesn't owe them six months' groceries. What'll it be?'

'Oh, gin and tonic, thanks.'

'We'll drop that cylinder down tonight or tomorrow,' the shop man said, satisfied that things seemed right again.

She wanted to say not to bother; no point delivering cooking gas for just one day; rental car company coming Wednesday. But he had already disappeared back through the brown door to the shop.

The gin tasted delicious, went to her head after three sips. Hadn't eaten. She remembered: the same on her last visit to Ireland, to Ballyshee just south of here – forty miles, the map showed. One came to Ireland to starve and drink gin.

'Where are you from anyways?' the bandana man, Charlie, asked.

'Don't tell him,' the baseball cap, named Martin, winked at her. Martin jabbed a thumb towards his friend. 'This lad'd want to know what you had for your breakfast, so he would.'

'Oh, and you wouldn't?' Bandana retorted.

'Will ye give it a rest, lads,' Nuala said, catching Susan's eye mischievously.

'Are you comfortable enough there?' Blue T-shirt, named John, asked. 'An' look, if those two are annoying you I'll shut them up for you fast.'

Susan laughed. 'No, I'm fine, really. Chin-chin, gentlemen.'

Martin removed his baseball hat and theatrically swivelled around to take in the lounge bar with its patterned carpet, the low, padded lounge stools tucked under the empty tables; a small, makeshift stage in the far corner. 'There are gentlemen here? Where are they? I don't see any gentlemen, do ye, lads?'

Charlie the bandana elbowed him. 'Ah, Martinín, will you give over; you'll frighten this nice girl away here . . .' To Susan he said, 'We were at hay all day; the sun gets to this young lad's brain . . .'

'But he's grand once he takes his tablets,' John chortled.

Martin threw a balled-up cigarette packet at them. It hit her in the side of the head.

'Sorry, miss,' he said sheepishly. 'It's just a fella has to stand his ground around these parts or they'd ate you alive, so they would.' He nodded at her empty glass. 'You'll drink another of them?'

'All right,' Susan said, already feeling the euphoric buzz of her brain. She'd had an absolutely horrid day, hadn't she? Besides, it was a downhill pedal all the way home to the house.

'Are ye all right back there?' Charlie yelled from the front seat.

'Fine,' Susan and Martin with the baseball hat chorused from the back seat, a cylinder of Kosangas propped between them, her bag of groceries at her feet.

John was in the passenger seat, holding onto the dashboard as the little car sashayed down the tarmac road.

Out the back window, the front wheel of her borrowed bicycle ticked around and around. She could hear the handlebars, or something, bumping off the inside of the boot. The car smelled of animal things – old hay, dung, something milky plus a whiff of beer.

'Hold on to your horses!' Charlie bellowed and swung off the main road onto the side road towards *Súil na Mara*.

Wisps of sensible thoughts floated across her gin-soused mind: never let anyone drive under the influence; your vehicle should be roadworthy; never take a lift from strangers, in a foreign country. Men. Especially men. On holidays . . .

She leaned out between the two front seats. 'Careful at this turn, Charlie,' she slurred. The little car was hurtling towards the gateway where, only this morning, she'd made smithereens of her rental car. 'Careful. Easy does it.' She mimicked steering a runaway car. The three men howled laughing. The funniest thing they'd heard all evening. Really, they'd never pegged her for such good *craic*. They had to admit there, that when she first appeared from the shop, they thought she looked a bit standoffish, like . . . but wrong. Oh, very, very wrong. Never judge th'oul book by the cover, hah?

'Brilliant,' Charlie announced, wavering slightly, the driver's door held open for her and her groceries. John had taken her bike from the boot and was propping it against the wall of the house. Martin had unloaded her gas cylinder and carried it in the house.

'Absolutely brilliant,' Charlie said again, giving her a military salute. 'Brilliant night.'

'Right!' John thumped the car roof loudly. 'We'll be seeing you, Susan Brown.'

'Wake up, little Susie, wake up . . .' young Martin serenaded her from the back seat.

In a shower of dust and pebbles, Charlie turned the car in the clearing before the house.

Calm. Must be calm, a suddenly sober voice said inside her head. Two eyes staring in the dark. She stood frozen between the rock garden and the front door. She was alone at the end of a road, the foot of a mountain in a treacherous place with some wild animal staring at her.

'Miaow.'

'Oh, God,' she said aloud. Exhaled for the first time in – hours?

A cat. A black and white cat. She let her grocery bag down to fumble in the dark for the door knob. Of course. The animal that had caused her car to crash, the disappearing flash of white fur over the wall.

'Miaow,' it said throatily, then rubbed, angled its head against her legs.

Tail in the air, the cat led the way daintily across the front room where the moonlight through the window made the grotty furniture, the fireplace, the old armchairs look oddly cosy. She lit the candle in the Chianti bottle on the mantel, then foraged around the room for others. Found a half-opened packet on a shelf, lit them and placed them around the living room.

The cat was already installed in the fireside armchair, its skinny little body tucked around itself and hollowed into the cushion in a way that told her this was his usual spot.

She sat cross-legged on the floor eating turkey slices from the packet, tore off hunks of bread from the loaf she'd bought, drank milk from the carton. The cat was eating greedily from a tin of salmon she'd given him. Click, click, click went the tin against the hearth, the black head, pink little nose buried in the feast.

'Horrid man, horrid man to abandon a cat,' Susan announced to the shadows that crept and shimmied around the walls.

Chapter 50

She arched her back. Stiff, but not as stiff as yesterday or the day before. The late morning sun was disappearing behind a funnel of clouds with ominous, purplish edges. Rain soon. Thunder. Could do with a reprieve from this heat.

The cat lay sprawled on the garden wall, a white paw dangling. They'd become friends, these past five days, her and this little animal. Fatter already, she noticed, the black, fur haunches filling out. Tins of salmon, tuna, warm milk.

Later, this afternoon, she would pedal up to the village shop for some people- and cat food.

The red roof of the rental car glinted beyond the vegetable garden wall. Had they completely forgotten about her? Friday already. Not the type of outfit to provide weekend services. It would be Monday now, at the earliest. And did she care? Where would she fit driving excursions into these languid, timeless days?

Like everything else, a shambles, this vegetable garden: thick weeds choking the ridges of carrots, potatoes, onions, a row of peas that nobody had bothered to stake up. Abandoned like the house and the cat.

The air was growing thicker, heavier, pungent with rising pollen and dug-up weeds. Butterflies drifted and lingered over the cabbage plants, a rhubarb patch under the wall.

The cat opened one eye to peer at Susan, made a little murmuring sound, then settled back to sleep.

Down below, the sea was turning a deep blue like a mussel shell, the mussel dishes she and Anna used to gorge themselves on on their Portuguese holidays, the south of France. Those spots – the Riviera and Algarve hotels – unimaginable now, here among this wilderness of vegetables and salty brown earth.

Compulsive, this morning gardening – her mind, her whole body anaesthetised by digging, kneeling in the cool, pungent clay, the numbing ritual of plucking, weeding, forking it all away.

Beep! Beep! She barely heard it at first. The rental car company? She scanned the horizon, the *bóithrín* beyond the wall. No car.

A woman with her hair flying behind her, waving at Susan, a moped speeding down the hill.

'Sorry. I meant to come yesterday, but it got busy. I knew you'd need stuff by now . . .' Nuala, the woman from the pub, was unloading parcels from the wire basket on the front of her black moped.

Susan said, 'Look, you didn't need to . . . I was going to come up this afternoon anyway.'

Nuala didn't hide her surprise at the change in Susan, this wild, unkempt Englishwoman standing before her – dirt smeared on the face, fingernails cracked and mud-rimmed, an old sunburn peeling under her open-necked shirt, the face, arms and legs growing suntanned. 'No trouble. Sure, an excuse to get out from the pub a while. Bit of a chat and a laugh. I'm not from these parts myself, you know. Seán – that's my husband that you met – he's the *native savage*. I'm from Kilkenny. Not many women my own age around here . . . Left Seán watching pub and shop. 'Twon't kill him for a while until we get busy for lunch.' Nuala looked to the darkening sky.

'*If* we get busy. This weather'll either keep them home altogether or flocking in off the beach howling for early lunch and soup.'

Susan said, 'I don't know what to . . .' *Women my own age around here.* She was flattered.

'Oh, and Seán said you'd want this. He charged it up for you.' Nuala produced Susan's mobile phone from her shorts pocket. A boyish stride, the ponytail bobbing behind her, Nuala crossed to the rock garden, the clearing before the house.

She called back over her shoulder, 'Jeez, haven't been down here in ages. Brilliant, isn't it? So, are you settling in, Susan, after all?'

'Tea?' Susan called from the front door.

'Naaah. We'll just sit here and have the chat.'

Her groceries packed away in the house, Susan came to join Nuala on a stone ledge that looked out across the bay. The clouds were growing turgid on the horizon.

'Look . . . I usually have a swim about this time; wash off all this dirt,' Susan said. She glanced skyward. 'This won't come for a while yet. And even if it does . . .'

'Ah, but . . .' Nuala smoothed her hand over her T-shirt and shorts. 'Aah, I didn't bring a swimsuit, like . . .'

Susan cocked a meaningful eyebrow at her.

Nuala's brown eyes glittered mischievously. 'Come on so for the *craic.*'

They splashed into the waves – first Susan, then Nuala, their legs, naked bodies glistening and goosebumped.

'Great, isn't it?' Susan called, her voice whipping on the breeze.

The rain came pattering noisily on the seawater.

'Freezing bloody cold!' Nuala shrieked.

Chapter 51

'Eeeee!' Micheál screeched. He pointed to a spot beyond Johnny's left shoulder. 'Eeeee!' he squeaked, the eyes startled but delighted.

Coming up a narrow path was a naked woman – a tanned girl with a pink towel over one arm, tousled hair. A small, black and white cat trotted ahead of her.

Johnny froze. He'd never seen a naked woman before, except on television programmes about the missions in Africa, but those ladies wore big beads and grass skirts and painted things.

The cat stalked past Johnny, stopped, turned to rub against his leg, then continued for the house.

'Oh!' The woman saw them, then looked wildly around. Johnny moved towards her, his arms spread as if to shield her. She said, 'You're early. I . . . I was just coming up to get things ready for you.'

Johnny fixed his gaze somewhere beyond her, at the sea, at a spot on the horizon where a cloud was moving towards the sun.

Micheál stared unabashed at her small, tanned breasts, the tuft of pale brown pubic hair.

'Is that a bellybutton?' he asked, pointing.

For an endless moment they stood as points in a triangle, Susan with the towel still over her arm.

The cat reappeared in the doorway; mewed impatiently.

'Lunchtime,' Susan said. She strode across to the house, and Johnny averted his eyes from the arch of her thin back, the curve of her bottom, the long, brown legs.

In the doorway, he shot his brother a look that said there'd be discussion about this later, some talk about respectable manners when you meet a naked woman striding up a cliff path.

They waited, one each side of the unlit fireplace, Johnny's thumbs twirling furiously, round and round, one direction, then back the other way. He signalled to his brother to straighten his shirt collar. Micheál fidgeted sheepishly. The cat was munching dry food from a dish under the front window.

They listened to the unaccustomed sounds of a woman padding from bedroom to bathroom – somewhere down the corridor at the back of the house. The sudden gush of water, the clank of a door handle, footsteps again, then another door.

It was a strange room, house – shabby, yet neat as a pin, rows of books on a bookshelf made from rough boards and building blocks, turf stacked drying against the hearth, a basket of still-muddy vegetables on the table. Green, ugly carpet, cheap furniture, but pretty candles and vases of wildflowers throughout the room.

The smell of lavender came through the open window, the salty whiff of the sea. A fishing boat had moved across the horizon, framed in the window like something painted, inanimate.

'Sorry about the delay.' She came at last. Her hair was damp, her feet in thonged leather sandals, a crumpled shirt over blue shorts.

Johnny stood to shake her hand officially, as if they'd all just encountered each other now. 'Lovely to see you

again, Miss Brown, and . . . sorry for your troubles –
the death of your father, God rest . . . Micheál!' He
eyebrowed his brother to follow suit.

'Susan,' she said. 'Please. Call me Susan. Now that
we're . . . Look, I'll go put the kettle on, fill a Thermos,
make us a picnic. Too nice a day to stay inside, don't
you think?'

She was different from the officious, bristling woman
they'd visited at her office in London with the revolving
glass doors, beeping and jangling phones, the cool,
snooty receptionist. Johnny had been terrified of that
Susan, her high heels, barely concealed outrage at news
of her family's indiscretions.

But he wasn't afraid of her now. Her face, her body
were thinner than he remembered, but sinewy, tanned.
Her broken nails were rimmed with dirt, and even after
her shower, she smelled like the sea and the hayfields
beyond this window.

His seersucker slacks rolled up to the knees, Micheál
was running along the edge of the tide, wheeling his
arms and trying to chase a seagull. Susan laughed.

'Sorry,' Johnny said. 'Sometimes my brother gets . . .'

'Johnny, sit. He's fine.'

Johnny sat back down on their picnic blanket under
a sand dune.

'Johnny . . . well, you worry too much about him.
He's doing no harm.' She squirted suncream into her
hand, then offered the tube to him. 'You should . . .'

'Oh.' He accepted, then rubbed the cream on his
arms.

The outgoing tide had left an expanse of wet sand,
where something skeletal had washed up, a swarm of
flies. Goat? Sheep? Youngsters in Technicolor swimsuits
splashed into the waves, little girls arm in arm, boys
threatening, chasing, squealing in the frigid water.

Up and down along this big beach, encampments of daytrippers, holiday makers – umbrellas, coloured blankets, a father in a beach chair reading a newspaper.

A toddler in a white sunhat and fleshy little legs came waddling across the sand towards them until its mother called it back.

'Was . . . there pain?' Johnny asked at last.

'What?' She couldn't fathom what he was asking.

'Your father . . .' Johnny crossed himself. 'God rest him.'

'Oh. No, nothing like that. Went in his sleep, actually. He'd been having trouble . . . Flu, then pneumonia. The Manor – that was the place he was in – telephoned me first thing the following morning. Peaceful, they said. Just . . . well, awfully confused towards the end.'

A room, a well-tucked bed, the antiseptic smell of a sanitorium flashed through Johnny's mind. Never far away, even after all these years. Gretta's face, voice. *My own manín, best little men in this parish.*

'Grateful,' she said. 'Grateful when they don't suffer.'

'Yes. Yes, we should be,' Johnny said.

They both shifted their positions, sat with backs erect against the dune, stared out to sea.

He watched the children plunge, bathe, rub water from their eyes. He liked the coconut smell of the suncream on his arms.

'So it's all gone then?' she asked, breaking their silence.

He studied her tanned face, the green eyes.

'Rathloe House,' she said.

'Yes. Ah, yes. They came and . . . well, everything just levelled. Nothing there now except getting ready for . . .'

Suddenly, he saw the questions across her features. Oh, he'd heard the talk, rumours, that she'd been seen with him, Mr McHugh, in O'Neill's pub, her car outside his cottage late one Christmas night. But just talk. And anyway, all that was back when the Preservation Committee was bustling with all its big plans and bravado.

The breeze rose, whistled and rippled through the dune grass above them.

'So he's . . . still at Rathloe then . . . And building his house? Mr McHugh, I mean?'

'Looks like it, Miss Br . . . er, I mean, Susan,' he said.

He knew now that the talk was true – oh, not accurate, of course, nothing around Rathloe ever was – but he saw it in the wistful eyes, the hollows of her cheeks. Now, he wanted to comfort, take away whatever torment she was suffering. Just as, two months ago, she had done for him.

She gathered her knees up to her chin. Smiled sideways, sleepily at him. Her words came out muffled, like a little girl. 'This place . . . it makes me feel better.'

Chapter 52

'Micheál!' Johnny sprang to his feet, shuffled across the sand behind the young mother who was waving her arms frantically. Micheál was crouching with the toddler in the sunhat, both studying the washed-up goat's body. Micheál was pointing at the skull, laughing his Micheál laugh.

A loud crack of a hand across Micheál's face.

'How dare you! Dare you!' the young mother screeched, looking wildly around her for a lifeguard, a *garda*, her husband who had woken up on a blanket and was racing across the sand.

'Fucking pervert,' the husband said, a fist slamming into Micheál's shoulder so that Micheál toppled backwards on the sand. 'Yez should be all behind bars, behind fuckin' bars.' Micheál lay spreadeagled, bottom lip quivering.

The father had backed up on the sand to take kicking aim. 'I'll kick your balls in. Kick the shite . . . you fuckin' halfwit pervert.'

'Bleedin' cops! A lifeguard! Somebody!' The mother clicked her fingers in the air.

The toddler, oblivious, poked a finger into the goat's eye socket. 'Dah!' the little girl said to her father. 'Dah, dah!'

'I'm gonna . . .' the father said.

'Going to what?' A stern, British voice. Susan.

'This fuckin', retard pervert . . . your friend here and my daughter!' The father's face was scarlet now – rage, sunburn.

Susan flashed him a stern, let's-all-act-civilised smile. 'Sir, I'd ask you to watch your tone and your language around us please. There's nothing actually wrong here, is there?'

'But . . .' the man blustered, advancing now towards Susan, a fist clenched. 'Interfering with . . . bleedin' interfering . . . my daughter.'

She held a hand up. 'But nothing. My cousin here' – she walked over to give Micheál a hand up – 'my cousin, Mr Monahan, was just showing your child the dead goat – a touch unsanitary, yes, but nothing perverted.' Cool, rational, Margaret Thatcher voice.

Micheál stood dusting sand from his slacks, blood coming from under his eye where the woman's ring had caught him. 'I'm sorry, Johnny,' he said, in a singsong voice.

The young mother chirped, 'But look, anyone can see that yer man here is . . .'

'Is what?' Susan faced her, arms folded. 'What exactly is *our* man, Mr and Mrs . . . sorry, didn't quite catch your names.'

The father dismissed the introductions with a thick, hairy arm.

'Something wrong here?' A young lifeguard arrived at last, skittish eyes that hoped that they'd tell him all was settled.

'Nothing a little common manners and an apology won't sort out,' Susan said, the voice defiant.

'Susan . . .' Johnny caught her elbow. 'We'll just . . .'

'Someone said you hit this poor man here,' the lifeguard said to the young mother. 'No fightin' or violence

on the beach. Or cursing either . . . I'll have to ask you
to leave. Rules is rules.'

'Shite! Shite! Shite!' The father kicked sand into the air.
'Apologise, my arse. A sad day, sad bleedin' country
when . . .'

'Dah!' The toddler reached her pudgy arms up to be
lifted, carried back across the beach to her blanket and
her toys. 'Dah!'

They marched towards their car, the family of three,
the baby's white sunhat bobbing above her father's
hairy shoulders. Mother, laden with blankets and beach
toys, delivered a final, poison look to the Englishwoman
and the two elderly gents.

'Rather untamed people, don't you think?' Susan
said, brushing her sandy hands together. 'Well, let's
head back, shall we? You'll stay tonight, of course. No
point in driving anywhere this upset . . .'

'Ow! Ow!' Micheál squirmed in his chair inside the
window. A bruise was forming under his left eye. Susan
swabbed at his cut with cotton wool and antiseptic.
Micheál flinched again. 'Ow!'

Nuala's moped was parked outside; she'd brought
treats from the shop: fresh soda bread, biscuits, smoked
salmon, goat's cheese from a local supplier.

She poked her head around the kitchen door where
she was rattling around making tea. 'How're things in
the casualty ward out there?'

'Micheál's being a terrible baby,' Susan said, laughing. 'Pulling my leg, as usual.'

'Ready,' Nuala said, the teacups, plates, clinking on
the tray. Johnny followed behind her with a plate of
bread, cheese, salad from the garden.

The cat, sniffing food, plopped down from its armchair and stalked, tail high in the air, across to the
table.

Áine Greaney

The twilight closed in around them, the little group gathered inside the window. A wafer of sun slipped down beyond the horizon.

A turf fire was taking hold in the grate, sparking and crackling through the house.

Chapter 53

'*Tráth* an' 'tis you that'll pay through the nose for hay this year, so you will,' Seamus said. He was basting a row of chicken quarters on the barbecue. A selection of Carraig men, plus Rita's brothers and brothers-in-law, were gathered, beer cups in hand, around the barbecue. McHugh felt his fists clench.

'Hen's teeth,' another man added. 'I don't envy you one bit . . .'

'I'm sure I'll find something,' McHugh said testily.

Under the back windows of the house, Rita and her sisters and woman neighbours stood around the white plastic patio tables sipping wine. Flowered sundresses, suncream and fixed smiles.

Some of the older women sat in the shade of a tree on kitchen chairs. Children squealed as they chased each other around the front of the house, then back again to the garden, ran among the tables, the barrel of beer, the wine bottles set in ice buckets, a banner pegged and strung across the clothesline: *Happy Graduation, Lorcan and Tomás.*

Dutifully, McHugh's nephews circulated, lingered on the edge of each group, joked amiably and accepted envelopes and cards from aunts and grand-aunts and neighbours. Came to talk county football and weather with the men.

'This brother of mine changes his mind like the feckin'

291

wind, so he does,' Seamus said. He flipped the last of the chicken on its back. A sizzle, then a plume of charcoal smoke. 'One day he's becoming the big rancher and building a mansion for himsel' above in Rathloe; the next he's haring off back to London; then he's back to ranching again, but without a pick of winter fodder . . .' He turned, barbecue fork in the air, his eyes simmering with perverse delight.

The other men, Sunday shirt-sleeves rolled up over sunburned arms, laughed.

A redhead with a peeling face slapped McHugh on the back. 'But sure, the divil's children, hah? That's what we heard ever. The divil's children have the divil's luck. And sure, isn't luck *go leor* you had beyond in England?'

Another man saluted McHugh with his plastic beer cup. 'I might have a few bales of hay for sale meself if you're interested . . .'

McHugh drained his beer. Walked away down the garden to where two girls, neighbour's daughters, were taking a fiddle and a guitar from their instrument cases.

They had been invited to play a few tunes after the dinner; lead the singsong at the party. A long evening and night in it yet.

The best day and night of his life, Seamus had declared as their guests arrived, women picking across the garden in their high-heeled sandals; men admiring the brilliant barbecue set up and the beer barrel. The best day of his and Rita's lives, with their two sons fully qualified and educated.

And brilliant for business, Rita said. A party like this. B & B guests need to see the bit of real Irish culture, right in the back garden.

'Been playing long, then?' McHugh asked the girls pleasantly.

'Ah . . . National School anyways,' one of them answered.

'I'll look forward to hearing you,' he said.

Lovín was circling, tail wagging, around Shep, Seamus' sheepdog. McHugh patted his thigh, and she came, delighted. More hot dogs and illegal food treats?

McHugh glanced over his shoulder towards his brother, his sister-in-law and the clusters of chattering party guests. He slipped out of the side gate onto the *boithrín* that led down the mountain to the main road.

He could still hear the burr of conversations, the children's voices, the thuck of a football. The barbecue smell.

'Stay,' he called to Lovín when they reached the main road. A line of cars came fast around the corner, beach chairs, suitcases, picnic coolers stacked in back windows, children in swimsuits and T-shirts.

At last, they crossed to the side road down to the beach, stepped up on the ditch to let another packed family car ease out onto the main road. Good. Only two cars left in the parking area off the beach. He wasn't in the mood for more talk, neighbours, the repeated clichés, the furtive eyes, the simpering for information.

The beach was almost empty. A young couple lay stretched on a blanket. Her tail wagging furiously, Lovín went to befriend a black Labrador pup who was strolling with its owners. The pup yipped and frolicked, then the two dogs raced along the sand.

Only half over and already an exhausting day.

He'd known that, hadn't he? His own fault. Should have steeled, prepared himself. Somehow found a way to dispel or disguise his own gloom.

Soon, it would be time for barbecued chicken, coleslaw and potato salads and cutting the iced graduation cake he'd seen in Rita's fridge. He'd have to hurry back.

The waves crept up the wet sand.

'Whee!' the couple whistled for their black Labrador pup.

It would have been different if she, Susan Brown, had come, even answered his written invitation. Of course, the graduation party had only been an excuse to see her. But she hadn't even returned his phone calls.

Why? If she was that vexed at him still, why, oh why had she decided to save him at the eleventh hour? Withdraw her funding support for Rathloe House?

The day before yesterday, Friday, he'd tried one, last tactic: telephoned her office. But the silky voiced receptionist said Ms Brown was away on holiday at the moment. No, not at liberty to say where. No, didn't know when she'd return.

He'd kept his gardens, his housing site, his land. Almost a year's hassle, all the to-ing and fro-ing, but now he'd won. Builders arriving tomorrow morning at nine.

So why this stultifying gloom?

He kicked off his moccasins, rolled up his trouser legs to wade along the water's edge. The sea was still cold, even in mid-July. He should take a holiday himself. Needed something, that was for sure. A fresh start. Bit of pampering. Mediterranean or Caribbean? Something even more exotic? Tahiti?

He burrowed his toes in the wet sand. Flexed one foot, then the other. Watched the wet sand seep, filter through his toes. Yes, definitely a holiday. Give his London travel agent a ring tomorrow. Find a dogsitter.

He had reached the end of the beach. The stream was gurgling over stones.

He really should go back. Huffy faces and snide

grudges if Uncle John missed the cake and the highlight of the party.

He turned to whistle for Lovín. She was digging beside a washed-up goat carcass, sand flying high in the air. He whistled again. She ignored him.

It beckoned, the little path up through the dunes to the hermit's point.

There was a bicycle propped against the gable wall. A makeshift clothesline with women's shirts, a T-shirt, lacy underwear.

The writer fellow back again. The vegetable garden had been freshly weeded, staked, pruned. The windows were open, curtains ballooning out over the sills.

A loud, frantic barking behind him. A black and white cat flashed past, then Lovín in hot pursuit.

'Lovín!' McHugh called. 'Lovin! Come . . .'

The cat, then Lovín tore across the front, then the rock garden.

The golden tail disappeared over the edge of the cliff. McHugh raced. 'Lovín!'

He waited for a man's voice behind him, a cranky face in the doorway.

'Lovín!' he called, furious now, his footsteps slipping on the steep, sandy path.

Chapter 54

He stood there, frozen. Susan Brown. Naked, sitting up in the sand, looking sleepily around her.

Lovín had abandoned the cat chase to nuzzle Susan's face, the tail wagging blissfully. She said,'Hello there? Where did you come from, then? Lost?'

Speak. His throat dry. Her hair was longer, wild.

She shaded her eyes.

Saw him up there. Reached for a pink towel and pulled it across her breasts.

He stumbled over a rock, then skidded, faltered on the pathway. She watched. An impossible apparition.

'You're here,' he said, his voice drifting on the breeze.

He flopped, knelt on the sand. She rose, so they knelt together now shoulder to shoulder, eye to eye.

'You're here,' he whispered again, then tasted the salt of her hard, brown flesh.

Epilogue

'Oh, Lovín, for Pete's sake . . .' Susan nudged the dog's nose away.

For the entire drive north and then west from Rosslare ferry terminal, the golden head had been stuck between McHugh and Susan, tongue lolling, hot doggy breath on their necks.

McHugh reached behind him to scratch Lovín's ears. 'Almost there now. Look, why don't you stretch out on your blanket?' The dog whimpered, then angled her rear end around on the back seat, tail brushing the backs of their heads. At last, she settled on a spot. Sat on her hunkers to stare out of the side window at the terraced houses, the streetlamps along a foot path.

'You think she remembers?' Susan asked, an elbow resting out of the passenger's window, the voice drifting on the passing breeze.

They had just checked into Ballyshee's Hermitage Hotel; McHugh staying in the car with the dog while Susan got a room, then carted their suitcases up the wide, antique staircase. Tonight, she would create a diversion while McHugh sneaked Lovín in the back way and up the stairs.

Now, the last of the Ballyshee houses fell behind them, then the road narrowed – stone walls, electricity poles, whitethorn bushes flashing past. In two hours, they were due for afternoon tea at the Monahans' cottage. Four o'clock on the dot. Plenty of time, Johnny had said on the phone to London, ample time to tour his and Micheál's flower gardens and new summer borders. Might even dine outside if the evening stayed fine.

Susan glanced across at him, her husband of two months – the chiselled profile, the trim, grey beard, his intense gaze.

Husband. Funny, incongruous word for this Irishman. And anyway, how could you have a husband without a wedding? Flowers and long dresses and confetti and top hats.

A Saturday morning two months ago, they had driven to a register office from their flat in Notting Hill. His friend and property manager, Jimmy, already waiting outside. Anna arrived at last, late and breathless. Two witnesses. Making it official. Say I do. To have and to hold.

Afterwards, champagne and a catered luncheon back at the flat, the distant hum of traffic beyond the rooftops, the faint whiff of Portobello Market through the high, open windows. His brother, Seamus and wife, Rita, arrived by car from Heathrow. Their flight delayed because of morning fog in County Mayo. Oh, and could only stay overnight; desperate busy season already, though it was only April. Absolutely chock-a-block at the B & B at Carraig.

Photographs, Peter from iTemps had insisted. Savita the receptionist stopped stroking the black and white cat in her lap – the adoptee from *Súil na Mara* in Carraig – to add to the clamor, the coaxing for an official wedding portrait. A bride and groom kiss? The champagne toast?

McHugh was sheepish but then relented. All right, there would be a photo. Just one. And look, he happened to have just the spot. John McHugh and Susan

Brown McHugh at the stone urn out on their patio. The
stone urn from the gardens at Rathloe House.

Ever since rolling off the car ferry, there had been
something poised and waiting about him, the long
fingers gripping the steering wheel. In the twenty-three
miles from Galway City, he'd changed the radio station
three times.

They hadn't been back since he sold out.

Three years ago, she had sat in a Dublin hotel lobby
waiting for him to return from the solicitor's office. The
final closing on the sale of his twenty-five acres. She had
watched him through the wide hotel windows, his tall
frame in a familiar slouch, hands deep in his pockets,
waiting for the traffic light to change. Even crossing
the Dublin street she saw it: something lighter in his
features, a weight off the shoulders, as if he had just
signed his own prison release.

Now, he nudged her, pointed up ahead on the left.
His old rental cottage, looking impossibly small, toylike
– the narrow gateway, the whitewashed walls and
green-painted windows. A car with a luggage rack
was parked outside. Behind it: the field where they'd
first kissed on a freezing December night.

That winter, back in Cripton and waiting for her
father to die, this field had become unreal in her mind.
Yet, here it was now, just a field dotted with young
lambs, sheep with their fuzzy blue markings – the first
initial of the farmers' surnames.

Lovín's cold, wet nose against her neck again. The dog
ears alert, eyes fixed on the road, the stone walls, the
farmers' gateways. A high house painted salmon-pink
with a white, balustrade trim. Another two-storey with
dormer windows and Italianate balconies. Two new
houses with landscaped gardens. One, then another in
various stages of completion – cut-out shapes of doors,
windows. In front, sand heaps and building blocks on

pallets. Here came the crossroads and the Rathloe school with its Venetian blinds pulled down, basketball courts and football fields deserted for the weekend.

On their left, the straggle of farmers' gaps and walls suddenly gave way to the high demesne walls.

Beside her, McHugh's face was deadpan, waiting.

She knew this man whose house and life she had shared for the past three years. Oh, yes, he would stoutly deny, but there it was – his little-boy shame before a place, a people who had borne witness. To what . . . ? His one-time attempt at . . . Something she, Susan, would never understand. Retribution for old wrongs. A past undone.

They pulled off the road into the clearing and the wide gateway.

On the right-hand pillar, a white rectangle with a black calligraphy sign: 'Rathloe Farm and Country Market.' The high gates were fastened back.

The Volvo bumped down the widened driveway. McHugh pulled further left to let an approaching car pass. Lovín growled at a sheepdog whose head was blissfully stuck out of the other car's side window.

McHugh and Susan waved back at the saluting driver, a woman with shirt-sleeves rolled up to her elbows. Two children were scrunched into a back seat that was filled with brown paper grocery bags and leafy, potted plants.

To the right was a checkerboard of pebbled walkways and tiny gardens. A sign with an arrow, 'Fresh, Organic Herbs and Vegetables.'

To their left, a line of sapling trees, between which were more pathways and signs, 'Nursery', 'Miniature Shrubs', 'Exotics', 'Herbaceous Borders', 'English Cottage Garden', 'Bedding Plants', 'Ornamental Trees'.

In the distance, people, families strolling, stopping to point to this plant or that, dogs on leashes, children running. A man was walking ahead along the avenue, trays of bedding plants stacked and balanced under his chin. In the distance towards the crossroads, a row of greenhouses, the glass roofs glinting in the June sun.

Again, they made way for an approaching, red delivery truck with lettering along the doors, 'Rathloe Farm and Market. Orders and Delivery 092-46718 www.rathloefarm.com'.

They slowed for the turn in the avenue, cleared now of the thicket of briars and overgrown trees. At last, they were in a wide car park, and there it was, where Rathloe House used to stand: a low, concrete building painted bright orange. A sign above a wide, chaparral doorway, 'Rathloe Country Market'. Bicycles with wire baskets propped against the wall, another waiting delivery truck.

Inside, voices, dishes and cutlery clattered and echoed beneath the high rafters. Casablanca fans whirred above the rustic counters with their craft displays, weighing scales, barrels, trays and crates filled with cabbages, rhubarb, carrots, broccoli. Pyramids of breads, muffins, cheeses, fish. Hanging displays of carrageen moss, dried flowers, herbs. Shining rows of homeopathic cures, jams, chutneys, relishes, organic honey. A smell of freshly roasted coffee.

Susan and McHugh strolled among the aisles, separated from each other to let two young men with buggies and shopping bags pass. McHugh went on ahead while she stopped to look at some bog oak sculptures.

Three stalls down, there he was, the face silhouetted against a lit-up display of pottery table lamps. He turned to watch her weave through the shoppers, the vendors with their crates and wheeling trolleys. He spread his hands. A lopsided, befuddled smile. The blue eyes twinkling. Here it was, then. The big house. His. And once, for a short time, her grand-father's.

'Arrah, look it! Is it a bloody charity shop we're running or what?' Babs Mannion was throwing away Sadie Sweeney's brightly coloured sign, 'Freshly Baked Tarts, €1.50.' Babs' pink T-shirt strained and stretched across her huge bosom. Sadie glanced up from where she was unpacking pots of jam from cardboard boxes. She made a face at her friend's back, then went back to her jam.

Pen in hand, Babs foraged under the counter for a marker to up the prices on their sign, 'Freshly Baked Tarts, €2.'

Gone. *Nada*. Blast it, the ink dried on the last of them. Oh, hold on! Andy, the lad with the bog oak things, would have some to spare.

'Back in a sec,' she called to Sadie.

A slight headache was forming behind Sadie's eyes. This morning, like every Saturday, she'd been up since six o'clock rolling out pastry, slicing fruit and setting things out to cool along the Sweeneys' kitchen windows.

Last night, this batch of blackcurrant jam had had to be labelled and dated for today's market. Saturday their busiest day. 'Make or break day,' the women of the Rathloe Altar Society called it – twice the revenue of any other day of the week. Yes, she was dog-tired, but tonight, she'd take a nice aromatherapy bath and go to bed early. But . . . she checked her watch. Still three hours to closing.

'Hey! It's the Sadie Lady!'

A hand on the small of her back; she straightened to see who it was.

'Arrah, Ingrid! Is it yourself? How's tricks?' Ingrid, a woman with dark eyes and long braids, was standing at the counter.

'Listen, Sade, you heading over this evening?' Ingrid

gestured her head towards the back of the market, the small, high windows that looked out on the rear gardens, picnic tables, a wine bar.

Every Saturday, Sadie and Babs or whoever was on duty at the Altar Society stall went for an after-work glass of wine or two and the *craic*.

'Yeah, deffo,' Sadie called back. 'See ye there.'

Oh, they'd had some wild times out in that winery.

Two years ago when the market first opened, she and Babs had been afraid to join all these youngsters when they all met for drinks on a Saturday evening.

An unusual breed, some of these vendors and growers – the men with long hair, ponytails, clogs like you'd see on a Dutchman, some of them actually Dutchmen or Germans or wherever they were from. And the women – some shaved as bald as an egg; others with big, grey mops down to their waists and slacks that ballooned out like parachutes.

Oh, yes, the older women had gone to peer in the bar door, eyed the little counter, the rough-cut tables with candles and people clustered around – bottles of elderberry and dandelion and blackberry and the devil knows what other kind of wines. And they had scurried away and settled for a hot whiskey up in O'Neill's.

Now, Sadie went back to stacking her pots of blackcurrant along the shelf.

Gosh, what kind of daftness or fear was on them? Listening to too much gossip and talk around the checkout counter up at Margaret O'Neill's supermarket.

But now . . . if herself or one of the other women was missing on a Saturday evening, the younger ones were always clamouring around and asking, 'Oh! Where's our Mrs O' this evening? Couldn't stop in for a bevvy, then? Confessions up in the church, had she? Oh, well. Wouldn't know too much about that, I'm afraid. But tell

her I said Hi. Have you tried the new Chardonnay yet?
A touch sharpish on the pallet but . . .'

Yes. Good times. Good friends. But, at her age, she'd
need a rest, a holiday soon. But there'd be time for that.
Sometime. A few years. When she retired. Maybe.

'Em . . .When you get a minute . . .'

'Oh, never saw you there, so I didn't,' Sadie said to
the woman waiting at the counter. A pretty woman in
a blue cotton shirt and white linen slacks.

Sadie wiped her hands on her striped apron. 'Now,
what'll it be? We've some lovely tarts, rhubarb, apple,
blackberry. Just hot out of the oven this morning. Or
a few muffins? Lovely with the cup of tea. Bran with
walnuts or stone-milled wheat with raisins.'

'I'll take a rhubarb and an apple, thanks. Oh, could
you put them in some kind of box? They're a present
for some friends.'

'Coming up. Not a problem,' Sadie said, a tart in
each hand, turning her back to the Englishwoman at
the counter to look for the pastry boxes.

Every Saturday they saw more and more tourists.
Some from countries she'd never even heard of. Not
to mention the blow-ins that had moved in around
the parish – Dublin, Glasgow, Rumania, Nigeria. She'd
lost track.

'Now, miss, that'll be . . .'

A man was standing next to the Englishwoman. Sadie
blinked at him.

Couldn't be. Yes, yes it was. And handsome. Suntanned arms, a white golf shirt. She'd never thought
of him as nice-looking. Mr McHugh of the big house
land. Only saw him as a snooty interloper. A man too
big for his boots. But here he was now, a hand on his
girlfriend's – no, she eyed the small wedding ring on
the woman's finger – his wife's elbow.

'Mrs Sweeney.' He met her gaze then started to study

the pies, the muffins and buns in the display case. 'Mrs Sweeney. How are you?'

'Mr McHugh. You're . . . you're welcome back.'

'Just a flying visit. We're around for the weekend, then first thing Monday, sign the deed on our new holiday home.'

Sadie's face puckered. Oh, please. Sacred Jesus, don't tell her that this hullaballoo with houses and her husband writing daft letters and telling lies and committee meetings and petitions and websites . . . Oh, please don't tell her it's about to start all over again.

He smiled at her. 'Just a little bungalow by the sea. Carraig, my home parish. Just came on the market . . .'

'Right.' Busily, she started to tie a ribbon around the pastry box. Her face, shoulders deflated. Relieved. 'Now, four euro there.' She handed the two boxes to the woman. Wasn't he going to introduce her to this wife of his?

'Well. So long then. Everything looks great.' McHugh nodded to the shelves of jam and chutneys behind her, then left and right to the other stalls with their crates, barrels and ringing tills.

'Mr McHugh!' Sadie was out of breath when she reached them. They were crossing the car park, the golden retriever's head pert and waiting inside the open car window.

Sadie pushed a pot of blackcurrant jam into his hand. 'For you.' Then, she nodded to Susan. 'And your missus here. A little thank-you . . . For what you did.'

Then, Sadie Sweeney retreated back through the market doors, where Babs would be huffing and puffing if she found their stall unattended.

'Well, isn't this the surprise of surprises.' Kitty O'Neill's lipsticked smile stopped short at her nostrils. The eyes narrowed. Hard. 'The usual, Mr McHugh, I suppose.'

'Hello, Kit. Yes. Just a quick one while we're passing. Pint of lager and a G & T, thanks.'

'And your friend?' Kitty nodded towards the unlit fireplace where Susan and Lovín were already installed. Another saccharine smile. 'She's keeping well, is she?'

On their usual bar stools, the four men sat staring at a Tom and Jerry cartoon on the telly.

Oh! Sacred hour, Mannion thought. If this wasn't the best, the bloody best yet. *The dead arose and appeared to many.* A boring oul' Saturday, with not a soul around the village and here comes some sport at last.

In the bar mirror, the four men watched the two below at the fireplace. Talking, laughing. Her nibs scratching th'oul dog's ears. Softer, Walsh thought. The woman looks softer now, more puffed out, like a heifer that finally puts on a bit of condition.

Mannion turned to smirk at Sweeney, who was perched on his usual stool inside the door. Jesus! The man's face was the colour of his gabardine hat. Grey. Pale as a ghost. Looked as if he might vomit or collapse. The eyes glued on the telly like a goldfish in a bowl, mouth opening and closing. No need to get that upset over it. Sure, 'twas only an oul' cartoon. And anyways, that little bugger Jerrín always got the better of th'oul cat.

'. . . A man about a dog.' Sweeney nearly toppled his bar stool over as he sprinted away towards the Gents'.

The men looked from one to the other. Whispered.

'A touch of diarrhoea,' Mannion said. O'Brien and Walsh nodded sagely. Ah, yes, since this bloody market below, the men had to cook their own tea now of an evening, or make do with green, weedy-looking things left in bowls for them. Give diarrhoea to a donkey, so it would.

The door clicked. Two teenage boys trooped in, crossed to the end of the bar to fill out the little printed forms, then installed themselves, one at each of the computer terminals under the back windows. Click, click, click. Mouse, keyboard, mouse. The familiar voice, 'You've got mail.' A sudden burst of tinny music. One of the boys giggling at something on the screen.

Kitty lifted a wire tray of steaming glasses from the glass washer, set them on the counter and kneed the stainless-steel door shut.

Oh, she wished nothing but misfortune on those two below at the fire. Or him anyways. Oh, yes, he, Mr McHugh, was the root of all her and her sister Margaret's problems.

Lunacy. Locked up and throw away the key. 'Twould be too good for him. For what kind of a man – only a lunatic would sell his pristine twenty-five acres to the lowest, not the highest bidder?

Three years ago, a development outfit from the other side of Galway arrived in the parish, all *biz* with plans for twenty semi-detacheds and a green in the middle. Brilliant news. Just the bit of jizz this parish needed, what with the disappointment over the big house, every cloud has the silver lining – young families, disposable incomes, lunches and Saturday night bands and Internet customers for Kitty. But then . . . Gentleman Jim himself turns the development outfit down. Sells it for half the price to some hippie with big leather boots and an earring.

She took a clean tea towel from a drawer. Started to polish her glasses. The wrong element in this parish now, that's for sure. In here nursing their miserly half-pints of stout and cocking up their noses at her and her pub. Demanding vegetarian menus. Ah, look, surely she had some vegan choices? They could help her out, if she wanted. No trouble. Advice. Recipes. Weekly supplies. Could even deliver. And look, didn't she have any naturally sweetened drinks for the children? Only fizzy, carbonated? Oh, no. Detrimental to children's emotional stability . . .

Last month, one of those women with the feathery earrings had the cheek to ask her if she, Kitty, realised that all that blue eye shadow was really quite damaging to the extra-sensitive epidermal layer around the eyes? God, Kitty wasn't long turfing that one and her friends out the door. And don't come back.

And that wine bar with its poisonous drinks and soups that looked more like stale porridge. Mandolin recitals, poetry readings and discussion groups and the devil knows what. Tourists racing past Kitty's door like ants. *The real, unspoiled Ireland.* Real Ireland my arse. God, she, Kitty O'Neill, always disapproved of such language, especially on a licensed premises, but look, hadn't they and that man below at the fire driven her to it?

And the plants and things they grew and sold there. God, she wouldn't like to think what the likes of them did to your insides.

'Ah, two bottles of Coke there, please. With ice.'

'Ha?' She hadn't seen one of the Internet boys standing waiting at the counter.

'Right.' She reached behind her. Flipped the caps off two bottles. Shoved a straw in each. 'Now. Two Cokes. And no spilling on my keyboards or I'll . . .'

Sweeney buried his face in his hands. He hadn't prayed in a very long time, but he was storming heaven now. Glory be. Hail Mary. *Oh, most gracious Virgin Mary.* He mixed up the verses, flithers of remembered prayers tacked onto bits of others. Oh, God. Surely those two were gone by now?

The toilet cover in the Gents' was hard and cold under his buttocks. What misfortune had befallen him today of all days? That bastard McHugh and that woman of his. Susan Brown Whitaker, the witch he'd lowered himself to write to asking for money. *Is now and ever shall be, world without end . . .* But worse, told all those lies around Rathloe about knowing her from his young days in London, in the Irish dance halls. *Deliver us, O Lord, and of thy bounty for which we're about to conceive . . .* They'd talk to her, of course they would, those three jokers out at the bar. Internment, interrogation without a cause. Especially that Mannion. Like an oul' woman, that fella, he was so fond of news.

Now, he pictured Mannion leaning in over the fireplace, th'oul tweed cap dipping forward on his forehead. She'd ask if he happened to know an old acquaintance of hers, a man she'd never actually met in person, but . . . a Mr Patrick Sweeney, the village historian and sort of philanthropist. Would he, Mannion, know where such a man lived in this village? She'd like to stop and say hello now that she was here . . .

Oh, they'd slap their thighs and bray like donkeys. Haw, haw, haw. If that wasn't a good one. The best yet. Ah, go on, go on, tell us a few oul' yarns from Sweeney's young days around Camden Town, back when the two of ye knew each other in the dance halls. Mr Twinkletoes himself by all accounts – at least, that's what Sweeney had led them to believe over here in Rathloe.

His eyes watered from the stench of Jeyes' Fluid. How long had he been in here now? Jesus, Mary and Joseph, how long would those two and that oul' sissy dog stay? *For these and all my sins I am truly sorry . . .* Once all his little fibs were discovered, he'd never be able to lift his head in this parish again.

'Ready?' Susan checked her watch. Ten to four. Just enough time to make it up to the Monahans'.

'Yeah.' McHugh drained his pint glass. 'Come on, Lovín. Up you get, girl . . .'

'Bye, then.' He nodded to the three men, to Kitty. She smiled acidly over the counter at him.

The fella in the monkey suit and dickie bow was singing a song into a microphone, swaying on his stool to the music. Mannion, Walsh and O'Brien cocked their heads to the side, watching the man's gestures, the song lyrics muted. An afternoon television programme for old people. This was their favourite game. Who would be first to guess what song he was singing, shout out the title before the white letters flashed across the bottom of the telly screen?

'*Tráth*, I think I know it!' Mannion shouted. 'Hold on, it's . . .'

'Look, someone should go in and see if poor Sweeney's all right,' Walsh said, his gaze still fixed on the singer.

'Hah? Arrah, leave him in there another *while-ín*,' Mannion said.

O'Brien muttered, 'Wait'll the song is over anyways.'